MATTHIAS

AND THE
KINGDOM OF KUSH

A NOVEL

DON SCHOFIELD

ISBN 978-1-0980-9318-1 (paperback)
ISBN 978-1-0980-9320-4 (hardcover)
ISBN 978-1-0980-9319-8 (digital)

Copyright © 2021 by Don Schofield

All rights reserved. No part of this publication may be reproduced, distributed, or transmitted in any form or by any means, including photocopying, recording, or other electronic or mechanical methods without the prior written permission of the publisher. For permission requests, solicit the publisher via the address below.

Christian Faith Publishing, Inc.
832 Park Avenue
Meadville, PA 16335
www.christianfaithpublishing.com

Printed in the United States of America

For Connie

The Christian Bible tells us that after the crucifixion of Jesus, the eleven remaining apostles replaced Judas Iscariot with Matthias, a dedicated follower of Christ. This is a version of that ministry.

Therefore it is necessary to choose one of the men who have been with us the whole time the Lord Jesus went in and out among us, beginning from John's baptism to the time when Jesus was taken up from us. For one of these must become a witness with us of his resurrection. So they proposed two men: Joseph called Barsabbas (also known as Justus) and Matthias. Then they prayed, "Lord, you know everyone's heart. Show us which of these two you have chosen to take over this apostolic ministry, which Judas left to go where he belongs." Then they cast lots, and the lot fell to Matthias; so he was added to the eleven apostles. (*Acts 1:21–26*)

PROLOGUE

House of John Mark, Jerusalem, Judea—circa 29 CE

Inquisitive brown eyes strained to recognize all who gathered within the walled compound of John Mark, a good friend to those now assembling in Jerusalem. The young man let his tired body rest against the stucco wall and carefully study the growing numbers as each mingled within the large, shaded courtyard.

"I miss him too," a familiar voice said as a firm hand reached out and touched the shoulder of Matthias to gently shake the young man out of his doldrums.

The nudge had its desired effect.

"I did not see you enter the compound, Nathaniel. Are they all here?" Matthias asked as he absentmindedly ran his fingers through his short, cropped black hair and a dark beard that barely outlined his face.

"As best I can tell," he was answered. "However, you can see for yourself."

Nathaniel was a well-built, middle-aged man with a full light-brown beard and weathered face that told of a hard yet honorable life.

"But of the eleven…"

"Yes, Matthias, all. Even Matthew."

The young man smiled and nodded slightly, acknowledging that he understood. There had always existed an unspoken friction between himself and Matthew, which neither attempted to hide yet which neither really understood. He again let his mind wander to the past for answers.

 The uncertain trail from Tiberius on the Sea of Galilee that circuitously followed the Jordan River on a route that eventually led to the city of Jerusalem was both hot and arduous. Compounding the difficulty was the press of ever-larger crowds that greeted their small band at nearly every village and place of rest. John, also called "the Baptist," had walked these same hills and valleys and drew similar gatherings. However, John's disciples were not nearly as enthused as those who followed this new rabbi, some who even came to join the venture. Matthias numbered himself among the latter.

 He had heard the words of John preached from the shores of the spring-fed river and understood his message of repentance. Judea desperately needed to be cleansed before she could be saved. It was not only the Romans who had polluted the Jew's special covenant with God; ultimately, the blame lie with the Jewish people themselves. Therefore, out of a longing to reclaim their unique identity, young men like himself left their homes and family to join the crusade. Yet John's message did not wholly satisfy; it came from a despondent and angry soul. That was until they listened to the words of this new rabbi who walked the same paths as John.

 Matthias was keen to recollect his first encounters with this man from Nazareth who tempered the call for redemption with love and forgiveness. At first it seemed a contradiction, beliefs that could only weaken the already-desperate Jew. Yet, with time, the evident power of the message grew stronger as the crowd of followers multiplied and the Nazarene offered what most sought: hope for Judea. Nevertheless, not all saw Matthias's place as one with them.

 Matthew and Simon (called by the others, "the Zealot") were vocal in their objections to Matthias joining their small band. The stated concern was principally that of being another "mouth to feed," which objection was ratified by Judas and, surprisingly, Philip. However, the Master gave no credence to the four and was amused by his, Matthias's, persistence. Therefore, Matthias was allowed to follow as a "disciple," similar to the circumstance of the women who also lived on the fringe as they traveled from village to village. Yet he, Matthias, did not object. In fact, the twelve soon found him useful in many small ways, including locating food and lodging while they and the Master preached the good news.

Now, one of the twelve was gone, as was the Master, and the most loyal of the disciples had remained in Jerusalem during this time of the festival of weeks to replace the unforgiven one...with him, Matthias, a candidate.

A hulking figure interrupted the silent musings of the dark-haired, young man.

"Are you coming?" a deep, gravelly voice asked from the fringe of consciousness as Matthias strained to make out the intruder who literally hovered over his body.

"Simon Peter!" the startled youth shouted as if exposing a long-forgotten memory.

The larger man with a wizened, furrowed face and graying beard merely smiled and gestured that Matthias should follow.

"Mary with the Master's brothers have arrived. The others are ready to begin the debate. Are you up for it?" the man asked.

Matthias nodded.

"I am. It is a journey I must complete."

"Then come," Simon Peter instructed. "We meet again in John Mark's upper room. And I am with you. It is how the Master would have it. However, we must convince the others. Matthew has doubts. As do James and Simon. I will do what I can"—the man stopped as he turned and looked into Matthias's inquisitive eyes—"Speak from your heart."

"I will," the young man assured the other. He could not do otherwise.

The gathering inside the exposed beamed, second-floor room had grown to where it was difficult to imagine how events would unfold. The problem was compounded by the sheer number within the confined space as the crowd divided into two distinct factions, each competing to outdo the other in attention and noise. Yet they had one common goal: to select a replacement for Judas, the betrayer. To this purpose the candidates moved among the factions as James, brother of Jesus, did his best to mediate. James, at least, succeeded in establishing a criteria for selection: each candidate had to have known the Master from his baptism to the time of his ascension with two names finally emerging—him, Matthias, supported by Simon Peter, and John Barsabbas, a man also of Matthias's age put forward by Matthew. The sole issue was how to decide an outcome.

"Do as it is done in the temple," one of those assembled suggested. "Cast lots."

The idea was immediately accepted.

Without waiting for further discussion, John Mark led three of his slaves to the center of the room as the crowd pushed in on the confined space with two slaves carrying small clay pots and a third holding what looked like several styluses and ink containers. When the two pots were placed in front of John Mark, the man bent down and, with a wooden mallet, shattered both into shards. Each slave then took several of the styluses and ink containers and stood to one side.

"Come. Inscribe a name," John Mark instructed. A fourth slave appeared and placed another larger pot among the shards. "Cast your lot here," John Mark said as he pointed to the third pot that had been placed at his feet. "Simon Peter, would you pray for us."

The large man stood silent for a moment and appeared almost distant, if not sullen, as he looked out at the gathered disciples.

"Oh Lord, who knowest the hearts of all, do thou show us which of these two thou hast chosen to take his place in this service and in the apostleship, from which Judas fell away and went to his own place."

Simon Peter then picked up a broken piece of pottery, wrote out a name, and cast it into the pot near John Mark. Other apostles were quick to follow suit.

After all had cast their lots, Simon Peter said, "Matthew, I could use your help," and held out a hand to his fellow evangelist.

Matthew walked slowly over to Simon Peter and took hold of a handle at the rim of the large pot as Simon Peter did the same. They then began to shake the vessel, slowly at first and then more vigorously, until one shard fell out.

"Who has been chosen?" someone asked anxiously.

James, the brother of Jesus, walked to where the two still held the vessel and picked up the lone shard. He looked at the name and then at the disciples.

"Well…" another asked.

"It is… Matthias!" James responded almost in a whisper.

Simon Peter smiled. He looked among the assembled gathering for his young friend. Finally, he spied the dark-haired youth standing by himself on the far side of the room as a sudden silence overcame the disciples.

For his part, Matthias did not know what to do…or say. He was too dumbstruck. Yes, he wanted to walk with the eleven others. He had earned the right. Yet so much had happened; so much had changed! He felt woefully inadequate.

Simon Peter made his way to the boy and put his arm around his shoulders.

"Come, join us as we rejoice in retelling of our time with the Master. You are now one with the others."

Matthias looked at his mentor and returned the smile, almost disbelieving what had just happened. In so doing, he caught what he thought were the cold, suspicious stares of Matthew and Simon as they stood in the shadow of a doorway. They then disappeared into the bowels of the house.

He could not worry about such things, Matthias thought to himself. He now had greater responsibilities. His life had but one purpose: to finish the journey to which he was called by the Master.

PART ONE

Mission

CHAPTER ONE

Caesarea Maritima, Judea, circa 31 CE

The two figures, silhouetted by the warm rays of a late summer sun, walked purposely down the center of the cobbled road that led to the heart of one of King Herod's greatest achievements, Caesarea Maritima. A sliver of blue stabbed the horizon in either direction, establishing the western boundary of Judea and the true beginning of the Roman Empire. Smells and sounds of a vibrant harbor permeated this world. The strangers studied the landscape carefully if only to locate their Caesarean contact.

"Out of the road, Jew!" a gruff, accented voice shouted over the clatter of fast approaching hoofbeats.

The taller of the two men who had a cloth bag slung over his shoulder pulled the other from the roadway into a crowd that was moving quickly to either side of the cobbled way. However, one young girl was not fast enough as she twisted her sandal in the uneven road and fell into the path of the approaching chariot, barely able to save herself from instant death. As it was, her right leg was run over by the unyielding chariot as angry stares followed both the driver and passenger who held the loose end of a red bordered toga in his right arm.

A tall, heavyset man holding tight to the hand of the obviously panicked child spit in the direction of the retreating chariot.

"Roman pigs!" he cursed.

"Never mind them," another responded, a man who had bent to minister to the injured girl. "Help us get this child to the side of the road," he pleaded. "Her leg has been badly splintered."

Matthias and his companion, Dracus, who only moments earlier were preoccupied with city landmarks, moved quickly to help.

"Dracus, hurry!" the shorter of the two shouted as the crowd turned its attention toward them. "Bring her to me."

The taller and more robust of the two strangers reached down to lift the now-unconscious child as three spectators stepped out of the crowd to help. An older woman dressed in a long brown garment looked on apprehensively as another young girl with uncomprehending eyes clung to the folds of her mother's long robe.

The injured child was lifted awkwardly out of the road to a cobbled walkway as other chariots and carts made a dash for the center of town. Each driver barely maneuvered around the crowd, some using whips to clear a way.

"Quickly! Find some binding. We need to brace the leg," the short, young, dark-haired Matthias ordered no one in particular. A woman tore the hem of her robe and handed several dirty remnants to the stranger. "Dracus, we are going to have to lift the leg. You will need to hold the child down as best you can while I work the bandages around her injury."

The taller man nodded that he understood.

Matthias placed his hand on the leg of the injured girl and mouthed something that went unheard. He then raised the child's injured leg as he quickly wrapped the wound in a tight bandage. The girl moaned in pain as the woman in the brown robe bent to caress the child's forehead. The girl only slightly evidenced recognition and then fell unconscious again.

"That's as good as I can do. The child needs to be taken to her home and a more-substantial brace applied. Are you the mother?" Matthias asked the woman who now knelt next to the young girl.

"Yes."

"Do you need help moving your daughter?"

"We can do that, stranger," a short, bearded man dressed in a white tunic interjected.

Matthias nodded, saying, "My friend and I will follow." He then tapped Dracus on the shoulder as both walked slowly with the crowd through the back streets of Caesarea to a destination near the outskirts of the city.

Once arrived at a three-stored, mudbrick structure, the child's mother pointed to a narrow outside stairway that led to an open second-floor door.

"There," the woman said repeatedly as she pointed above their heads.

With one man awkwardly carrying the child up the stairs, the injured girl was placed on a bed of straw covered with coarsely woven blankets.

"Let me look at her," Matthias requested.

Those in the cramped, unlit room stepped to one side as the young disciple and his companion came forward.

"Bring me some clean water. I'll also need wooden braces to put on the leg," Matthias directed. He then bent over the child and placed his hand on the wound as he mouthed some unheard prayer.

"I'm going to help you, child," Matthias said, smiling, as he slowly took the unclean bandages off the leg and cleaned the open wound with water from a bowl held by his friend.

He next applied two wooden splints which he tied firmly to the injured leg. The child opened her eyes momentarily and smiled up at the stranger as her grip dug tight into the palm of her mother's hand. Matthias returned the smile and then closed his eyes again as he mumbled another prayer while his body shook imperceptibly. He then sat back as a look of serenity came over him.

"She should improve," Matthias said to the mother. "However, you must not let her walk until she is able." And he again gently placed his hand on the splintered leg.

"How can I ever thank you?" the mother asked.

Matthias merely smiled and said, "No need. The child's smile is payment enough."

"At least come eat with us," another voice, new to the crowd, added, "and stay the night. Both you and your companion. It is getting late, and my wife and I live with my daughter not far from here. We have room for two more."

Matthias thought for a moment and then acquiesced.

"And how are you called?" the stranger was asked.

"I am called Matthias. And this is my friend, Dracus."

"And what brings you to this part of our Roman world?"

"We go where our Master sends us. And he brought us here."

"To what purpose?"

"We do not know," Matthias answered as he again smiled in an attempt to dispel the troubled look in several eyes. "But come. We will go and eat, and I will tell you of my adventures. I believe you will find them at least interesting."

The crowd that remained began to walk slowly out the low-cut doorway with Matthias and Dracus being the last to exit. Matthias looked over his shoulder at the injured child with the mother kneeling next to the girl, washing away the dirt of the day. Once again, the strange smells and sounds of the coastal city overwhelmed his senses.

Why, indeed, he wondered, had they come to Caesarea? And as asked, "To what purpose?"

The eight reclined closely together in a horseshoe configuration inside the small mudbrick room as they reached for bits of dried bread and sauce while listening to the stories of the man who two days earlier was a stranger.

"And what of this Nazarene? Is it not blaspheme to claim to be the 'Son of God'!" one asked almost in indignation. "Surely the Sanhedrin had no choice but to order his execution. He was not thinking as a Jew and could only cause trouble with the Romans!" One or two in the gathering nodded in agreement.

Matthias listened respectfully. He knew that what he had told them of the life and trials of Jesus challenged everything that these men and women knew of their faith. He did not want to push too far, at least not yet.

"I understand," he said. "However, I was there and witnessed most of what I have told you. And at first, I did not believe. Then his words set on my heart, and I took up his way. I *saw* the empty tomb and was with the others when the Spirit came and spoke to us in strange and wonderful words. Our hearts were on fire! Even Dracus, my friend, here"—Matthias put his arm around the shoulder of his companion—"came to understand. Although, as a slave, he had his tongue cut out by the Romans, he also heard the Word and witnessed the crucifixion. Now he follows the way of our Master."

Matthias looked to Dracus for assurance and was not disappointed as the man nodded and looked into the eyes of others in the room. There was both amazement and disbelief.

"Do not be afraid of what I say. I do not ask you to understand, only to listen. I am not taking of rebellion. Jesus's message was one of love, not vengeance and war. Remember, he was a Jew and respected the words of the prophets. His kingdom is not of this world."

"And that is precisely the problem. He thought himself a god! It is blaspheme!" the man second to Matthias's right shouted.

Matthias held up his left hand and said, "I do not wish to cause trouble." And then, attempting to change the focus of the discussion asked, "And how is the young girl with the injured leg? I have heard little of her in the three days I have been in Caesarea."

"She improves beyond anyone's hope," Matthias's host answered. "Some say it is a miracle. Of course, you would know nothing of this."

Matthias was tempted to answer; however, at the last second, two women hurried into the room as one bent and whispered into the ear of the man seated directly to Matthias's left. He stood immediately.

"We have visitors," the man said in a low monotone.

Suddenly the silhouettes of three men, two in black-and-brown uniforms with swords drawn, and a third dressed in a long white robe with black piping, overshadowed the gathering.

"We come for the one who calls himself Matthias," the man in the long robe exclaimed.

The others in the room moved quickly into the shadows as both Matthias and Dracus stood but did not respond.

"Are you Matthias?" the white-robed official asked.

Matthias pushed Dracus to one side as he identified himself, "I am Matthias. Who are you, and what is it that you want of me?"

"Come with us. The high priest has ordered that we take you to him," the official responded. No other explanation was given.

The two armed guards then tapped Matthias on his shoulder and pointed to the doorway. Matthias did not argue.

"Find those we seek and let them know what has happened. They will know what to do," Matthias said to his companion as he was escorted out the door.

Those who had backed into the shadows remained hidden and silent.

CHAPTER TWO

The large room was framed by a west-facing, columned patio that looked directly out to the busy Judean harbor and azure sea; from it and to the left Herod's great palace was clearly visible. It was as if the structure was built to be one of several defensive barriers to the royal residence, and perhaps it was, considering that the building was used as both the office and official residence of Caesarea's Jewish high priest and the principal Jewish center for worship. Floor-to-ceiling diaphanous curtains billowed from the patio, stirred by the building's proximity to the harbor.

The room's furnishings were sparse: a writing desk and chair; two additional chairs set side by side in front of the desk; and a wooden bureau cluttered with papers and scrolls centered directly behind the desk with another table covered with open scrolls positioned against the north wall. It was obvious that, by design, the center of attention was the desk and its occupant; and on this particular occasion, that space was occupied by a bearded, priestly figure in a long, flowing white robe with black piping who also wore a turban made of the same fabric as his robe. Three other figures stood in front of the desk, two adult males and a young man, who watched intently as the priest wrote his thoughts on a single piece of parchment and then looked up, unsmiling, as he handed the parchment to a figure standing closest to his right hand.

"This should satisfy anyone who questions your cargo," the priest said to the adult male standing at the elbow of his clerk. And to the clerk he added, "Have it copied and give the original back to our friend here from Kush."

Again, the priest looked to the visitor, only this time he attempted a smile.

The obviously foreign visitor who was dressed in a flowing orange-and-brown robe with matching turban reached out to a youth standing to his right and was handed a cloth purse, which he carefully placed on the corner of the priest's desk.

"A gift of gratitude from my queen," the man said in halting Aramaic as he bowed slightly.

The two foreigners then turned and started to walk out of the room. As they did, a uniformed guard hurried past, leaned over the desk, and whispered to the high priest.

"Bring him to me," the priest ordered as he walked to an opening in one of the curtains while looking out at the busy Caesarean port.

A uniformed escort of two guards and another dressed similar to the priest entered the chamber with Matthias trapped in the middle as they hurried past the departing delegation. The older foreign male nodded slightly as did Matthias. The room was then empty but for the two priests, Matthias, and guards.

A bearded priest who had stepped away from the windows and sat behind the large wooden desk spoke first.

"So you are a follower of the Nazarene?"

Matthias did not respond but looked past his examiner at the billowing curtains while the guards held tight to his upper arms.

"And do you not believe the Sanhedrin when it says that those who incite others to follow this heretic will be punished?"

Matthias again answered with silence.

"The penalty could be your death." This was said with obvious contempt for the prisoner.

Still no response from Matthias, however.

"What do they call you?" the high priest asked.

When Matthias again gave no answer, the guards in unison pulled on both arms of the man and brought their prisoner to the floor by striking the back of the man's knees with their fists.

One then said between clenched teeth, "Kneel in the presence of the high priest. He asked your name!"

Matthias looked up slowly at his inquisitor who had come to stand in front of him, thought again of defying this display of authority, decided it was not "the way," and answered, "Matthias."

"And do you follow the Nazarene?" the high priest asked.

"I follow the way of Jesus of Nazareth. We mean you no harm."

"Others in your household say to the contrary. They say you preach of the resurrection of this heretic, and that is treason!"

"He is with us no more. He has gone to the Father. How does this harm you?" Matthias asked, throwing back his head.

The high priest studied his prisoner for a long moment before returning to his desk.

"It matters not to me. The Sanhedrin has determined this to be treason. And you condemn yourself by your very words!"

"I have done nothing wrong!"

"And what of the girl? And the spell you have cast on her?"

"Spell? She walks again! Is this such a threat to the Sanhedrin?"

"It is if you indoctrinate her and others like her in the ways of the Nazarene."

Matthias looked deeply into the eyes of the priest and actually saw fear! He decided to say no more.

The high priest sat back in his chair as the guards pulled the young disciple to his feet at a subtle, silent command from their overlord.

"What to do with you?" the priest voiced out loud. "I could have you executed. However, I do not want to give your followers another martyr." Then, after some thought, he added, "Let Jerusalem handle its own problem. I have enough of my own. In fact, it is probably in everyone's interest that you be passed to higher authority. I will have to think on it."

The priest then looked away from his prisoner as his left hand slipped over the bag of coins given by the representative from Kush.

"Take him to the prison, and I will make my decision known later."

The guards bowed slightly and then tugged again on the arms of Matthias as they pulled him to his feet and turned to exit the high priest's chamber.

The outcome was predictable.

CHAPTER THREE

Matthias twisted uncomfortably as he attempted to adapt to his circumstance on the fourth day of his imprisonment. The rock-hewed cell was barely large enough for a child to maneuver its small body, let alone an adult; standing was nearly impossible. And the straw thrown on the hardpacked dirt floor in an attempt at some degree of comfort would have been bearable if it had not been days since new straw was added. The stench of human excrement was overwhelming. However, the issue which most bothered Matthias was the matter of food which, although each prisoner was daily provided with a pasty gruel meal, still most depended on outside help, which Matthias had none.

While bemoaning his fate and contemplating some avenue for relief, a faint noise reverberated from the hallway which grew steadily louder. Finally, the barred door to his prison opened, and three indistinguishable figures bent into the low doorway. Light from a torch held by one of the intruders made identity impossible. Eventually one of the figures spoke.

"Dracus," a baritone voice commanded in a distinctively Roman dialect, "take the key from the guard and remove his shackles."

A silent figure first reached to his rear and then hurried into the cramped space as the man pulled at Matthias's feet.

"You've come!" he said touching the arms of Dracus who struggled with his friend's restraints. "How were you able to get the high priest to agree?"

The crouching figure said nothing but looked to his rear as Matthias followed Dracus's line of sight. Both men focused on a stocky individual dressed in a white tunic with a red cloak attached at the shoulders. A short daggerlike sword that hung in a scabbard at the man's waist said the stranger held an important position in the Roman army. The stranger could not miss Matthias's puzzled stare and attempted to answer some of the obvious questions.

"I am Cornelius, a friend of Simon Peter," he explained. "Dracus told us of your confrontation with the authorities. Being a centurion in a Roman legion has some value," and the man smiled as he put one hand on his sword. "But come quickly as our 'friends' are not known for their patience."

Matthias smiled hesitantly as he turned to Dracus for help standing. Once on his feet, the four figures moved away from the cell and down a tight, dark hall that smelled of rotting flesh and human waste until they entered an alcove of an exterior doorway. The centurion removed a large wooden crossbar that kept others from entering the prison as Matthias with his two companions hastened into a busy alley that intersected with the building.

"This way!" the centurion motioned as he hurried down the narrow passageway toward a central street that bisected Caesarea. "We will go to my house where Simon Peter waits."

Matthias had many questions but felt Dracus tug on his arm and knew that this was not the time for explanations. Therefore, with nothing said, he followed the others toward the outskirts of the city and to more-spacious dwellings. They stopped in front of one of several walled structures where the centurion motioned Matthias and his companion inside.

"Quickly!" he warned. "I do not trust the Jews." His face reddened with his last remark. However, Matthias understood and smiled knowingly.

The three entered a short hallway with access to other rooms, which eventually opened to an atrium.

"My slaves will take you to their quarters," Cornelius said as he pointed at Matthias. "There you can change out of that rag. And join us when you are finished." The man nodded at a room to their right off the atrium.

Matthias was compliant and changed quickly. He then rejoined the others where three figures stood from couches, two of whom were familiar.

"Welcome back to the world!" a stoutly built, steely eyed man greeted as a strong hand clasped Matthias on the left shoulder. "You survived the hospitality of our local hosts, I see."

Matthias smiled up at the tall man and said, "I did! Not that our friend, the priest, had anything to do with it. And you, Simon Peter, why do you come to Caesarea?"

Matthias let his gaze move across the room to where two other men stood, both half-hidden by shadows, one vaguely familiar but the other a complete stranger who distinguished himself by dressing in a rust-colored robe embroidered with golden threads on both the sleeves and neck. Simon Peter saw the inquisitive look in his friend's eyes.

"Remember, the Master instructed that I now be called Peter," the robust man said, correcting Matthias. "And this is an ambassador from Ethiopia, a treasurer of their royal court, who our brother, Philip, sought to teach in the ways of the Master," he said, holding his hand out toward a dark-skinned, slender man with a black goatee while gesturing that the stranger should step out from the shadows. "And you know Barnabas, of course."

The stranger from Ethiopia stepped forward and bowed slightly, which was reciprocated by Matthias. The other also stepped into the light and politely acknowledged the young disciple. However, this man, although dressed more simply than the Ethiopian, remained erect and slightly more regal, which seemed to challenge the underlying authority of everyone. Peter and Barnabas could have passed for brothers.

"The grace of our Lord to you both," Matthias answered as he bowed slightly and smiled awkwardly in welcome.

He turned again to the foreigner whose gaze remained fixed on him, and it was then that he recognized the man as being the same who he had passed in the sanctum of the high priest. Matthias tensed at the unexpected meeting.

Peter stepped between the centurion and Matthias to explain.

"The peace of our Lord be with you also, my brother," he began. "And I am sure you have many questions," he added.

Matthias nodded affirmatively.

"All will be answered in due time," Peter explained. "However, most importantly, we have come with a mission we wish you to undertake."

The large man looked over his shoulder and back at Barnabas who remained rigid and silent in the dabbled light of the room.

"Our friend, the Ethiopian, is to return to his people. He has finished his mission here. However, our Lord has worked a miracle and has led our new friend"—he turned and smiled at the foreign stranger—"to seek instruction in our ways. Our brother, Philip, helped him to understand certain passages of our holy script and took it upon himself to speak of Jesus. After more discourse about our Lord, the Ethiopian asked to be baptized which, Philip did. Now our new friend wants his queen and her people to hear the good news of Christ! So Philip came to me in Jerusalem, and as I and Barnabas were coming to Caesarea, we accompanied the Ethiopian to the centurion's home who is also a follower of our Lord."

Matthias looked slowly around the room and at the men who appeared as interested by the narrative as he.

"It was another miracle of our Master that we found you at this place," Peter continued, "with the hope that you will undertake this mission."

Matthias did not speak or move. He knew that Peter was the closest disciple to the Master and often spoke for him in counsel. The correct response was silence.

"It is the wish of our brethren that you escort our new friend back to his people and teach him and others like him in the ways of our Lord."

The Ethiopian again bowed slightly but said nothing.

For a moment the young disciple was speechless. Only this morning he was imprisoned for sedition against his own people, and now, freed from his cell, he was being asked to minister to potential multitudes in a foreign land. It was much to take in for one day.

Peter sensed Matthias's apprehension.

"We need you and your talents, brother Matthias. It is the Lord's will." He stepped forward and placed one hand on Matthias's shoulder. "You are indeed fortunate that the Master chose you for this mission. Our Master's words need to be told not only to the Jew but also to others such as Cornelius here and to our friends in Kush."

Neither Peter nor the centurion exchanged glances, but both nodded in unison.

Matthias did not know what to say. Under the circumstance, how could he do anything but accept, and he looked first at Dracus who was standing to his right and then back at Peter.

"When?" he asked hesitantly.

"That has yet to be determined," Peter answered. "It could be as early as the next two or three days. Cornelius has orders to send a detachment of his men to the fortifications south of Alexandria, and he awaits transport. Here, take this." He handed the young disciple a small, scrolled papyrus. "It has the name of the man you are to contact in Alexandria. He is a well-known merchant. He is also known to be sympathetic to our cause."

"And I have had dealings with this Egyptian in the past. He is to be trusted," the gray-bearded Barnabas added.

Matthias took the scroll and opened it.

"Andronicus Phylos?" he said with obvious question. "A Hellenist?"

"Yes. Well, not actually," Peter answered. "He, like others in Egypt, take on the pretense of being descended from Athens or cities like it. However, he is a Jew known to James and others in Jerusalem."

"And as for your transport," the centurion interjected as he stepped to the left side of Peter. "It will probably be a cargo ship. Rome has committed everything else to fight pirates off the coast of Africa. I will have an answer by tomorrow."

Matthias still was confused. He looked at each of the others for a sign of hesitation, or at least some discussion. However, none was forthcoming.

"I will do as you ask," he finally replied. "Rather, Dracus and I will go," and he put his hand on the right arm of his silent companion.

"And you will remain here until all the arrangements are made," Cornelius added. "No use in tempting our local authorities again," he said and smiled. "You have made enough of an impression."

Matthias nodded in agreement. However, an *agreement* as to what was still mostly to be determined.

The calm sea splashed rhythmically against the wooden hulls of the broad beamed ships moored in the cramped quarters of the man-made harbor as men hurried purposely up and down the stone and wooden wharfs to ready each vessel for that day's journey out to the unpredictable waters of the open sea. It was not quite dawn when the eight men approached one of the ships, careful not to interfere with a preoccupied crew, mostly slaves, who were busy loading several large clay jars into the hole of a large, single-masted vessel.

"This is the one Cornelius spoke of," the gruff but well-intentioned Peter said to the others. "I will go onboard to let the pilot know of your arrival."

His companions nodded their assent as the large man hurried up a narrow wooden gangplank to the deck of the moored ship.

Within moments both Peter and Cornelius came down the gangplank, awkwardly sidestepping slaves carrying supplies onto the ship, and walked over to the three men awaiting instruction.

"The pilot says you are to board as soon as possible," the well-muscled Roman soldier said to Matthias and others wanting transport to Alexandria. "He will depart as soon as the tide turns. My men are already onboard."

Matthias signaled his understanding. Then, looking at his companions, his gazed settled on the stranger from Ethiopia. It occurred to him that the man had said very little all morning but merely followed the others, including his four slaves, to the harbor. Matthias's stare must have been unsettling as the man held up his right hand and attempted a smile.

"It is well," he said in his heavily accented speech as he maneuvered toward the gangplank behind his slaves each of whom carried a large chest. "You follow."

Matthias attempted to return the smile as he and Dracus also moved to board the ship, each carrying a small cloth sack crammed with what little provisions the centurion could spare. Although he would never question Peter, he had to wonder if, indeed, he was the right person for this important undertaking.

CHAPTER FOUR

Alexandria, Imperial Province of Egypt

After a journey of nearly one week on a rolling sea, Matthias finally stood sure-footed on solid ground near the intersection of the Heptastadion, a man-made causeway linking the island of Pharos with the city of Alexandria and its grand east-west boulevard, the Canopic Way, attempting to take it all in. Progress from Caesarea to Alexandria was relatively uneventful with only one squall to disturb their passage. However, because of their cramped quarters, there were instances when he thought the short tempers of the seven crewmen and the Roman soldiers were going to boil over into open conflict. Fortunately, the boat's pilot had a calmer head and kept all in check. Nevertheless, sighting of the Alexandrian lighthouse came none too soon.

The latter was a wonder of the age, which inspired Matthias to look north and to the entrance of the harbor with curiosity. The lighthouse towered majestically over the shipping lanes that were vital to the commerce of Alexandria. Indeed, it was said that every ship which entered its environs was required to give up all books in order that each be copied, catalogued, and then placed in the renowned library situated not far from the royal palace. Without a doubt, Alexandria was built to impress, with a myriad of marble temples and colonnaded plazas, all busied with a citizenry going about their uniquely cosmopolitan business. Matthias could easily understand why Alexandria claimed to be the second city of Rome.

This was all a distraction, however, from his purpose, and Matthias refocused his attention to the business at hand. Because their ship had docked at the westerly end of the grand harbor,

Matthias, Dracus, and the Ethiopian had the entire breath of the city to navigate in order to reach "the delta," the Jewish quarter of the city. As a consequence, the Ethiopian, who was familiar with Alexandria, joined the throngs that crowded the grand Canopic Way in search of two sedan chairs while Matthias and Dracus remained at the busy intersection of streets, looking lost and uncomfortably foreign. Finally, the silhouette of their tall, dark-skinned companion was spied working his way through the crowd with slaves and transport.

Matthias watched curiously as the man and his entourage approached.

"You were successful?" he asked, knowing the answer.

The Ethiopian smiled and pointed at two canopied chairs and bearers.

"Yes. This will make our venture much more enjoyable," he said in broken Aramaic.

Matthias noticed that the four chests carried by the Ethiopian's slaves were already tied to the front and at the foot of each chair. This certainly was a different world than crossing the deserts of Judea.

"I do not have the means to repay your kindness," Matthias cautioned, meaning no disrespect to their tall benefactor.

The comment was waved off.

"This is at the expense of my queen. Besides, it will get us to our destination much faster and without wearing ourselves to exhaustion."

Matthias was grateful. The voyage from Caesarea to Alexandria had worn on everyone.

"I appreciate everything you've done. And you speak our language very well," he said as he walked over to one of the chairs and hesitated.

"Sit," the Ethiopian instructed as he gestured with both hands. "I as others learned from your Judean traders. Now, where do we go?" he asked.

Matthias pulled aside a curtain that enveloped the chair. As he did, he also pulled out the scroll given to him by Peter and read the name inscribed: "Andronicus Pylos," he said aloud. "He lives in the

Jewish quarter and does business with the Romans. I suggest going to a forum in that district and inquire."

The Ethiopian nodded and also climbed into a chair. Matthias noticed that the man's four slaves watched both take their positions of relative comfort with indifference. Dracus also tried to remain inconspicuous. Matthias suggested that he join him; however, the man signed, "no." Therefore, the two chairs set off down the long, crowded boulevard, with Dracus and the Ethiopian's slaves walking alongside. Matthias, however, could not shake his slight discomfort with this unexpected extravagance.

The trek down the Canopic Way was uneventful even if the expanse was crowded with an exotic blend of human endeavor. The greatest draw appeared to be the myriad of temples that lined the way, each emitting an assortment of smells from large incense altars, many used for the sacrifice of animals, with white clouds of smoke permeating the many adjoining forums. Matthias was grateful that his faith did not depend on such a display.

Their progress down the thoroughfare was steady if not fast and came to a stop only once to let a passing caravan of caged wild animals, some very strange and unfamiliar to Matthias, pass through an intersection of roadways. The noise from the caged beasts and curious onlookers was almost deafening.

"Why are they brought into the city?" he shouted, having climbed out of his chair to stand next to the Ethiopian.

"For the games," he was answered.

Matthias noticed that the tall, dark-skinned man's attention, however, was more focused on the last wagon in the caravan than on his question.

"And them?" Matthias asked, pointing at the barred vehicle which held several well-muscled men chained at both their legs and arms.

The Ethiopian paused for a moment while his eyes never lost contact with the silent prisoners.

"For the games too, I presume," he finally answered. The man then let his gaze drop and turned his attention back to Matthias. "We should move on," the Ethiopian suggested as he climbed back into his chair.

Matthias did the same, however, not without noticing that his compatriot had again focused on the caged prisoners and on one man in particular, a dark-skinned individual with strange tattoos and welts on both his back and chest. For a moment Matthias could have sworn that the two men recognized each other, then the caravan resumed its slow progress down the wide roadway and disappeared as the Ethiopian turned his attention back to their small band. He gave a silent signal to his slaves, and Matthias was abruptly lifted, and their caravan moving again through the busy throngs. He could barely make out the eastern ramparts of a wall that surrounded Alexandria and suspected that their chairborne journey was nearing its end.

Matthias was correct. The bearers turned up a roadway that led to the northern limits of the city, a community locally identified as "the delta," and finally came to a stop in front of the entrance to a forum where Matthias could distinguish familiar tongues from the mix of population. Both he and the Ethiopian climbed out of their chairs and made their way to the center of the columned enclave where several distinct groups of men stood in animated discussion. It did not take long to discover where their next contact, Andronicus Phylos, conducted business, and both men started in that direction, with Dracus walking close to his friend as the Ethiopian's slaves followed, each again carrying a locked wooden trunk.

CHAPTER FIVE

"I am he," a tall, thin, bearded man answered in response to a question put to him by Matthias. "And why do you seek me out?"

Matthias was amused by the man's formality. Andronicus Phylos was not at all what Matthias expected; although it was obvious that the Egyptian was the center of all things under the roof of the large open complex where they now stood. Workmen, presumably slaves, went about their tasks in a very deliberate manner while struggling against the heat of a midday sun, with Phylos watching every movement without making it too obvious. Matthias was impressed by the seeming efficiency of it all.

"We come from Judea with an introduction from Simon Peter," Matthias offered as he handed the man a scroll that he took from a small cloth bag that was tied about his waist. "The Ethiopian and I"—he nodded toward the dark-skinned traveler who took two steps forward—"we need your help in going south to the land of Kush."

Matthias waited for a reaction; however, nothing registered but a continued hard stare. The man finally read the scroll and then looked back at Matthias and his companions.

"Simon Peter says that you follow in the way of the Galilean. This interests me. However, what of your friend?" He turned to face the Ethiopian. "Is he why you go to Kush?"

Matthias nodded and said, "It is the will of those in Jerusalem who also follow our Master that his teachings be made known to those of that land. The Ethiopian is a high official from Kush."

Phylos nodded slightly, indicating that he understood, and started to respond when he was interrupted by one of his workers.

"Take all the grain from the first five silos," the Egyptian instructed, "and bring it to the four ships in the harbor that I pointed out yesterday. They will transport everything to Rome."

The worker acknowledged the order and hurried off into the interior of the complex. Phylos again turned to his visitors.

"Now, to your problem," the Egyptian said. "Of course, you must first come to my house, and we will discuss your needs in detail. I am not sure that you are aware Rome and Kush have been at war and only recently resumed trade. It seems the ruler of Kush, who is a woman, by the way"—he looked curiously at the Ethiopian—"likes to tweak the Romans with periodic incursions into Egypt. Which is not necessarily the wisest of things to do. You will need to clear your travel with the imperial representative here in Alexandria, which may take some time. I can help in that regard."

"And we can stay in your home for those few days?" Matthias asked uncomfortably. "We do not wish to be an inconvenience."

"Absolutely," the Egyptian replied. "We have much to talk about. I want to hear all about Jerusalem and this new prophet. How well did you know him?"

"I followed him before and after his crucifixion. Indeed, because of his death…"

The Egyptian held up his right hand and looked curiously at Matthias, saying, "Not now. We will discuss this later. First, you must rest." Again he looked around his establishment. "Ah, Antonius," he said, spying another worker standing to one side in the shadows. "Come here. I am going to leave for the day, so I want you to take charge of sorting out the grain shipment. Remember, it's grain from the first five silos. And we'll have to be quick about it as the Romans are getting impatient. I will be at my residence should you need me." He waved at Matthias and his companions to follow.

Matthias obligingly walked back into the heat of the congested roadway that passed directly in front of the Egyptian's complex, accompanied by Dracus and the Ethiopian. The pace was slow; yet it was not long before they were again enveloped by Alexandria's mixed citizenry.

It seemed they meandered the back streets of "the delta" for an interminable period of time with the unrelenting heat of a midday sun and the din of city noises contributing to their exhaustion. Nevertheless, they finally reached the outskirts of Alexandria near its northeastern wall where Phylos stopped at an ornately carved wooden door, which was set deep into a large mudbrick enclosure that fronted a crowded street with three small, wood-framed slots cut into its exterior wall high above eye level. The door opened slowly as the Egyptian stepped briskly inside and directed that all should do likewise.

"You will be shown to your rooms," Phylos said as he clapped his hands twice, and three male slaves appeared from seemingly nowhere. "Take them," he ordered as two slaves moved effortlessly and gathered up the strangers' belongings and moved toward a large, open courtyard highlighted by two narrow marble stairways that extended down from a second floor. However, everything came to a temporary halt when two young women, one tall with flowing, dark hair and the other short with her light-brown hair braided and wrapped around the sides of her head in two coils, came rushing toward them from the courtyard.

"Father!" the taller and prettier of the two women hollered as she approached. "I'm glad you came home early. We can…" and then stopped abruptly when she noticed the strangers. "I'm sorry. I thought you were alone," she said.

"Philomena," the Egyptian responded, "this is our friend, Matthias, from Judea whom James wrote about," and he nodded at the short, dark-haired man. "And this is…" he hesitated, not knowing how to introduce the Ethiopian then, after some thought, added, "an official from the land of Kush who travels with Matthias and is returning home."

Both strangers bowed slightly in acknowledgment. Matthias's eyes, however, never left the taller of the two females.

The woman returned the stare.

"Father, Dorca's cousin is sponsoring a day of games. Will you take us?" the daughter asked, changing the subject.

"We will see," was the curt reply. "Right now, I want you to help make our guests comfortable. And I, for one, would like to hear all the news from Jerusalem. Matthias is a follower of the Nazarene who was crucified."

The latter comment sparked an interest that was obvious by the curious reaction of both girls.

"Perhaps he can be persuaded to tell us of his experiences." The Egyptian looked apprehensively at Matthias.

"It would be my honor," Matthias answered. "In fact, it is this mission that Peter and the others would have me take to the land of Kush. I am to speak to all of my time with the Master."

There was a momentary silence before the Egyptian reached out and patted Matthias on his back as he nodded toward the stairway in the middle of the atrium.

"There will be time enough for that. For the moment, you and your companions need to rest. Follow my servants to your rooms, and we will talk later." He emphasized the latter by motioning that they should move farther into the courtyard and toward the stairway.

Matthias was more than happy to accept the suggestion and moved quickly across the columned atrium with Dracus at his side. It did not go unnoticed that the two girls watched their progress with more than curious stares.

"So you are a prophet?" the tall, pretty daughter of their Egyptian host asked coyly.

Matthias was momentarily jarred by the question and turned abruptly to face his inquisitor who sat with him on an ornately carved stone bench near the center of the atrium. The early morning sun was just beginning to cast indefinite, opaque shadows on a polished marble floor.

"Not at all," Matthias replied. "It is the Master who gives me the words. I am nothing without Him."

The girl looked at Matthias with a puzzled but interested stare and said, "I do not understand. And I am not trying to be rude. It is just that what you told us last night was beyond anything we expected. I can understand why the priests in Jerusalem are upset with you. To think that there is one who actually considered himself the very Son of God! And you served him! It is, well, what some might consider heresy!"

Matthias smiled as he shook his head slightly. His right hand reached out and touched the upper arm of the girl.

"No, it is not. You had to be with him to understand. Believe me when I say that I did not choose this life. He chose me."

The two looked at each other for a long moment. It was the girl who broke the silence.

"It does not matter. Unlike my father, I will not press you further. Do you intend to stay long in Alexandria?"

"That all depends…" at which moment both were interrupted by the Egyptian.

"Daughter, I need your help at the granary. There is a shipment due in, and I need a person who I can trust to give an accurate account of what is received. The Romans sometimes keep a heavy thumb on the scales." He looked at Matthias and realized that the young man did not understand his concern. "Taxes. The Romans take their cut from the amount of grain I receive," he explained. "They also take an assessment when I ship the grain to Rome. They get it both coming and going, in other words. Not a bad system if you're on their end. However, I try to watch as carefully as I can and somehow manage to make a small profit."

Matthias merely smiled as he looked obliquely at the ornate furnishings that surrounded him. A "small profit" went a long way. He also marveled at the seeming trust the older man placed in his pretty, young daughter. *Unusual*, he thought.

"Certainly, Father," the girl answered.

"Good," Phylos responded. "I need to escort our young guest and his companion to the prefect's office and will return as soon as I can." He then turned to Matthias. "Are you ready?" he asked.

Matthias had momentarily forgotten about the Ethiopian who at that moment entered the atrium followed by Dracus.

"We need time to gather up the necessary documents," Matthias said, and the Ethiopian agreed.

"Then, say we meet back here midmorning," the Egyptian replied. "I do not know how long this interview will take, perhaps all day. It depends on the mood of our Roman friends. However, it is useless to argue," and the man moved quickly toward an adjunct of the atrium as Matthias and the Ethiopian returned to their second-floor rooms.

Hopefully, this was a day that Rome wished to demonstrate its benevolence.

CHAPTER SIX

Royal Palace Complex, Alexandria.

The Egyptian was as good as his word, and the party of six took a direct route to the prefect's residence after leaving the Egyptian's home. However, it was easy to see how the man had accumulated his fortune, as there were no luxuries such as sedan chairs used to cover the distance. Instead, they walked the entire route at a fairly brisk pace, so much so as to almost leave the Ethiopian and his entourage behind. However, within half an hour of walking through "the delta," they turned into a complex of buildings and temples that became more overwhelming as they approached what appeared to be a large portico. The Egyptian stopped abruptly in front of one of the more-imposing edifices.

"We must first find my friend, Gaius Quintinnius," Phylos said matter-of-factly. "He is known to speak for the prefect, and I conduct most of my business through him. He usually can be found over there," and he pointed to one of several smaller buildings seemingly attached to others by a long, colonnaded walkway.

Without waiting for comment, Phylos walked up several steps and started down a covered passage while the others followed compliantly. Once at the designated complex, the Egyptian walked confidently through an open wooden door that revealed what appeared to be a large reception hall. There was activity everywhere with a noticeable presence of military; Phylos, however, was keen to find only one person.

"Ah! There he is," the man said and hurried off to his right. Matthias and the Ethiopian did the same. "Gaius Quintinnius, my friend!" the Egyptian shouted probably louder than necessary.

However, he caught the attention of his quarry who was surrounded by several men dressed in unadorned togas. "If you have a moment," he continued.

A portly, round-faced man with a nearly bald head and short, stubby arms turned slowly.

"Phylos," the man said hesitantly. "I thought our business with the shipment was concluded."

He looked truly surprised and gave a half-shrug.

"It is," Phylos replied. "That is not why I sought you out. It is other business of which I need your help."

He smiled as he looked obliquely at both Matthias and the Ethiopian.

"Well," Qunitinnius answered, "I suppose we can talk for a moment. However, not here." He turned to his circle of companions, said something under his breath, then nodded at an unoccupied corner of the hall. "Over there," he said and walked off, followed by Phylos and those with him.

"What is it? However, be quick about it. The council meets shortly."

It was apparent that the balding man was short on patience.

"I need you to approach the prefect with another request," Phylos began haltingly. "My two guests"—he nodded at both Matthias and the Ethiopian—"wish to travel to the land of Kush. I know that Rome has had its problems with that kingdom, and these two hope to get the prefect's permission to travel there."

"To what purpose?" the other asked immediately. "These things are not routine."

"I know. However, the one returns home." He indicated the Ethiopian. "The other," he added, now looking at Matthias, "is for business. He wants to make contacts for future caravans out of Judea."

The short, stocky man studied his petitioner suspiciously and said, "Maybe. However, these things have to be handled very carefully. Rome is still smarting from renegades who continue to attack our southern borders. Are your friends prepared for the costs of such a venture?"

Phylos smiled and said, "I will ask," and he turned to the two mute onlookers.

"Can you afford this service?" he asked matter-of-factly.

Matthias and the Ethiopian stood silent for a moment. The Ethiopian then reached into a large pocket concealed by his robe and pulled out a drawstring handbag, which he handed to the Egyptian.

"Take for permission," he said in halting Greek.

The balding man did not hesitate but snatched the purse from the Ethiopian and handed it to Quintinnius.

"I will see what can be done," the man said and started to walk away. Phylos and his guests watched in silence.

"Now we wait," the Egyptian said as he began to walk out of the large hall.

Approaching the colonnaded passageway, Phylos was stopped by a short, dark, bearded man carrying several tightly bound scrolls.

"Phylos," the stranger said. "What brings you to the palace?"

The Egyptian turned abruptly.

"Business," Phylos answered. He noticed that the stranger was carefully scrutinizing both Matthias and the Ethiopian; therefore, he added, "And these are my house guests, one from Ethiopia and the other from Judea. What brings you to the palace, Rabbi? I thought your business was at the museum?"

"It is. However, sometimes they let me out to see how the real world functions," and Rabbi Jonas smiled, pleased with his attempt at humor. "So, Judea. Jerusalem?" he asked.

Matthias took a step forward and said, "Caesarea Maritima most recently. However, I have lived in Jerusalem. We hope to go the land of Kush," and he nodded at the Ethiopian who stood silently to his left.

"This all sounds very interesting. I would very much like to visit with you and your friend," the stranger said with obvious curiosity. "Do you have the time?"

Matthias looked at Phylos.

As he was not interrupted, he asked, "When?"

"At the moment, I am caught up with other matters." The rabbi looked down at the scrolls he carried awkwardly in the crux of one arm. "Tomorrow?"

Again Matthias looked at his host and, with no contradiction, assented.

"Good. We will meet here about this same time tomorrow morning. I will then personally escort you to our beautiful library where we can talk without all this traffic. Phylos, will you be joining us?"

"No," the Egyptian responded. "However, I think my friends will enjoy the outing."

"Until tomorrow then," the rabbi said as he turned and walked briskly toward one of the smaller buildings adjacent to their walkway.

Matthias looked curiously at the Ethiopian who tugged on the sleeve of his cloak and whispered in his ear. The young disciple turned to the Egyptian.

"It seems that my friend has other business he needs to conduct while in Alexandria. Therefore, only Dracus and I will take the tour."

The Egyptian merely shrugged as he started retracing a route back to his enclave. For better or worse, Matthias and Dracus would have a day to themselves.

Matthias considered the afternoon and evening spent alone as almost providential as he was able to gather his thoughts and take time to consider the journey that lie ahead. It also afforded him the opportunity to meet with and to discuss the life of the Master with several families associated with the Egyptian's household as arranged by Dracus. Matthias supposed that some might have considered his preaching's heretical. However, it felt good to talk of the past, as it was the reason why he was being sent to the land of Kush. Nevertheless, he knew that he could not maintain this profile for long, or he would run the risk of endangering his mission, even being incarcerated as he had been in Caesarea. Therefore, he welcomed Rabbi Jonas's invitation as a distraction to the environment in which he felt most comfortable.

The venture began early as two of the Egyptian's slaves escorted both him and Dracus back to the columned walkway in front of the complex of buildings that surrounded the royal palace. There they were left alone for nearly half an hour until their host arrived as one with a crowd infiltrating the forum.

"Have you waited long?" asked the short, bearded man dressed in a white unadorned toga.

A raised black cap centered on his head made him stand out from those around him.

Matthias politely shook his head.

"Good. Then follow me. It is not far. The palace has a direct route to the library," the man said and started down a columned passageway.

The rabbi navigated with a slow but steady pace through crowds gathering around the palace and its adjoining buildings. Actually, Matthias welcomed the chance to be out on his own without obligation to anyone, at least for the moment. However, he also recognized that this "moment" would not last—nor did he want it to. His mission was elsewhere.

CHAPTER SEVEN

The Library of Alexandria

The three men walked a relatively short, circuitous distance from the complex of palace buildings toward the western half of the city also divided by the broad expanse of the Canopic Way. To Matthias it was all a maze of temples, forums, and shops whose sole purpose seemed more to confuse than to instruct. However, Rabbi Jonas moved undistracted through the crowds and noise until nearing their destination where he stopped, balanced the scrolls he was carrying in the crux of his left arm, and raised his right hand to point directly ahead.

"Alexandria's renowned library," he said with pride. "Quite impressive, is it not?"

Matthias studied his surroundings carefully. Usually the urban areas of cities left him claustrophobic; however, there was something open and almost inviting about the space they just entered. The walkway on which they traveled had suddenly blossomed into a large stone-paved forum dominated by two expansive, columned buildings more Greek than Roman in design with statutes of both Egyptian and Greco/Roman gods standing as silent sentinels. The site was an obvious gathering place for Alexandrians who congregated in clusters as men engrossed themselves in animated discussions. It reminded Matthias of the temple in Jerusalem.

"It is impressive, Rabbi," Matthias responded. "Is this where you study?"

"Yes," the man answered and then started immediately up a tier of broad steps. "Come."

Matthias and Dracus followed dutifully as the rabbi led them into a large, open, three-storied rotunda also congested with numerous assemblages of men, all attempting to outtalk each other. Another statute—this one considerably smaller than those in the forum, but creped in gold with a human form and the head of an ibis—dominated the center of the hall from its place of honor on a black-and-gold-speckled pedestal surrounded by marble benches. The walls of the rotunda were painted with brightly colored murals depicting Egyptian gods in various poses with the ibis-headed figure predominant. Incongruous to this and just inside the entryway was a slightly larger-than-life statue of Julius Caesar, standing proud in his Roman robes, pointing to the various halls and rooms of the library, as if claiming all as his own. And in a sense, it all was, or at the very least, a significant addition to the treasures of Rome.

The rabbi stopped, paid no attention to the arrogant Roman as he gathered the scrolls he was carrying into his lap, and sat on one of the marble benches that surrounded the central statuette. Mathias did likewise, with Dracus standing discreetly to his right.

"If you look carefully, you will see that everything radiates from this one location," Rabbi Jonas said as he turned slowly to emphasize his point. "There are areas of the library dedicated to science, others to the arts, philosophy, historical matters, and one to those that can't be quite categorized." Again, the man nodded his head in different directions.

Matthias looked carefully and saw multiple hallways leading off to other large library spaces, each containing shelves and shelves of scrolls.

"My area of endeavor is located down the hall of philosophy where I suggest we go."

The man stood and abruptly started walking through the columned rotunda toward a hallway off to their right. As they progressed further into the building, Matthias could make out other large, open rooms, each furnished with floor-to-ceiling shelves on which innumerable scrolls were stored. Tables were scattered throughout the open spaces, with men studying unrolled parchments while speaking to others in muted discussion, seemingly oblivious to all other activities that surrounded them.

Finally, the rabbi stopped at an entrance to a large alcove that led off a hallway the man said was dedicated to philosophy, with several tall cabinets built into three of its sides and two large tables anchored at the middle of the room. A dozen or so men of all ages, some in long robes and others in short tunics, milled about the space much the same as those in the other rooms of the library.

"Come," Rabbi Jonas directed. "This is my study area and school. I will introduce you," and he walked past Matthias to stand in the middle of the alcove. His presence caught everyone's attention.

"My friends. If you will give me your attention for a moment." All eyes turned toward the speaker.

"This is Matthias." Rabbi Jonas indicted with his left hand the stranger at his side. "He and his party have recently arrived from Judea. And if I understood him correctly, he is familiar with the one they called a prophet who the Romans crucified."

No one spoke a word. However, it was obvious that all wanted a more-detailed explanation.

Rabbi Jonas smiled in response and turned to Matthias, saying, "If you would introduce yourself and explain your journey, it would help us to understand the events you have experienced."

Matthias took a moment to collect his thoughts. He noticed that Dracus had maneuvered himself to stand just outside the entrance to the alcove.

"My companion and I," he said and nodded in Dracus's direction, "have come from Caesarea Maritima located in Judea at the request of our community. We journey to Ethiopia."

Again, curious stares greeted the commentary. Then one of the men standing at the back of the alcove stepped forward to ask a question.

"From what community do you come? Are you a follower of this prophet?"

Matthias thought carefully before he answered, "I have been sent on a mission to Ethiopia. And yes, the community of which I speak are all followers of the one we call the Master."

A distinct murmur came from those who now surrounded Matthias and the rabbi.

"Why do you call him 'the Master'?" another asked. "He is dead is he not? Are you not a Jew?"

Matthias smiled. He could spend a day answering the three questions just posed to him.

"Yes, I am a Jew. And yes, 'the Master' died. However, he is not dead."

The questioner's response was immediate. "You speak in riddles. How could he still live if he died?"

"That is the wonder I observed. His tomb was empty and He appeared to us in Galilee."

There was a distinct murmur before a tall, robust man stepped forward from the crowd that encircled Matthias to make his statement. "I also understand that he called himself the Son of God," the man charged.

"Yes," Matthias replied with some hesitation.

A moment of silence was followed by audible gasps of disbelief.

"That is blaspheme!" the tall man responded.

Those around Matthias began to move closer as Dracus stepped in from the hallway and inched toward his friend as a measure of protection. Matthias looked to the rabbi for extrication.

"You see, my young friend, this has been a subject of our recent debates," the rabbi explained. "To be a Jew and to also say that this Galilean is the Son of God is incomprehensible! It is contrary to all we teach."

"And what about the stories of his followers eating the flesh and drinking the blood of their sacrificed victims?" another anonymous voice shouted from within the alcove.

Matthias did not respond. However, it was impossible not to sense the hostility that was rapidly developing.

Dracus moved even closer and stood partly between his friend and the rabbi as he put one arm around the waist of Matthias to pull him out of the alcove and into the open hallway. At the same time, another voice was heard above all others, which momentarily broke the tension.

"Rabbi Jonas! Another of your lively discussions, I see. I will have to attend one of your lectures just for its stimulating value."

The speaker was a good-looking, dark-haired, young man with the deportment of one who was used to the exercise of authority. Another, an obvious friend of the interrupting stranger, stood silently at the intruder's elbow and watched the confrontation with obvious interest.

"Gaius Correllius," the rabbi greeted. "I would be honored to have you as a student. Do you know my young friend?" he asked.

"I have not yet had that pleasure," the intruder replied as he smiled over his shoulder at Matthias. "However, I have been sent to rescue him from your cerebral surroundings and bring him back to more mundane matters. Phylos, the merchant, needs his immediate return," and with that, he held out his right arm as he pointed to the exit.

"Certainly," the rabbi answered and stepped back as Matthias and Dracus made a quick move for the open hallway led by Correllius and his friend.

The crowd that circled Matthias hesitantly moved to one side as they followed the departing strangers with angry stares. Rabbi Jonas merely smiled and nodded his acquiescence.

"Quickly!" Correllius instructed in a whisper as he walked ahead of Matthias toward two figures waiting in the shadows not far from the rabbi's classroom.

"Your friends insisted on coming," the unfamiliar male said as he patted the second stranger on his right arm and looked over Matthias's shoulder at the two hidden shapes.

Matthias slowed his pace as he also studied the two cloaked individuals. It was not until they both dropped the hoods which shielded their faces that he recognized Philomena accompanied by her cousin, Dorca.

Before he could say anything, Philomena held out her hand and pointed to a nearby passageway.

"No time for explanations. We just need to leave and quickly. Women are not particularly welcome," she said, and she stepped ahead of the others as they all raced toward a bright light that would be their way out, however, not before taking the hand of the man who called himself Gaius Correllius and squeezing it affectionately.

Matthias was surprised how much the gesture bothered him.

Once outside the building, the two women stopped in front of the columned complex and turned to Matthias.

"Father wants to see you as soon as possible," Philomena explained. "Besides, I suspected your reception by the rabbi and his friends might not quite be what you would have hoped for. Gaius and his friend agreed to help."

She smiled at the taller of the two young men who stood to Matthias's right.

Matthias did not argue. He had come to expect controversy. Actually, he welcomed the interruption as apparently the merchant had received a quick reply from the prefect. They hurried through the busy streets of Alexandria to learn the pleasure of Rome.

The six waited anxiously inside the large canopied shop of Andronicus Phylos. It was apparent that Philomena was not used to suffering the delays of others, including her own father, and she had no hesitation in verbalizing her complaint.

"Where is he!" she demanded. "He said he'd be right here. I have other things to do." She looked obliquely at her cousin as her gaze came to rest on Matthias.

"I forgot to introduce my friends," she said, changing the subject. "The man who rescued you is Gaius Correllius, the son of one of the counselors to the prefect or something like that." She waved her right hand at the dark-haired, young man standing to Matthias's left. "The other is his friend, Leander Aschyllis. We call him Aristotle."

Matthias smiled a greeting while he took a mental assessment of both. The man called Gaius Correllius had distinct, almost-chiseled features, which were accentuated by a too-large nose. Nevertheless, he presented himself well and was obviously held in some esteem as evidenced by his reception at the library. The other, a much smaller, almost-wiry individual with an oblong face and dark-brown eyes that flashed intelligence, was more of an enigma as the man remained mute through most of their encounter. Both returned Matthias's smile and nodded a greeting.

"Ah! Here comes Father," Philomena interrupted.

"Good morning, my children. Or at least I believe it is still morning," the man said hurriedly as he looked past the shadows and at the sunlight that illuminated the street that ran parallel to his shop. "I have good news."

Everyone looked at the man apprehensively.

"The prefect has approved your travels to Kush," the Egyptian explained as he held out his open hand to Matthias. "It seems that your 'gifts' to both my envoy and the government helped expedite matters considerably." Phylos bowed slightly to the Ethiopian.

"This is good news," Matthias responded. "When can we leave?"

The merchant turned from a momentary distraction to confront Matthias again, "I have a caravan leaving for the garrison south of Alexandria in four days. From there, you and your party can travel down to the Nile without much difficulty. In fact, my daughter with a number of my clerks are traveling with the caravan to take inventory of supplies stored at the oasis. It would be opportune if you traveled with them."

"Of course," Matthias responded as he looked back at the Ethiopian, who smiled his approval.

"Good," the Egyptian replied. "It's settled. Until then, I suggest that you experience one of the great cities of the Empire."

Matthias shrugged and said, "Perhaps later. Dracus informs me that there are some in Alexandria who wish to hear of my friend, the Nazarene. I will visit them first."

"As you wish. Now I must get back to more mundane matters. Rome has little patience. Be prepared to leave in four days."

Matthias politely nodded. He would leave today if he could.

CHAPTER EIGHT

The Stadium of Alexandria

Matthias sat conspicuously silent amid a crowd of over fifteen thousand animated spectators as they watched the carnage enfold between wild beasts and gladiators. Although his eyes were wide open to the spectacle, Matthias was consciously focused on the past three days, which were more suited to his temperament.

Through the persistence of two slaves, Dracus was persuaded to bring himself and his mentor to a secret meeting of those interested in Jesus's ministry which discourse convened in a multipurpose, ramshackle building not far from the Egyptian's enclave. Matthias spoke at length of the wonders he had observed. However, what drew the most attention were those experiences immediately leading to Jesus's crucifixion, the resurrection, and Jesus's later appearance to the apostles. Matthias had no explanation for events other than a telling of each as he had witnessed them in as much detail as possible. Although the attendees were acutely aware of the danger in listening to the heresy preached by Matthias, his circle of listeners grew more numerous with each telling so that by the last meeting, more than fifty people crammed themselves into two small rooms to hear the message. Matthias recognized this to be the work of the Master and wanted to continue but knew this was impossible. Consequently, he nursed his regrets until a loud commotion startled him from his musings.

Those seated next to Matthias began to stand and cheer with obvious approval of what was happening in the arena directly in front of them as loud chants of, "Hercules! Hercules!" overtook the crowd. Because the games were financed, in part, by a friend of the

Egyptian's family, Matthias had a position of honor not far from the prefect's representative and his entourage. And he noticed that Philomena and her friend, Gaius Correllius, had joined those who stood waving excitedly while his Ethiopian friend, who was seated to Matthias's right, also stood but remained silent and almost motionless while staring straight ahead.

Matthias strained to see what was causing all the commotion but could only see glimpses of animal carcasses. Then the crowd quieted as the presiding official stood and slowly looked around as shouts of, "Hercules! Hercules!" began again. The official finally signaled that the object of all the attention should step forward as he tossed a ringlet intertwined with leaves to a young, dark-skinned man whose body glistened with sweat and stood below the royal box flanked by two Roman soldiers armed with spears.

"You are their hero, gladiator," the official proclaimed. "Enjoy the moment."

The official then sat down as the crowd again roared its approval.

The one called the gladiator slowly picked up the laurel crown and held it loosely at his side. One of the two guards standing beside him watched the gesture and immediately pulled the man's arm up to his head where he forced the accolade to be displayed. The gladiator did not resist but instead stared expressionless straight ahead. The crowd's roar continued.

Matthias watched the spectacle with curious interest until he noticed that Dracus, who had been standing to his right, was carefully stepping between spectators as he made his way to a nearby exit.

"Where are you going?" Matthias called after his friend.

However, the noise made it impossible to be heard. At this same moment, Matthias caught two armed guards leading the laureled gladiator past a cart that was half filled with dead animals and parked against the wall near an exit close to their section of the stadium. Suddenly shouts of panic erupted from nearby spectators as the arena responded in loud shrieks, with Matthias pushed aside as Philomena and her friend, Gaius Correllius, stumbled toward him. At least three guards also pushed past with swords drawn.

"Out of the way!" one of the armed men shouted as he shoved Matthias into the stands and climbed over a stone bench toward an exit congested with spectators.

Philomena and Correllius were transfixed, as was Matthias who watched the scene unfold: the dark-skinned gladiator had used the cart positioned next to the stadium wall to catapult himself into the stands and make a run for freedom before anyone realized what had happened. It did not take long for the gladiator to sprint over and around bystanders and out the nearest passageway.

Matthias's instinct was to do likewise. However, a hand on his shoulder held him back. The Ethiopian tightened his grip as he imperceptibly shook his head, not to follow but to remain. Matthias did not understand yet complied while others ran in all directions. Moments later the government's official and entourage were escorted past Matthias and out of the arena; it was only then that the Ethiopian relaxed his grip.

"Are you coming?" Philomena hollered over her shoulder. "All the excitement seems to have passed," she added when the noise finally quieted. "Besides, we need to get back and start preparing for tomorrow."

As she spoke, Gaius Correllius took her hand.

Matthias felt guardedly uncomfortable; however, he smiled and nodded that he understood. The Ethiopian had already slipped around him and was walking slowly toward an exit near Philomena. Matthias started to follow when he noticed that Dracus was nowhere to be seen although the man knew they had to make plans for the journey that lie ahead. *How odd*, Matthias thought to himself and then also moved toward a curtain that separated his seat in the stadium from a vaulted passageway. Then something else struck him: the tattooed markings and welts on the body of the renegade gladiator were the same as those of the man inside the cage that greeted them on the streets of Alexandria when they first arrived! A coincidence? Matthias was too much a pragmatist not to be skeptical.

Dracus was beginning to doubt his decision to listen to the pleas of the Ethiopian. In point of fact, it was much more than *listen* as Dracus had agreed to be party to a plot to help free the one they called the gladiator. It appeared that on watching the man parade down the streets of Alexandria, the Ethiopian immediately realized the significance of the welts on this person's chest, marking him as a high official in his own land. Beyond this, the Ethiopian would say nothing more.

The Ethiopian first approached Dracus through his slaves about finding a means to help the gladiator effect an escape. Then the matter became much more personal when, at a meeting of those discussing the life of Jesus, the Ethiopia approached and spoke of the upcoming gladiatorial games. It was suggested that this would be their best opportunity to free the man, and he laid out the broad outline of a plot to bring this about. Dracus's role was simple yet dangerous: he would wait outside the spectator seats with another who would have a hooded robe which Dracus would give to the gladiator and then lead the man out of the arena to a safe hiding place. And all was to be done without the knowledge of Matthias who the Ethiopian did not want to involve for fear of risking the man's mission.

As a consequence, Dracus now stood hidden immediately outside the curtained seats of the stadium. His whole focus was how to get the gladiator from this point to the nearby shops, sites previously used for discussing the ministry of Christ. However, doing all this without the knowledge of Matthias made Dracus feel uncomfortably disloyal.

While reflecting on his conspiratorial role, the passageway from the arena suddenly began to crowd with spectators running to find a stairway as a dark-skinned man burst through the curtained section and hesitated. Dracus immediately pulled the young man to one side as he handed him a cloak. The gladiator slipped into the garment as he pulled the hood over his head, and both ran with the panicked crowd toward an exit.

Once outside the stadium, Dracus grabbed the tall black man by his arm while pointing to an intersecting alley. The two sprinted the short distance to a narrow alley entrance and followed its course through the labyrinth of city buildings as they weaved around shops and stalls until Dracus stopped in front of an establishment crowded with baskets and large clay pots.

They then disappeared into the interior of the shop where they were motioned to a curtained doorway and told to conceal themselves behind the numerous baskets scattered haphazardly about the dirt floor. Noise from the outside world grew as if a violent storm approached and then, as quickly, subsided, leaving them finally alone. An elderly woman who smelled of beans and onions found them and pointed to a stairwell that led to a second-floor room. Both men quickly climbed the stairs that opened to a small, cluttered living area where they were greeted by another holding two bowls of stew and bread. Dracus waved off the proffered food. He wanted nothing more than a return to normalcy, knowing that eventually he would have to give an explanation for his absence. Once he had experienced a similar circumstance, and Matthias had been his means to escape. He had now fulfilled a similar obligation, and the black gladiator was free. Therefore, from this moment, the mission, whatever that entailed, would have to be his paramount concern.

PART TWO

Illumination

CHAPTER NINE

Outside the Eastern Wall of Alexandria

Even at the earliest hours of the day, Alexandria could not escape the heat of a scorching sun as a haze of hot air and dust defined the space occupied by man and beast. Matthias had come to accept this inevitable inconvenience as he searched the horizon for anything familiar until he felt a nudge on his left shoulder.

"Yes, I see him," the young disciple said as he turned to Dracus. "It seems that he is as anxious as we to leave Alexandria."

With this, Matthias started to walk south along a well-traveled path that followed the eastern wall of the city populated with open-air bazaars and shops, which hung heavy with the fragrance of exotic smells and animal dung. Dracus walked only footsteps behind until they finally came to an expansive field where a large herd of camels grazed bordered by a lake that was Alexandria's southern boundary. Their Ethiopian friend was spied near the tethered, humped animals engrossed with a tall robed man, and failed to notice their arrival. When he finally turned and saw Matthias, it brought a smile to the Ethiopian's face.

"This one drives a hard bargain," he said in broken Aramaic. "However, we have come to an understanding." He pointed to the multitude of camels that claimed one area as their own. "I have reserved eight for our use, two for you and your companion. I don't think he trusts many, especially foreigners like myself," to which the Ethiopian volunteered another smile.

Matthias did not have a ready response. He was not used to travel by any means other than by foot. The cost for such a luxury was beyond his experience.

"I am most grateful. However, again, I cannot repay you," Matthias said with considerable embarrassment.

The Ethiopian shook his head and waved Matthias off with a dismissive gesture.

"My queen has the necessary resources and desires to meet knowledgeable men like yourself. She would insist that I pay." He then turned to scour the horizon. "However, I do not see our Egyptian friends. Do you?"

Matthias carefully studied the surrounding shops and staging areas and also did not see the entourage promised by Andronicus Phylos.

"No," he said curtly and then looked at Dracus, as if the man would have an explanation.

Dracus, however, also shook his head.

"Are you bothered by something?" a familiar female voice asked from the interior of a curtained sedan chair that approached down the same footpath used by Matthias. A man on horseback rode close to the woman. "You look puzzled," Philomena continued as she drew back the curtain.

Next to her Gaius Correllius stood out in the full regalia of Alexandria's elite while holding a staff with what appeared to be a red banner wrapped around a pole.

"Not puzzled as much as waiting to be told where to go," Matthias responded.

Philomena shook her head slightly and said, "Our caravan will assemble at the far end of the lake," and she pointed to the distant horizon. "Look for a flag that Gaius will plant at the site." She looked over at her companion, who briefly held up the staff in his right hand. "Expect to leave at noon," Philomena continued. Hearing no objection, she let the curtain fall back, which apparently was a signal to move on, as her two slaves lifted the conveyance and started for the staging site. Correllius followed, acknowledging neither Matthias nor the Ethiopian.

"Did you hear what she said?" Matthias asked his Ethiopian companion, who nodded and then turned abruptly to his right in search of the camel trader.

Then, thinking out loud, Matthias observed, "I really did not expect Philomena's fancy friend to be traveling with us. He just doesn't seem up to the hardships of the desert," and then turned to follow in the way of the Egyptian's daughter.

Dracus picked up his two bundles of supplies and bag of herbs. Still, he had to ask, exactly what were Matthias's true feelings for the girl and her "fancy companion"?

In the time it took Mathias and Dracus to walk the distance to where Gaius Correllius had planted a red banner, quite an assembly was taking place. Several riders on horseback, two or more dozen camels with numerous herders, even a small herd of goats, had congregated at a staging site, all seemingly under the watchful eyes of Philomena and Correllius. Matthias noticed that most of the herders and riders approached the woman first; even the Ethiopian, who appeared from seemingly nowhere, first paid his respects to the girl before setting about his tasks.

"I guess we'd better do likewise," Matthias said over his shoulder to Dracus as he nodded at Philomena and her aide who had positioned themselves under a large canopy.

"Don't want to offend anyone. Why don't you find the Ethiopian and see what needs to be done," Matthias suggested as he quickened his pace to join the growing caravan.

As he turned to walk up a slight incline to greet their Egyptian hosts, Matthias noticed that the Ethiopian was engaged in an animated discussion with one of the herders. Matthias also noticed that, as the two talked, the listener removed his turban, which exposed a head of oddly sculpted, dark hair. The man's stature and commanding bearing reminded him of the gladiator who had escaped from the arena only yesterday. Then Dracus walked up to the two and was greeted warmly by both. *Surely not!* Matthias thought to himself, *the risk would be far too great!* The three men then parted, each going toward other slaves and the camels that surrounded them while Matthias gave his attention to Philomena and her "friend." The young disciple decided that, in this particular matter, his best course of action was to turn a blind eye to everything.

The girl and her male counterpart were deep in conversation when they were distracted by Matthias.

"Are you and your companions ready?" Philomena turned and asked abruptly. "We start shortly. It should take ten to twelve days to get to Lake Moeris. Probably the latter."

She continued.

"My father has arranged to have a contingent of Roman soldiers travel with us, maybe as many as fifty men, which should dissuade the bandits who frequent our route south."

Matthias smiled politely. He simply could not imagine Correllius involved in any situation other than polite local intrigue in which he held the upper hand, certainly nothing that was life-threatening such as fighting off armed bandits.

"I will be ready," Matthias answered in as reassuring a tone as he was capable. "As will the Ethiopian. We appreciate being allowed to travel with you."

"It is as Father wishes who will be here as soon as he can get away to see that all goes well," Philomena responded, unintentionally seeming to dismiss Matthias as an unwelcomed burden. Trying to correct herself, she added, "We will talk more once we are beyond the city. There is still much I would like to hear of your Master and the events in Judea."

Matthias again nodded politely. He then turned to locate his friends and felt a sense of exhilaration as the journey to the land of Kush was about to begin in earnest.

CHAPTER TEN

Matthias looked up at the expansive night sky that enveloped the desert which surrounded him and for a moment longed to walk again with the Master and his disciples as they crossed the Judean hills on their journey to Jerusalem. There were similarities between that experience and this, not the least of which was the sense of awe at being connected to all things as the words of the Master gave reassurance and hope to a new life. "Follow me!" was the mantra so easy to accept; now Matthias was overcome with doubts. Why him, the son of another poor Galilean, being sent on such an important mission far from any world he knew? What could he offer? The questions persisted, and only the stillness and beauty of the night gave him the peace he so desired as he recollected a similar world in fellowship with Jesus.

The three-day journey to their present encampment had not been particularly difficult with the last vestiges of city life and lush vegetation passing away, with only occasional suggestions of a forgotten monument or structure on the horizon. Now their world was built of sand enveloped by the cobalt blue of a night sky perforated by stars and a waning moon. Matthias understood this world, and it gave him peace.

The solitude was suddenly disturbed by the excited shouts of a female.

"Help me, someone!" a woman cried. "He has been stung by a scorpion!"

The outcry came from Philomena, who came running from her tent toward the center of the compound. Several men already surrounded the girl by the time Matthias arrived.

"Help me, please!" she implored as she watched the young disciple join the circle of onlookers.

"Who has been stung?" Matthias asked as he ran with the woman to her tent.

Once inside and an oil lamp was lit, he found Gaius Correllius laying prone on a carpet with his right leg raised and a very noticeable red wound rising on the man's lower calf. He was in obvious pain.

"The pain won't stop. Can you do something?" Correllius was barely able to ask through clinched teeth.

"Stand back, please," Matthias said as he motioned the curious away while searching the tent for Dracus.

"Has anyone seen my friend?" he asked, to which there was no response.

Not knowing what else to do, he asked Philomena for a sharp knife and said, "We need to open the wound and suck out the poison."

At that time, two men entered the tent, one being Dracus who was closely followed by a tall, young, dark-skinned man dressed only in a long, flowing robe with his sculpted hair uncovered. It was the same person that Matthias spied talking with the Ethiopian on the day they left Alexandria; Matthias was also certain that this was the same man who escaped from the Roman games.

The two moved closer to Correllius as the dark-skinned stranger opened his hand for the knife proffered by Philomena. The girl was near panic.

"Who is this person?" she asked behind tears.

Matthias stared up at the stranger as the Ethiopian appeared and reassured Matthias of the man's skills.

The young disciple signaled for Philomena to let the man have the knife, and she hesitantly complied.

"I feel we can trust this one," Matthias said, looking into the eyes of the stranger, as Correllius moaned in pain. "Now, we all need to move away. Please!" He motioned again with both hands that everyone should step outside the tent.

Matthias remained, as did Philomena and Dracus while they watched the tall black man bend over Correllius's leg and cut into the inflamed wound. The man then sucked the incision for a short period of time, spitting each mouthful of saliva and poison onto the carpeted floor. He then looked around at his surroundings and, on spotting a bowl jumped to his feet, grabbed the object and raced out of the tent. Philomena began to brush Correllius's forehead and arms with cool water from a basin she had earlier placed next to a sleeping pallet as Correllius continued to moan in pain; only now the man began to sweat profusely, which Philomena answered by redoubling her efforts.

Then, in what seemed an interminable period of time yet was probably only minutes, the dark-skinned stranger returned with a bowl full of what looked like paste and dirt and began to apply the mixture to the wound; after which he tightly bound the application with strips of cloth torn from a robe hanging in the tent. Correllius lied back, barely conscious.

"What now?" Philomena asked meekly. "Could you use your special powers to help."

Matthias noticed the desperation in the woman's voice.

"Of course, I will say prayers for him," Matthias replied, sincerely concerned. "Perhaps you, also, can soothe the pain by continuing to administer the cool cloth."

The stranger affirmed this suggestion by stepping between Matthias and Philomena and pantomiming the wiping of a wet cloth across Correllius's forehead. Philomena repeated the process immediately. At the same time, Matthias bent down and touched the bandaged wound as he whispered a silent prayer. Then, stepping outside the tent, he found the Ethiopian standing alone and watching the scene unfold while carefully observing the comings and goings of the few Roman soldiers who were interested in the event.

"Who is your friend?" Matthias asked, nodding at the dark-skinned man who remained inside the tent as he hovered over his patient.

The Ethiopian did not respond; he just stared at those around him. Eventually he turned to leave.

However, before returning to his assigned area, he managed a smile and said only, "He is one who knows. You can trust."

He then walked into the shadows of the night.

Matthias was now even more confused. He had no better idea of who the dark-skinned stranger was than before other than he was known to the Ethiopian and had some pretense to medicinal cures. Of course, Matthias hoped that the man's efforts proved successful.

He also hoped that the Romans never had the same suspicions as he of who traveled with their small band across the deserts of Egypt.

Early next morning Matthias's first priority was to check on Philomena and her companion. There had been no further disruptions, which Matthias hoped was a good sign.

On reaching Philomena's tent, he stopped near the closed flap, looked for assurance from one of Philomena's slaves who was busy cooking over an open fire, and was given an approving nod. So he entered as unobtrusively as possible. Philomena was sleeping next to Correllius, his head cradled in her lap, balanced against a pillow, both looking at peace. Matthias did not want to disturb either, so he turned to leave.

"Wait!" Philomena snapped as she gently laid Correllius's head on the pillow and stood.

"He slept all night," she began, "but I know when he wakes, he will be too weak to travel. What can we do? The Romans are not going to wait," she added.

"I will have to check with the Ethiopian. How long do you think it will be before he can travel?"

"At least two more days," Philomena replied. "I will do my best. He is lucky to be alive. Speaking of which, where did that tall black man learn such skills? He is a treasure. Is he traveling with you?"

"He's with the Ethiopian. I know nothing more. And I will get back to you when I have spoken of this to my foreign friend."

Philomena nodded as she turned to Correllius and brushed his forehead. The man moaned and tried to raise his right arm but was too weak to do much more than open his eyes. The girl called to one of her slaves, who brought a bowl of hot broth into the tent; the contents of which were prescribed by the stranger which Philomena raised up to Correllius's lips as she tried to spoon the liquid into his mouth. She was only partially successful.

"I will return as soon as I have an answer," Matthias said as he pushed aside the flap to the tent. "What I do will depend on what the Ethiopian says."

As for himself, without saying it to Philomena, he had mixed feelings.

Surprisingly, the Ethiopian was agreeable to hold back for at least two days in order to give Correllius an opportunity to recover. This also afforded the stranger an opportunity to continue his medicinal treatments. It was debated whether it would be wiser for Philomena and Correllius to return to Alexandria rather than continue on to Lake Moeris. However, if Philomena decided to return home, the Ethiopian did not want to follow. He wanted to continue on to Kush.

As it turned out, Philomena agreed to continue south if only because no one would escort her back to Alexandria. Even three of Correllius's friends who had attached themselves to the caravan opted to continue on with the Romans, a calculation most likely made in hopes of protection from bandits. This meant that Matthias and the Ethiopian would join Philomena and Correllius with their contingent of slaves and herders along with a friend of Correllius who remained to face whatever dangers that lie ahead. It was a precarious situation, yet doable. Matthias calculated that with the Romans gone, they at least would not be questioned about the dark-skinned stranger—which in itself was a blessing.

CHAPTER ELEVEN

After three days of inactivity, Gaius Correllius insisted that they break camp; although it was obvious that he barely had the strength to ride. Therefore, the caravan of camels and horses moved slowly across the desert in the early hours just after dawn taking advantage of the coolest part of the day. Philomena did her best to maneuver herself and her horse as close to Correllius as possible in order to help steady his gait, which was made all the more difficult as Correllius did his best to fend her off. Regardless, they made slow but steady progress toward Lake Moeris and had hopes of reaching the Roman enclave the following week. Matthias especially came to appreciate the organizational skills of the man Philomena called Aristotle, the one friend of Correllius who remained to help navigate their weary lot through the desert. Now, as they were about to make camp at a fortuitous oasis, a different, more-ominous problem arose brought home by one of the herders who pointed anxiously at two dark, stationary figures silhouetted near the top of a distant dune.

"Bandits!" the man hollered.

"Quiet!" the one Philomena called Aristotle responded. "We can see for ourselves," he snapped as he shaded his eyes and looked to where the herder was gesturing. "Actually, they've been watching us for some time. Obviously, they're in no hurry."

Aristotle then turned and entered a small tent erected next to Philomena, with both adjacent to the Ethiopian who claimed his piece of the oasis by unrolling two rugs under a palm tree. The rest of the crew, including Matthias, were scattered haphazardly around an ancient well, finding whatever shade they could as they watered, fed, and hobbled their animals and prepared a place to rest out of the sun. A goat cut from the dozen or so remaining was sacrificed for an evening meal. Nevertheless, the earlier alarm was never far from anyone's thoughts.

In short order the Greek reappeared with Correllius stumbling after him as both looked toward the eastern horizon. Philomena followed but said nothing.

"I don't see anyone," Aristotle said. "They're either in hiding or have given up for the day."

"Unlikely," Correllius speculated. "This would be the perfect time to lay a trap. What do you think we should do?"

Before Aristotle could answer, another herder came running into the center of the camp and pointed south.

"Someone's coming!" he yelled.

Aristotle took a step forward. Before he could comment, two men on horseback were among them, scattering several herders away from the well, while others backed into the shadows of late afternoon. Correllius, Philomena, and Aristotle watched silently, as did Matthias and the Ethiopian.

"Romans!" someone was heard to say under their breath as Aristotle started after the two figures. However, Correllius caught him with his right arm and held him back. He would confront their visitors.

"Welcome, my friends," he said, raising his hand in a salute as he approached the two riders who had dismounted and were washing their faces with cool water. "Do you journey far?"

There was no immediate response. One of the two men finally turned from the well and carefully studied his environment.

"We will camp here tonight," the uniformed man said to no one in particular. Then, turning to Correllius, he continued, "You and your lot will have to move to allow for my men. Whose tent is that?" he asked, pointing at the one raised by Philomena and shaded by overhead palms.

"It belongs to myself and my companion," Correllius replied as he motioned at Philomena. "My name is Gaius Correllius, and this is my friend, Leander Aschyllis. My other associate is the daughter of an Alexandrian trader. We travel from Alexandria to Lake Moeris on the warrant of the prefect in the hopes of trade." He added the latter to set the boundaries of his position. "Make whatever use you want of this site. We continue on in the morning. And once you have established yourselves, why don't you and your companion join us for a meal."

"Perhaps," the man answered. Then, noticing that the other rider had remounted and was riding slowly toward the south, he added, "I have twenty men to bivouac. When that is done, we'll talk." Wasting no time, he also mounted and rode slowly south as the silhouette of a line of men marching toward the oasis barely came into view.

Correllius turned to Aristotle and Philomena and said, "I guess we're going to have company. At least we don't have to worry about an attack." Then, noticing Matthias and the Ethiopian standing off to his right but within earshot, he added, "I'm sorry. However, you'll have to move. The Romans aren't ones to debate the niceties of 'who was first'."

Matthias shook off any objections, as did the Ethiopian. They both were used to accommodating others. Besides, there was some consolation in the safety of Roman protection—whether Rome knew it was being provided at its expense or not.

The Ethiopian was quick to return to his property and order its relocation to the boundary where the oasis began. Matthias did the same. They both were more concerned with completing a journey that lie more than a thousand miles to the south.

The night passed uncomfortably for most. As expected, the band of twenty Roman soldiers and their two leaders displaced the site previously occupied by Matthias and his fellow travelers. Only Philomena, Correllius, and Aristotle were able to keep their original claim intact. The soldiers even confiscated the goat that had been sacrificed and skewered for that evening's meal. Gambling and drinking went on well into the night with the occasional loud outburst of laughter, disturbing any real hope of sleep. However, the most disquieting circumstance was the unspoken threat to Philomena who, being the only woman in camp, naturally drew the soldiers' attention, especially as the level of alcohol consumption increased. Innuendoes were inevitable, and on several occasions both Correllius and Aristotle felt the need to remind the two Roman leaders of their positions within the government.

Eventually the hint of dawn broke on the horizon, and a quick decision was made by Correllius to break camp and leave for Lake Moeris as soon as possible. Correllius noted that although the night might have been difficult because of the Romans, they, nevertheless, did not face the threat of bandits, and that in and of itself was reward enough. Regardless, no one questioned that an early departure was in their best interest, and all set about the task of breaking camp accordingly. By the time a new sun blazed over the dunes, the small caravan of traders was well on its way to Lake Moeris.

CHAPTER TWELVE

Both Gaius Correllius and the one called Aristotle were relieved that a day had passed in open desert without incident or even the suggestion of trouble; the night hours were more of the same, where a quiet monotony gave reassurance of safety. Therefore, it was somewhat startling when early the next morning one of the herders and a forward scout reported sighting several riders paralleling their trek. This did not bode well. However, for the time being, both men opted to keep the warning to themselves so not to panic others. Nevertheless, it was not long before everyone knew of the unidentified riders and began to question their significance.

"Are they bandits?" Philomena asked pointedly as she rode up on her horse to confront Correllius.

"I don't know," the man answered truthfully as they both reined to a stop. "I suppose it's possible."

"What are we going to do about it then?"

"What can we do?" Correllius replied, leaning forward with one hand on the withers of his horse for balance. He still felt occasional pain from his wound. "We continue moving south, I guess. Perhaps they decide that we have nothing worthwhile to steal."

"So you do believe that they are bandits," she countered. "Shouldn't we at least prepare and arm ourselves? Maybe there are more of us than they want to take on."

"Anything is possible. However, moving closer to the garrison at Lake Moeris is probably our best defense. They already backed away once."

"We had Romans in our camp then. And we still have at least two more days to travel," she added pointedly.

Correllius nodded and said nothing in reply. He knew he could not win this argument; in fact, he was as worried as she but did his best to hide his concern.

They both started a slow ride as the caravan moved past, looking to the horizon to assess the danger. Nothing stood out.

"Have they gone?" Philomena asked, somewhat surprised.

Correllius merely shrugged his shoulders and remained silent as he continued to survey the dunes. The only thing he noticed was a slight breeze from the west that was a welcomed relief. Philomena took his failure to answer as a rebuke and spurred past him in order to ride nearer to the head of the column. For Correllius, this was another burden he did not have to deal with, if only temporarily.

Although vigilant, the caravan's movement continued without incident until they finally stopped in the early afternoon for a brief rest. Aristotle joined his friend as they assessed their circumstance.

"I think I know why we lost our traveling companions," Aristotle said as he led his horse next to Correllius and offered the animal a bucket half-filled with water.

"Why is that?"

"The herders are worried about the wind that has been blowing our way. They say this could mean trouble. They also suspect that the bandits believe the same and have moved on."

"You are full of good news, aren't you?"

"I do my best," Aristotle replied and smiled.

At that same time, a gust of wind with blowing sand swirled through the stalled caravan.

Correllius looked west and suddenly lost all the color in his normally ruddy face. A brown-gray billowing cloud that stretched as far as the eye could see was approaching fast. One of the herders came running in panic while pointing to the horizon.

"Storm!" was all that could be understood as the man hurried off to warn others.

"We need to take cover! Fast!" Correllius snapped as he climbed up on his horse and rode for the head of the column. In route he passed Matthias, Dracus, and the Ethiopian who already had taken shelter behind camels while pulling robes over their heads. Correllius rode on until he reached Philomena, who had dismounted from her horse but stood transfixed by the approaching phenomenon.

"Pull your horse down and lay beside it!" he hollered. "This is not going to be good. Try to cover the horse's head with something. You do the same." To emphasize what he said, Correllius dismounted and led his horse to Philomena and motioned for her to follow his example. He was able to pull his horse to the ground; however, Philomena had to let her animal go. They struggled to pull a robe over their heads and another over the horse.

Sand whipped by an unrelenting wind began to bury the band of traders in dunes indistinguishable from the desert that surrounded them. It took nearly an hour for the storm to abate. Finally, Correllius was able to dig his way out of the windswept sand, as did Philomena.

"You all right?" he asked as he awkwardly pulled his horse to its feet.

"Yes," Philomena answered. "However, I had to let my horse go. It fought too hard."

"It happens. Why don't you stay here and help the herders reassemble the column? I'll ride to the back of the caravan and see how much damage was done."

"All right," she replied while brushing her clothing and taking her first hard look at their environment.

It seemed that they were in a valley surrounded by mountains of sand as Philomena watched camels and herders slowly emerged into the daylight. It was miraculous that anything survived, she thought.

Correllius, on the other hand, had been through storms such as this before and knew that survival meant quick action. Camels were accustomed to the vicissitudes of the desert and could take it all in stride. However, that was not the same for other stock such as horses, which could easily be suffocated by the blowing sand. He was thankful that his horse did not bolt. Philomena and Aristotle were not as fortunate. At least there was no loss of life and very minor damage to property. For this they needed to be grateful. Indeed, one could almost say that the gods had looked down on them favorably, which made him momentarily consider the presence of Matthias and his companion. If he was a religious man, he would perhaps see more to this coincidence than was actually warranted.

For his part, Matthias was well aware of the danger they had providentially avoided but said nothing to suggest that he attributed their good fortune to anything other than the quick thinking on the part of both Correllius and his friend. He did not want to distract from his sole purpose—to get to the land of the Ethiopian. Yet he knew firsthand the powers of the Master and how events could be altered. Indeed, he had witnessed many unexplained incidents, including the feeding of the multitude, the healing of the sick, even the raising of the dead. However, if he took the opportunity to draw conclusions, he might endanger the mission, even lead others to accuse him of sorcery. After all, this was Egypt, where life itself was subservient to magic and stone-headed gods. And he did not yet have a taste to challenge these ingrained superstitious beliefs. He would wait. In two days, they should arrive at Lake Moeris. The Ethiopian said from there they would find a boat to take them up the Nile River. To Matthias's way of thinking, it was all in the Master's hands anyway.

Surprisingly, the trek to Lake Moeris went as predicted and took the balance of one day and most of the next to complete. There were no surprises, no bandits to threaten the caravan's progress; although everyone was on edge and on guard. Both Philomena and Aristotle had to suffer the indignity of riding camels to complete the journey, which did wonders for their dispositions. It all came to an end when, during late afternoon on the second day out from the storm, the fractured column approached the outskirts of Arsinoe located on the southern bank of Lake Moeris. It almost became a race to see who could reach the gates of the city first, where the camels could be unpacked and led to fresh water in the surrounding pastures.

For the moment, at least, their desert existence had come to an end.

CHAPTER THIRTEEN

Dockside at Arsinoe on the Nile Tributary

Almost too quickly Matthias, Dracus, and the Ethiopian with his entourage were dockside, ready to board a relatively large boat that would take them up a tributary of the Nile River and closer to the kingdom of Kush. In fact, it was shortly after their arrival in Arsinoe that Aristotle announced his family had a long-standing arrangement with a local pilot to provide transport when needed to the upper Nile, specifically the region near the first cataract of the river. It seemed that family business included trade from the surrounding hills and beyond.

Therefore, Aristotle was anxious to continue their journey; and having offered passage to Matthias and his Ethiopian friend, at daybreak the following day the three along with the gladiator stood conspicuously out of place near the loading platforms of several boats. It took the intervention of Aristotle to point out their transport, a large vessel constructed in the traditional Egyptian manner with raised bow and keel, a large paddle for steering, and a sail affixed to a mast midship. Men were already loading supplies and odd-shaped containers when Aristotle suggested that they also board.

"The pilot wants to get into the channel before the others," Aristotle said almost apologetically. "It can be tight going down this tributary of the river. However, it has been done for ages. I told him we were ready."

He looked apprehensively at the small group standing in the center of the dock as everyone nodded in agreement.

"Good," Aristotle said as he turned to locate his friend, Correllius.

Philomena had opted to stay with her father's emissaries in Arisone, which disappointed Matthias.

"We will be in contact," Aristotle said, holding out his arm to Correllius as a gesture of friendship.

The man grasped the other's forearm and said, "To the future."

"To the future!" Aristotle enthusiastically responded as he turned quickly and started for a gangplank that led to the main deck of the boat.

Matthias and the Ethiopian did likewise as slaves carried the last of the supplies onboard. At that same time, a contingent of ten Roman soldiers boarded the vessel. Then, as fast as the gangplank could be pulled onto the boat's deck, five slaves pushed the vessel away from the dock and into the tributary's main channel. The crew then raised the one large sail in order to harness favorable northerly winds as the boat slowly began the journey south.

Matthias stood silently on deck, watching the crew's efforts as the vessel glided away from Arsinoe and Lake Moeris. Their short stay did not afford him the opportunity to fairly judge their environment other than that it was an obvious Roman outpost with extensive cultivated fields radiating out from a large saltwater lake. Stone temples and monuments abounded with the most notable being dedicated to a local crocodile deity. Matthias had not seen evidence of these so-called river monsters that were said to infest the region. However, he took no chances and avoided the waterfront until absolutely necessary. Now, watching the banks on either side of the narrow waterway brighten with the dawn of a new day, it was obvious that they were entering a strange and unfamiliar world.

"Not like anything you've ever experienced before, is it?" the vaguely familiar voice said in Matthias's right ear. "I've taken this journey many times, and each has been a wonder in its own right." The speaker was the bearded face of the trader, Aristotle, who moved closer to Matthias before leaning against a rail on the starboard side of the boat.

"For instance, take that complex of buildings over there," he continued and pointed to three structures anchored to the desert and just beginning to be illuminated by the morning sun as the surrounding landscaped morphed into lush green vegetation fed by waters from the narrow tributary. "I cannot remember seeing any one of those before, and this is just a foretaste of what is to come. Wait until we begin the journey up the main channel of the river."

For his part, Matthias did not quite know what to say. Until recently, the trader had remained relatively aloof; and when he did converse, it usually was with others present—certainly not a one-on-one encounter.

"I don't know what to make of it," Matthias finally replied, looking straight ahead and not making eye contact with the trader. "You are right, though. This land is unique."

Aristotle watched Matthias silently for a long moment.

He then turned his back to the passing landscape and observed, "You know, there is talk that you and your god had more to do with our safe passage through the desert than is realized."

Matthias did not reply immediately but instead watched the facades of three more monumental buildings blossom into giant multicolored depictions of Egyptian deities and kings. He then slowly turned and looked squarely at the Alexandrian.

"I am no different than any other man. It is the Master who uses me if he so wills."

Aristotle was not sure what to say, but he responded, "All I know is that Correllius should not have recovered so quickly. And both the Roman soldiers and the sandstorm saved us from certain attack by bandits. It was as if we were destined to complete our journey. I could not speak to my gods and expect the same results."

Matthias merely smiled and shrugged his shoulders. He was glad to be interrupted by Dracus who offered him a large piece of bread and some fruit.

"Eat well, my friend," Aristotle said, pushing away from the boat's rail. "We will talk more later," he said and strode off toward the bow of the boat.

Again, Matthias's attention was drawn to the passing landscape and the myriad of monuments and structures that appeared to float effortlessly past as the boat cut a path through the narrow channel to the south. Men were stirring along the banks of the tributary as they began their daily chores of gathering water into basins and jars or lifting the life-giving fluid by weighted mechanisms into irrigation ditches. It was a foreign world, which momentarily drew on Matthias's curiosity. Then, as they moved further downriver, the thought occurred to him that this land was ruled over by an untold number of cold stone deities, and he asked himself, "Would men like Aristotle ever learn the truth?" He had many more weeks before he could begin to tell the Master's story. Patience was what he needed at the moment.

It took two days of careful sailing, avoiding collision with boats maneuvering themselves upriver, each laden with grain and other supplies, to reach the prosperous administrative community of Oxyrhynchus. Matthias was informed that the town was named after a local sharp-snouted fish that was worshipped by the locals; it also served as another garrison for the Romans. Many temples, especially those influenced by the Greeks, dominated the site. Their arrival signified that the journey down this tributary of the Nile was nearly half over.

"We will be here two days," Aristotle informed him. "You might warn your Ethiopian friend that the Romans routinely check all foreigners for contraband and runaway slaves."

Matthias appreciated the caution, and he would discuss the circumstance with his Ethiopian companion. However, as important was the respite gave him a chance to wander, again, on dry land. He hated to admit it, but confinement to the perimeters of a boat, even one as large as the one they sailed, had no appeal for him.

The first day in port was uneventful, which Matthias used as an opportunity to visit the local Jewish community and cautiously discuss his association with the Master. He also discussed what to expect further upriver. The Ethiopian said that he would use the time to replenish his store of supplies which Matthias and Dracus opted to do likewise. However, it was the second day that almost ended the trek to Kush.

From the beginning, everyone did their best to avoid contact with the Romans. However, the man that the Ethiopian had befriended and taken under his wing chose now to confront a slave auctioneer in the heart of the city, who was offering several black men for sale. It seemed that the Ethiopian's friend knew the tribe from which two of the slaves were captured and wanted to disrupt the sale by any means possible. The commotion not unexpectedly drew the attention of a contingent of Romans, and it was not until the intervention of Aristotle and his repeated assertion of a connection to the prefect with a promise to administer twenty lashes to the disruptor that the soldiers released the gladiator back into Aristotle's custody. It also helped that several gold coins passed from the Ethiopian to the Roman authorities.

Early next morning, before the break of dawn, the boat slipped dock and headed into the channel that would take them south. For most, including Matthias, the continuation of the journey did not come any too soon.

CHAPTER FOURTEEN

Nile River

The large vessel lumbered slowly up the Nile River as both passengers and crew adjusted to the routines of river life. It had been four days since they departed the garrison at Oxyrhynchus and made the transition from tributary to the Nile proper and began the less-lugubrious trek upriver. The prevailing northerly winds held, and the boat moved with relative ease, counter to the natural current unlike other vessels moving downstream, which had to employ oarsmen in order to navigate. At dusk they made landfall and awaited dawn before continuing south in order to avoid hidden obstacles such as tree limbs, hippopotamus, and crocodiles.

Matthias found himself alternating between both sides of the boat as he considered the sights that presented themselves to the passing traveler. He, as many before him, was overwhelmed by the sheer number and colossal scale of the monuments erected by the Egyptians over the centuries. However, he also reminded himself that this was a land where Jews were once enslaved and only escaped through the intervention of God. Indeed, to Matthias's way of thinking, the magnificence of the passing temples and obelisks erected to commemorate dead kings and stone-faced gods in actuality offered little; and he could not help but wonder, as they sailed farther from the world he knew into this strange, bewitching land of gold and demons, what he, one man, could offer to counter the traditions of centuries.

"At it again, I see," a now-familiar voice said over Matthias's shoulder.

Matthias turned and smiled. Aristotle stood to his right dressed in a loose, nondescript full-body robe not unlike the one worn by himself.

"Impressive, aren't they?" Aristotle continued. "Makes one wonder how they could have managed to build such magnificent structures."

As he spoke, the boat passed two large pharaohs carved in granite, guarding the entrance to another temple. It was obvious that at one time all were multicolored and inscribed with various hieroglyphs.

"Where do you worship your god?" the man asked, obviously curious. "Is it the same temple that Philomena speaks of in Jerusalem?"

Matthias thought for a moment. It never occurred to him that others might consider Christ to be one of a pantheon of gods; in fact, he never really thought of the Master as "a god," period.

"We really don't think of the Master that way," he answered. "Our one God is the same as that of the Jews, so I suppose that the temple in Jerusalem is our place of worship too."

"Then what is there about this Christ which makes you so dedicated? I saw how you behaved in the desert, remaining apart from the others, and to be honest, you are woefully out of place. Even the Romans and my people, the Greeks, have come to terms with this lot." Aristotle waved his right hand at the passing sights revealed at the river's edge. "We at least pay some homage to the local deities."

Matthias just smiled although deep in thought. He could not explain the extraordinary bond he felt with the Master or the sense of purpose, even obligation, he had for his "mission."

Aristotle awaited an answer which did not come.

"That's all right," the man finally said. "I won't push you on the matter. Besides, the pilot informs me that tomorrow we come into the waters around Thebes, which once was the center of all life in Egypt. It seems that we are fortunate enough to arrive at a time when the god, Amun, is to be honored. I hope you and your companions won't be so put off that you refuse to accompany me to the festival that takes place here every year. It is quite a spectacle."

Matthias hesitated for a moment before he accepted the invitation.

"Good!" Aristotle responded as he slapped his new friend on the shoulder. "Until tomorrow then," he said and walked off to enjoy the shade offered by the canopied center of the boat.

Matthias again stood alone as he watched the Greek depart into the shadows and then turned to the passing shoreline and the inevitable panoply of monoliths and colonnaded temples. Perhaps he was "woefully out of place," however, at one time or another, so were all who followed this same path.

Early the next morning, barely at the break of dawn, Matthias and Dracus stood near the bow of the boat with the Ethiopian to their right and the black gladiator to their left. All watched with anticipation as other boats began to anchor nearby and discharge passengers who crowded a well-worn footpath that snaked along the eastern bank of the river and terminated within the environs of Thebes.

"What do you know of this place?" Matthias asked the Ethiopian, surprised that he was insistent on witnessing this spectacle to an Egyptian god.

However, before the man could answer, Aristotle appeared from under the boat's canopy dressed in a scarlet robe intertwined with silver threads and accented by a silver cord tied at the waist. He also wore a small black brimless hat trimmed in silver. It was as elaborate a costume as Matthias had even seen the man wear.

"I surprise you, my young prophet," Aristotle said, standing back a bit and letting his wardrobe have its full effect. "I dress for the occasion, so to speak," he said and laughed. "Have you heard of the god Amun?"

Matthias shook his head.

"I thought not. He is one of the principal deities revered throughout Egypt, and we are approaching his temple. The celebration that began yesterday or the day before is called the Opet Festival, which marks the beginning of the rise of the Nile River and the high holy days of Amun, a god of strength and fertility. It is a joyous time for all Egyptians."

Matthias stood silent as he listened to his new friend. The man was obviously sincere in his excitement and expected a similar response from everyone else. This was truly a momentous occasion and not only to this Greek. Both the Ethiopian and the black gladiator were similarly enthused.

"So are you still coming ashore?" Aristotle asked in a tone that warned of finality.

Matthias nodded affirmatively as he pointed Dracus toward a narrow board that led to the riverbank. Aristotle led the way surrounded by two slaves with Matthias and Dracus close on their heels. The Ethiopian and the gladiator navigated the plank somewhat more cautiously in part due to the elaborate robe worn by the Ethiopian in honor of the occasion. Once on shore, all followed Aristotle as he joined the crowds heading south along the footpath that paralleled the river.

After a short distance, Aristotle stopped and pointed to the top of a steep embankment.

"We need to get up there," he said as he broke away from the others and hurried up the high slope. Everyone from the boat followed.

Once on top of the man-made hill, what laid before them was breathtaking by any standard. Although the upper heights of several gateways to multiple temples could be seen from the river, nothing prepared one for the spectacle at hand. From north to south, for almost as far as the eye could see, was an expanse of columned buildings with soaring pylons and massive stone-hewed representations of kings and gods standing guard over each. The distance between three of the complexes was measured by seemingly hundreds of either ram-headed or human-headed sphinxes. Bright colors illuminated the exploits of gods and man while columns of white smoke emitted from exterior altars pierced the bright morning sky. And people, to be numbered in the thousands, either crammed the open courtyards of the largest temples or pressed to stand as near as possible to a sphinx-lined walkway that connected the two complexes with a boat slip not far from where Aristotle stood. Then, from seemingly nowhere, a large, elaborately decorated boat with a white curtain canopy appeared with loin-clothed men holding bronze swords standing guard so to prevent the curious from boarding. The prevailing atmosphere was one of joy and celebration even at this early hour, and Matthias noticed that both Aristotle and the Ethiopian raised their hands and bowed slightly on witnessing the spectacle.

"We should try and get as close as we can to the anchorage over there," Aristotle said, pointing to another man-made dock in front of a smaller temple located some distance downstream. "That is where they will come," he said without further explanation.

Matthias had no clue as to what the man was referring; however, he allowed himself to be caught up by the excitement of the moment and followed dutifully. Once near the slip where they had a view of both the dock and a promenade that led to the lesser temple, Aristotle stopped and again pointed toward the river.

"They will dock here," he said matter-of-factly, "and the gods will be carried up that walkway."

As he spoke, he swung his arm toward a columned temple to their left as the crowd grew rapidly. However, everyone seemed attentive to each other. This was a day of celebration, not confrontation.

Matthias stood silent, as did Dracus who watched without questions. Matthias really did not know what to ask. Then all attention turned toward the promenade that led from the smaller temple to the nearby dock as a contingent of loin-clothed soldiers—some carrying spears and others swords—led a parade of who Matthias presumed were priests, all dressed in white robes with two cloaked in leopard skins, down a brick walkway to the river. Once at the dock, the contingent stopped with the soldiers positioning themselves on the river's edge to face the crowds as the priests looked downriver. Matthias noticed that three tripods with bronze-colored basins had been placed strategically at the edge of the promenade, away from the slip, each emitting a trail of white smoke. The sounds of excitement rose in unison as the whole assembly pushed toward the river's edge, and Matthias was no different as he strained to see what had caught the interest of those around him.

Looking over the heads of many, he caught glimpses of a golden boat moving slowly upriver toward a dock that led to the smaller temple. He was perfectly positioned to witness the large vessel maneuver into a slip that had been cut from the Nile and anchor with white-robed priests again facing the raptured crowd. Earlier he had seen the boat from a distance; however, he was unprepared for the extravagance of the vessel's outward appearance. Both panels of the bow and stern were painted with various scenes depicting Egyptian deities; two side panels affixed to the stern, one of a lion and the other of a cow, appeared to be made of solid gold. And like their boat, an enclosure had been built around the mast. However, unlike their vessel, the enclosure was both painted with scenes of gods in various poses with gold outlining the whole. Golden masks of unrecognized images decorated the tops of two large rudders.

As soon as the boat anchored, one of the priests wearing a leopard skin went onboard and greeted another also dressed in white with a leopard skin draped around his shoulders. The two men disembarked and turned to watch as three small golden barks each with a golden statuette were lifted by four loin-clothed bearers and carried ashore. A procession immediately started up a grand promenade that terminated at the smaller temple, led by soldiers and followed by priests carrying incense vessels. Other priests carried the three golden statuettes ensconced on golden barks as all began to chant some unintelligible verse.

The crowd was deliriously raptured as once again both Aristotle and the Ethiopian held up their hands and bowed as the procession passed with Aristotle's scarlet-and-silver robe shimmering in the full light of day. Matthias could barely make out that one of the statutes depicted an Egyptian male wearing the crown of a pharaoh while holding a staff of office, another was a woman crowned with a vulture headdress, and the third image was of a mummified young man holding a golden rod.

Aristotle turned to his young friend.

"In case you wonder, the first statue is Amun, our creator. The second, his consort, Mut, the Egyptian mother goddess. And the third, Khonsu, their son, a god of healing. Is your god revered like this?"

Matthias did not know how to respond. He had spent much of his youth following a man others called "the Son of God," and now he was one of the appointed called upon to deliver Christ's message. Silence to Aristotle's question was perhaps the best answer.

As it turned out, Matthias did not have to reply.

"We had better get back," the enthused Greek said, starting to backtrack on the footpath that led to their overlook of events. "I have a feeling that our pilot will want to continue our journey south as soon as possible."

He would get no argument from Matthias. Undoubtedly, the ceremony and rituals they had just witnessed were designed to impress—which they did. However, for the benefit of three golden statues? Matthias was somewhat surprised that not only the Greek but also the Ethiopian were engrossed with the display. Yet this was the culture they knew, and both reveled in its extravagance.

Matthias eagerly followed Aristotle back to their boat and the respite it offered from this ancient celebration of lifeless golden idols and stale but ingrained beliefs. However, based on what he had witnessed, Matthias did not underestimate the challenges he faced and the difficulties that lie ahead. What he had to offer were words and the promise of eternal life. Whether this was enough to compete with golden idols would take a far-greater power than he possessed to answer.

CHAPTER FIFTEEN

First Cataract, Nile River

"This is where the journey ends, my friend."

As before, Aristotle had caught the young Galilean off guard as he watched their boat moor near the southern end of a busy quay at a site the Greek called Elephantine Island situated in the middle of the Nile River, a journey that had taken them only three days from when they left Thebes.

"This is where my father maintains a warehouse," Aristotle continued, "and the crew will unload the rest of the supplies for the Romans garrisoned here." He pointed to several large walled building up an embankment to their left. "My father's warehouse is not far. This also marks the border of the Roman Empire with the land of Kush—the island of Meroe, as the Romans call it—where you go."

Matthias looked at his friend briefly and then turned his attention back to the boat from where a gangplank was being lowered to the island community, which was little different than the multitude of other towns and villages passed on their journey upstream each with their myriad of temples and statuary dedicated to ancient kings and strange beliefs.

"Thank you for all you have done," Matthias said.

At this time, the Ethiopian and Dracus came and stood next to him, both anxiously watching the activities dockside.

"It was my pleasure," Aristotle responded. "You and your companions made the journey quite entertaining. I have never before traveled with a messenger from the gods! I only have golden statutes as a reference. In that regard, you should know that the island on which you stand is where Khnum resides. He is the ram-headed god and protector of the Nile. So be on your best behavior." Aristotle smiled as he spoke, obvious that he was playing with his new friend.

An awkward moment passed before the Greek spoke again as he offered his arm in friendship. Matthias responded with the customary grasp. The Ethiopian followed their example without saying a word.

"Take care. I am off to find hidden treasure."

Matthias smiled, hesitated, and then turned to the Ethiopian.

"Where do we go?" he asked.

The man turned and pointed south toward the river and said, "There. Philae."

Matthias was not quite sure to what the Ethiopian was referring; however, he would follow whatever course was suggested. In point of fact, he could do little else.

Matthias was amazed how quickly the Ethiopian secured the service of a boat to transport him and those in his party to the nearby island of Philae. Granted, it was an odd-shaped vessel with a flat bottom and little to distinguish the bow from the stern. Its appearance was more like a raft, but large enough to accommodate the Ethiopian and his entourage of slaves and cargo. A rudder was affixed to the stern with four slaves equipped with long-handled paddles employed to navigate the short distance over waters churned by hidden boulders.

It soon became obvious why the flat bottom was an advantage as the oarsmen struggled to keep the boat afloat in churning pools of water. For the most part, they were successful, and only on occasion did the boat come dangerously close to a boulder or a sandbar in the middle of the river. Finally, after navigating around a bend, the island of Philae came into view, another Egyptian monument to the pantheon of gods.

The Ethiopian was anxious to go ashore as was the gladiator, and although cautioned, both stood to watch the highlights of Philae ascend on the horizon. However, as they did, the boat took a violent turn to the right as the oarsmen paddled to avoid another obstacle. Consequently, both men lost their balance and fell to their knees, the Ethiopian able to grab hold of the side of the boat; however, the gladiator was not as fortunate. Momentum threw him overboard as the boat lurched backward.

Matthias saw the danger and hollered for the crew to paddle toward the floundering man as reptilian eyes watched from the bank of another island just west of Philae. Yet there was no indication that the oarsmen heard Matthias as they were too busy keeping the boat from drifting into other boulders.

Without considering the consequences, Matthias jumped into the water and swam the short distance to the panicked gladiator and grabbed him by the nape of his robe in an attempt to pull the man back to the safety of the boat. Fortunately, Matthias felt the handle end of an oar jab him on the shoulder and took hold while pulling the gladiator as close to himself as possible. He next felt the hands of two men, one of them Dracus, grab him by his robe and pull him into the boat as two others took hold of the gladiator and did the same. A third man splashed water with his paddle in an attempt to ward off the approaching danger, which barely succeeded as the tail of one crocodile hit the side of the boat and almost capsized it.

"I warned you about standing near the edge! I warned you!" the boat's pilot shouted at the gladiator in an incomprehensible tongue.

"Yes, we heard," the Ethiopian responded in broken Egyptian. "Now, please, just get us to Philae, and I will compensate you for whatever damage may have been done."

The latter seemed to placate the man as the oarsmen again began the tiresome task of paddling the boat along the coastline of Philae to a dock on the south side of the island. There several larger vessels were already discharging their cargoes as the small, flat-bottomed boat glided to an anchorage. The occupants could not disembark fast enough, and Matthias was no exception.

"You risked a lot back there," the Ethiopian said in passable Aramaic. "You could have been killed. Here, take this."

He reached for a gold band crafted with a lion's head that circled his upper right arm, unclasped it, and handed it to Matthias.

"That is not necessary," Matthias said as he tried to hand the armlet back.

"I know," the Ethiopian replied. "However, I would be grateful if you accepted it as it is the custom of my kingdom to reciprocate a great service with a gift."

The man's expression pleaded for him to accept.

"Thank you," Matthias finally responded as he handed the armband to Dracus who quickly put it into one of their two small cloth bags. Then, changing the subject, he asked, "Now what?"

The Ethiopian did not reply immediately but instead started down the gangplank. "Follow," was all he offered.

As Matthias stepped onto the gangplank, he felt a hand grab him by the left shoulder and pull him to a stop. It was the gladiator who hit his left breast over his heart with his fist and then bowed slightly to Matthias. The meaning was obvious.

"Again, no thanks is necessary. You would have done the same for me," Matthias said, knowing the man did not understand. And he had no doubts that the latter was true. "Now I suggest that we follow your friend," he said and nodded toward the wharf and at the disappearing Ethiopian.

The entourage slowly began to assemble behind the Ethiopian as they moved further into the environs of Philae. Matthias saw no difference from other towns with a temple located at what appeared to be the center of the island flanked by large inscribed pylons which dominated everything. However, the Ethiopian did not appear to be headed in that direction. Instead, he remained close to the southern bank of the island and buildings that fronted the river.

As was Matthias's habit, he stumbled dutifully behind.

It was not long before the Ethiopian revealed their destination. He stopped in front of a large building with four boats moored near an open entrance as crews from each vessel hauled supplies and goods into the open-fronted structure. The Ethiopian studied his environment for a moment and then disappeared. Matthias and the others could only wait patiently on the dock for further instruction.

It was not long before the Ethiopian reappeared with another dark-skinned man who the Ethiopian introduced as the overseer of the warehouse and explained that the man would arrange for a boat to transport them farther up the Nile. More than that, the overseer agreed to let them use an unoccupied space within the building for lodging until he could procure a boat, which at the earliest would be midday tomorrow. Almost as an afterthought and somewhat sheepishly, the Ethiopian said he would spend the night with the overseer, as it seemed the two knew each other from past business dealings, which called Matthias's attention to an intangible that had been bothering him since they first arrived at this first cataract of the Nile River. There was a noticeable change in the bearing of the Ethiopian, especially as pertained to his interaction with others. Matthias was not quite sure how to assess the difference other than that the Ethiopian appeared more aloof and at times more abrupt in his actions. In this regard, the overseer was noticeably deferential to his Ethiopian counterpart almost to the point of being obsequious.

For whatever reasons, Matthias was just grateful to be on solid ground before starting the next phase of their seemingly endless journey. And if anything was bothering the Ethiopian, the man did not let it interfere in his relationship with the young Galilean, for which Matthias was sincerely thankful.

CHAPTER SIXTEEN

The island of Philae was within the spillway considered the first cataract of the Nile River; where Matthias now stood was where the cataract began. He and Dracus had been instructed by an assistant to the warehouse supervisor that the Ethiopian wanted to reembark for Kush early. This meant that they would have to walk around the obstacles that created the cataract and board a vessel upriver where the cataract began. However, this was not necessarily a bad thing. They did not have far to walk once they set foot on the mainland with their way marked by a well-defined bricked trail. What concerned Matthias was the absence of the Ethiopian.

Nevertheless, Matthias was as anxious as any to continue the journey; although it seemed the farther upriver they traveled, the more disoriented he became to the world about him. Even the Jewish synagogue at Philae, although serving a small community, included a shrine to the local goddess, Isis, the consort of Osiris, the god of the underworld. Matthias longed for nothing more than to talk with others about the Master and his ministry of how uncomplicated life could be, life based on the promise of goodness and sharing. Yet he had no idea of when their journey would end, and now Dracus called an even more worrisome matter to his attention.

Tied to a pier and presumably to be used by them as they maneuvered upriver was a vessel far more elaborate in its detail and fixtures than the boat they had sailed thus far. Yet what caught Matthias's attention was not the boat itself but rather two muscled guards who stood silently at the pier-side end of the vessel's gangplank. Dracus had attempted to board and was unceremoniously rebuffed. Matthias also noticed that two of the Ethiopian's slaves were huddled not far from the pier, also prevented from boarding, and could not imagine why an empty boat required armed protection. Contemplating this and other imponderables, Matthias and Dracus leaned against one of the larger boulders that littered the site to await their Ethiopian benefactor.

Their wait was not long as a parade of two sedan chairs led by two spear-bearing guards advanced along the stone trail from Philae toward the pier. Matthias recognized the occupant of the second chair as the Ethiopian while walking beside him was the gladiator now dressed in a short brown tunic tied in a knot at the left shoulder. However, the occupant of the lead chair was unknown but obviously the person in charge, judging by his actions on arrival. Once this individual had slipped from his elevated seat, Matthias could see that the man was a short, rather rotund, dark-skinned individual unafraid to dress ostentatiously, wearing an ankle-length, fringed, multicolored robe. He had rings on almost every finger, a gold band with blue stones on his upper right arm, and a gold headband that circled his moon-shaped head.

The man immediately began to give orders to several slaves as all slowly made their way up the gangplank, carrying various shaped boxes and trunks. The Ethiopian also started up the gangplank, gesturing that his slaves including those huddled on the riverbank should follow, and on noticing Matthias and Dracus, motioned that they, too, should board.

"I want you to meet our benefactor," the Ethiopian said once all were on deck. He then called out a name which caused the rotund man to stop, turn, and take a step backward. "These are the two I told you about," the Ethiopian said, gesturing at Matthias and Dracus. "I met them while in Judea. They come to Kush in hopes of preaching of a new god. I thought the Candace would be interested."

The rotund man said nothing but held out a bejeweled hand, apparently expecting either Matthias or Dracus to perform some ritual of respect. Instead, the two stood silent, staring at the short, heavyset stranger.

"No matter," the man finally responded as he dropped his arm to his side. "We need to depart as soon as possible," he said and turned from the Ethiopian and his two companions as he started for the enclosure at the center of the boat.

"Pay no attention to my little friend," the Ethiopian said. "He sometimes gets too full of himself. He is descended from kings, his ancestors once being pharaohs of Egypt, which explains his name, Aspelta, an early ruler of Kush. His family is also one of the wealthiest in the kingdom. Lord Aspelta may blow wind in your face. However, he will do you no harm."

Matthias took it all stoically. He did not want the Ethiopian to suspect that he felt out of his depth. He was a simple man who certainly did not know the protocol in dealing with kings or even their descendants. And he certainly did not want his mission embroiled in such matters. He could only wait and see where the Master led and hope that he did not stumble on his own inadequacies along the way.

"Perhaps we should get settled," the Ethiopian suggested. "I believe that the pilot is as anxious to get underway, as is our wealthy friend. Other boats upstream want to start their journey down the rapids."

Without waiting for comment, the man turned and walked in the same direction as the bejeweled merchant and disappeared under a canopy that hid the central structure of the boat. The gladiator was never far from his mentor.

"I guess we should follow," Matthias said as he picked up a small bag and headed for the bow of the boat.

Any unoccupied space between cargo and fixtures would be home for the next untold number of days.

On the second day of their journey upriver, the resplendent boat seemed to settle into a routine that suited all onboard. The wind was brisk and billowed the large white sail, which made navigation that much easier and less strenuous for both the pilot and his crew. The principal objective was to maintain a proper course in the river's channel and thereby avoid hidden obstacles such as boulders and fallen trees floated downriver with the rising waters. With oarsmen used as spotters and others constantly adjusting the rigging of the sail, the vessel maneuvered faultlessly through the silt-rich Nile waters. As for the passengers, none were more prominent than the merchant who, early each day, dressed in white linen with an appropriate Egyptian-styled headdress, perched himself into a chair raised on a dais at the stern of the boat, with the Ethiopian sitting on a stool placed near the merchant's right elbow as both reminisced about Kush and the glories of the merchant's family. Every so often this same presupposing man would flick an ivory-handled, horse-haired whip, which was held loosely in his right hand, and then settle back to assume his unquestioned position of authority.

Matthias stood afore deck and carefully took it all in. It was not an unpleasant world; there were no storms on the horizon. Even the Nile cooperated, offering near-still waters that invited passage to foreign lands. Perhaps it was the latter that most bothered him: the world he knew, even the temples and obelisks of Egypt, was passing away as he now entered a different realm, a world he knew little to nothing about. His only life adventure was with the Master and the journeys he and other disciples took within the very limited boundaries of Judea and Galilee. What did he have to offer that could compare?

The way ahead was defined by a blue ribbon that snaked through the sands of an unknown and alien land yet a place to which Matthias felt inextricably drawn.

CHAPTER SEVENTEEN

Napata, on the Upper Nile River beyond the Third Cataract, Kingdom of Kush

On the sixth day out from the island of Philae, the wind turned and began to work against the vessel's course. The boat's pilot immediately ordered the single large sail to be dropped and the oarsmen to begin the tiresome task of paddling south against the current. However, the strain told in the not-so-hidden exhaustion of the crew, men who, only days before, had pulled the vessel through two cataracts of shallow water and boulders. Now they had to fight the mighty Nile itself. It was little encouragement that throughout the ordeal, their overlord remained perched on his golden dais, even while navigating the cataracts, as all onboard disembarked to help pull the boat upstream. The man was immovable while volunteering the occasional order. However, it was doubtful that anyone listened then or now as the boat drew nearer to what appeared to be a substantial settlement on the right bank of the river.

Matthias watched from the bow as the boat set a course for what appeared to be a small community of vessels moored on either side of two piers jutting into the Nile. The piers were located at the far end of what once must have been a thriving port but now was little more than the shell of a city, with its walls breached and ruins predominant throughout. Observable activity centered near the few observable, undamaged structures that radiated inland. In the distance, clusters of small pyramids faced with large pylons dominated what the desert had not reclaimed.

The pilot expertly maneuvered their vessel alongside a man-made embankment where two gangplanks were extended from both the stern and bow to shore. Almost immediately slaves began to carry cargo hidden within the boat to one of several structures that fronted a wide walkway that ran alongside the river while the merchant, led by a phalanx of guards, exited down the rear gangplank. The Ethiopian with his gladiator shadow followed, as did Matthias and Dracus, as all stopped on the pier, awaiting direction. As if on cue, a short, heavy-set man wearing an Egyptian-style kilt and headdress came from seemingly nowhere to greet his visitors.

"Lord Aspelta!" the man shouted as he took the extended hand of the rich merchant and lowered his head to touch it with his forehead. "We did not expect you back so soon! I hope all goes well?"

"It does," the merchant answered perfunctorily. He then noticed that the man was carefully examining the others who had disembarked with him. "As you can see, I have guests," he explained. "Our Lord Treasurer"—he pointed to the Ethiopian—"travels to Meroe as do his companions. We will help with the arrangements. And I need all my belongings brought to my villa as soon as possible."

"Certainly, my Lord!" the greeter replied obsequiously. Then, as if planned, two sedan chairs arrived and stopped just short of the merchant and his party. The short, round-faced Napatan pointed the way.

"Oh, we are also visited by Prince Teritegas," the man added almost offhandedly. "He arrived yesterday."

The merchant stopped immediately, turned and glared as did the Ethiopian.

"Why did you not say so sooner!" the merchant demanded. "Is he with my daughter?"

"I do not know, my Lord," the Napatan answered.

"Come, we must go," the merchant said as he climbed into one of the chairs while the Ethiopian took a place in the other.

Without waiting, the merchant signaled to proceed to a distant walled compound that fronted on the river. The Ethiopian waved his slaves to do the same as Matthias, Dracus, and the gladiator walked briskly alongside. It was obvious that the Ethiopian was adjusting comfortably to his return home.

The trek to the far side of the partially razed city, a consequence of Roman retribution, did not take long; however, the difference between sectors was astonishing. Whereas the city just northwest of the docks was a jumble of toppled columns and mudbricks, the city to the southeast where the small band of travelers now headed was a hub of activity within a walled enclosure with multiple-storied buildings protruding above the city's ramparts.

The caravan moved quickly toward a gate nearest to the river, and once on the other side of the wall, the weary travelers stumbled through crowds that congregated on either side of a narrow thoroughfare that meandered through the community. The merchant stopped near a structure that fronted on the river as two guards accessed a large brick enclave. Inside was a world not unlike that of Andronicus Phylos's home but far more ornate.

The entire motif was Egyptian-themed with large murals of various deities painted on each wall from which multiple doorways opened onto a wide hallway that circumscribed a large rectangular atrium. The latter was circled by columns topped with lotus-inspired capitals. At least three fountains fed numerous gardens where flowers and blossoming trees grew in profusion. White diaphanous curtains hung between several of the columns at the far end of the atrium, where a large staircase climbed to a second floor. It was on a landing midpoint on the staircase that Matthias noticed three individuals, two females and one male, all carefully watching their progress into the home. On seeing the merchant, one of the females broke away from the others and hurried through the open garden.

"Father!" shouted a dark-skinned beauty with curled black hair embellished with gold strands that hung from a ringlet that circled her head.

The girl's dress was a simple white garment that fell to her ankles and was tied at the waist by a braided gold belt; her jewelry consisted of a large golden vulture worn around the neck highlighted with semiprecious stones.

The merchant stopped and opened his arms for an embrace as others in the party stepped back so not to interfere with the reunion. The male who accompanied the daughter also hurried to greet his host. The third figure, another female, came up more hesitantly and stopped an arm's length away from the others. However, it was the male who was most anxious to be noticed.

"Greetings, Prince Teritegas," the merchant said warmly as he looked past his daughter and at the young, handsome man smiling broadly to his right.

The man wore a short brown tunic covered in part by a leather breastplate. He carried a scabbard on his left hip and wore a wide gold band on each arm. The merchant maneuvered his daughter to the side as he bowed slightly while the young man clasped the merchant by both arms and smiled.

"We did not expect you back so soon, Aspelta!" the young man said with a broad smile. Then, looking past the merchant and at the others, he stopped, and his face brightened. "My Lord Treasurer!" he exclaimed as he took a step forward to greet the Ethiopian. "We are indeed full of surprises!" he said as the two embraced.

The Ethiopian pulled back slightly as he studied the exuberant young prince and said, "You look fit. And how are your mother and father?"

"They do well and will certainly be glad to hear from you. Was your journey fruitful?"

"We will talk of that later. First, let me introduce you to my companions." The Ethiopian swung an open hand as he pointed to both Matthias and Dracus. "They come to Kush from the land of the Jew sent by their god." He then extended his arm toward the gladiator. "And this is a man you will recognize as coming from beyond the river." He nodded at the distinctive markings on the man's chest and his sculpted hair. "He was a slave of the Romans. Your mother will be most intrigued by it all."

The young man looked perplexed.

"I will explain after we are settled," the Ethiopian explained.

There was a brief pause before the merchant understood that he was now expected to react and finally pointed to the interior of the atrium.

"My servants will make the necessary arrangements," he said in an authoritative tone as he clapped his hands twice, which attracted four males from behind a curtained wall.

Matthias noticed that the one called Prince Teritegas and the young girl dressed in white immediately turned away and hurried for an exit behind another curtain that billowed to one side of a large staircase. The other female, however, remained as she studied each of the new arrivals. Like the other girl, a gold ringlet circled her brow; however, that was about the only similarity. Although of the same height as her companion, she appeared far more athletic and well-toned. Even her dress was more suited to outdoor activity as she wore a leather breastplate over a multicolored tunic that came down to her knees and carried a sheathed short sword on her left hip. Suddenly her mouth opened into a broad, appealing smile.

"Lady Asata!" the Ethiopian exclaimed. "I did not recognize you. Come here, child," he said as he held out both arms.

The girl quickly complied and then turned to the others.

"This is my favorite niece!" the Ethiopian said in Aramaic for the benefit of Matthias as he pulled the girl toward himself and tightened his embrace.

Matthias bowed slightly. He could not help but notice that the girl kept her focus on him.

"Now, go find Prince Teritegas and Lady Nasaisa and enjoy the rest of the day," the Ethiopian said and gave the girl a gentle pat on her back as she broke away and ran out of the room. "Shall we go also?" he asked.

The merchant again pointed further into the atrium and headed toward the stairway. The others followed. For Matthias, however, no matter how hard he tried, he could not shake the memory of the radiant smile and the flashing dark-brown eyes of the young woman who at that moment turned to face him again and then disappeared behind a billowing white facade.

CHAPTER EIGHTEEN

Sleeping arrangements were unlike those of the past: whereas the Ethiopian, his slaves, and the gladiator were usually billeted in one room, with Matthias and Dracus teamed in another, here Matthias was paired with the Ethiopian while Dracus and the gladiator were escorted to the slave quarters, at least for one night. Matthias would have preferred to have accompanied his friend, but the merchant insisted otherwise. The young disciple reluctantly complied and followed the Ethiopian and two of his slaves into a sparsely furnished room located on the second floor of the merchant's large house just to the west of the stairway.

Actually, considering the ostentatious nature of their host, Matthias was surprised by the simplicity of furnishings. A canopied bed occupied the center of one wall with a small table and two collapsible stools nearby; a large wooden, unadorned trunk stood at the foot of the low-slung bed presumably for storage and personal items. Apparently, the merchant had alerted his slaves to the room's dual occupancy as both a rug, a small round pillow, and a blanketlike throw were neatly stacked in one corner. Matthias had to smile as he had endured much more while with the Master. However, one could tell by the not-so-muted grumblings of the Ethiopian that the man expected grander accommodations to be provided by their rich host.

After taking time to get situated, the Ethiopian, once he had changed into a clean robe, suggested that they return to the atrium where they would rejoin the others and partake of a traditional Napatan meal. As Matthias understood the custom, this particular endeavor was to be as elaborate as the host could arrange to show his appreciation for the visit. In this regard, Matthias had no doubt that the merchant would go all out as he had a goodly number of the Kush royal court under his roof. However, for his part, Matthias only wanted enough to sustain himself before retiring to bed. And he hoped that Dracus was able to do likewise.

The assembly of guests cushioned on overstuffed couches was as Matthias anticipated, with the addition of the merchant's wife and two additional couples who were obviously close friends of both the host and hostess. The meal was also as Matthias had been led to expect, with elaborate plates of roasted lamb, fruits, and freshly baked breads placed before the guests on silver and gold platters. Matthias reposed at the far end of the dining area out of earshot of the merchant who, with his wife, was holding court with his royal guests, dutifully paying homage to each. Matthias kept to a diet of bread and fruit while his eyes occasionally wandered to the court visitors, especially the female friend of the merchant's daughter, who every so often would look his way and smile. However, any attempt at conversation was rebuffed by his failure to comprehend the language.

Near the end of the meal, when Matthias was about to give his excuse for leaving early, the gathering was interrupted by a member of the household staff who whispered in the merchant's ear. The merchant shook his head, mouthed something very softly to his wife, and stood.

"Please continue. I'll be gone only a short while," he said and then followed his servant through a curtained exit out of the room.

At that same time, the gladiator pushed past the two departing figures and hurried over to Matthias, where he put a hand on the young disciple's shoulder and pointed to the doorway. He also nodded at the Ethiopian and mouthed a few unintelligible words. Matthias could tell by the latter's expression that the message had startled the man.

For a moment Matthias hesitated, as did the Ethiopian.

"Something is going on," the girl called Lady Asata who was seated almost opposite Matthias said to no one in particular as she rose from her couch. "I'm going to find out what."

She hurried to an exit followed by Matthias and her uncle.

"I guess we should go too," Prince Teritegas said. "It seems that we'll be left to ourselves if we don't."

He also stood from his couch with the merchant's daughter at his heels. The wife and her friends continued in conversation seemingly oblivious to the sudden departures.

Where they all hurried was to a large, columned room on the opposite side of the atrium with a raised dais located at one end and an elaborately carved, stately looking chair positioned at the center of the dais. As Matthias and the others entered, the merchant stood in front of the chair with the servant who had interrupted the meal standing to his right. Everyone approached cautiously, uncertain of what to expect next.

Suddenly a commotion was heard at the entrance to the room as three men wielding short swords brushed past and entered, escorting two men between them. One was Dracus who stumbled as he pressed a large, red-stained cloth to his left side!

Matthias started toward his friend when he felt the strong hand of the Ethiopian pull him back.

"Bring them both here!" the merchant commanded.

The three guards complied and hurried the two men forward as they pushed each to their knees on the hard stone floor.

"What have these men done?" the merchant asked as he looked to the man standing to his right for an answer.

"They were fighting in the slaves' quarters. Over this," the man said and held out a golden armlet. "It has the royal insignia on it."

He handed the object to the merchant, who took it and examined it closely.

"I didn't steal it!" the man on his knees next to Dracus shouted. "He must have." He pointed at Dracus.

"And you," the merchant said, looking down at Dracus, "what have you to say for yourself?"

With some effort, Dracus shook his head as he continued to stare at the floor and hold tight to the stained cloth that shielded his left side. The merchant nodded at one of the guards who pushed Dracus with his knee and told him to speak.

"He cannot talk!" Matthias shouted to the surprise of everyone. "His tongue was cut out by the Romans! Tell him that!" Matthias demanded as he looked to the Ethiopian for help.

The Ethiopian glared disapprovingly and then turned his attention to the merchant where he focused on the golden armlet.

"Hand that to me," Prince Teritegas said as he stretched out his arm.

The man slowly complied as both the prince and the merchant's daughter stepped forward while Teritegas examined the band. At the same time, Matthias and Lady Asata rushed to Dracus.

"This man has been injured!" Lady Asata said as she gently pulled back the cloth from Dracus's left side. "He's been stabbed!"

At the same time, Matthias tried to assess the extent of his friend's wound while the man attempted to communicate.

"Is this what it's all about?" Prince Teritegas asked as he held up the golden armlet. "This has the royal mark on it. I don't understand why either of these two men would have it."

As he spoke, Dracus continued to communicate with his hands but had difficulty expressing himself due to the pain.

"As best as I can understand," Matthias said, "this man," and he pointed at the other individual kneeling on the floor, "attempted to steal that armlet from Dracus, and a fight broke out. This man stabbed my friend and started to run off when he was stopped by the guards and both were brought here."

The Ethiopian interpreted as Matthias spoke.

"But why would your friend have something that clearly belongs to the royal house?" Prince Teritegas asked as he again fingered the armlet.

"I can explain," the Ethiopian said as he stepped forward, turned, and addressed the prince. "I gave my armband to this man"—he pointed to Matthias—"for saving my life. There is no theft except, perhaps, from our wounded visitor."

Prince Teritegas looked at the merchant as he handed the armlet to the Ethiopian.

"Take him!" the embarrassed merchant ordered as he pointed at the kneeling slave and stared sheepishly at his royal superior. "I promise that he will be dealt with severely!"

"And while we talk, this man is slowly bleeding to death!" Lady Asata interrupted as she tried to help Dracus to his feet. Then, turning to Matthias, she said in broken Aramaic, "Take him to my room. My slaves will care for him. I have dealt with injuries like this before."

She looked up at Lord Teritegas, and both smiled as some unspoken yet familiar experience passed between them.

"I need to go with him," a confused Matthias added.

"As you wish," Lady Asata assented again in Aramaic. "However, let my slaves look to his injury. They have the experience."

Matthias nodded and hesitantly followed as Dracus was lifted from the floor and slowly escorted to Lady Asata's apartment. For the first time since their journey began, Matthias felt both he and the mission were at risk.

CHAPTER NINETEEN

Matthias bent to comfort his friend by applying a damp cloth to the man's forehead. Earlier Dracus was carried by a litter out of Napata and conveyed by boat to a site near the tall grass on the west bank of the Nile River. It was early morning with the sun barely warming the desert, which seemed to invigorate the slaves as they assembled a caravan of carts and animals for the trek south to the city of Meroe.

The previous night had passed with considerable apprehension as Dracus's condition fluctuated from stable to serious during long, uncertain hours. Their friend, the gladiator, made some effort to help but was largely rebuffed by Lady Asata and her slaves who meticulously ministered to the stricken man. Near daybreak Darcus's condition seemed to improve, allowing him to be carefully maneuvered across the Nile, where they now awaited an enclosed wagon promised by their host, which would transport the injured man on the last leg of their journey south.

Matthias opted to travel with his friend; Lady Asata insisted that she do likewise. Matthias had to marvel at the resourcefulness of this young woman, not the least of which was her rudimentary knowledge of Aramaic, which she explained was a result of being tutored by court officials as potentially useful in future trading expeditions, the lifeblood of Kush. He also had no doubt that his friend owed his life to the skills of this unique stranger.

"Look! They come!" Lady Asata shouted from the saddle of her chestnut mare as she pulled hard on the reins to turn her horse back from the deep grass that ran parallel to the river.

Matthias turned from his friend and looked toward the east bank of the river where a large raft was conveying a cumbersome wooden wagon across the Nile. Four slaves on either side of the raft were having difficulty steering the craft through the current, having only long poles to propel them.

Then the girl spoke to him, "Have your friend ready to be moved as soon as the wagon is on shore and hitched to the horses. The caravan is about to depart for Meroe. I will join you later."

She waited for no response and rode farther inland toward the head of the assembled party. Matthias noticed that another, presumably Lord Teritegas, rode toward her, each wearing an elaborately tooled breastplate and brandishing a sword at their side. This was their element.

Matthias stood and looked in all directions as the ubiquitous slaves scurried to ready the camels, donkeys, horses, and carts for the trek south. As for the boxlike wagon, it was now just about off the raft with several slaves arduously pulling it onto dry land where two horses stood at the ready. Matthias also had difficulty putting out of mind the grizzly sight of the impaled severed head of the man who stole from Darcus conspicuously displayed on a stake near the main gate to the city where it was certain to be noticed by the prince.

The merchant was good to his word, Matthias thought. And their journey would not begin again any too soon.

The young disciple pushed himself against the wooden slats of the wagon and braced himself as he watched his friend turn on his side to sleep. It had been a hard three-day ride across a barren landscape, with hardly any escape from unrelenting heat other than shade offered by their boarded enclosure, which had its own drawbacks. For one, the uncirculated air inside the wagon was stifling, which Matthias tried to remedy by prying off two boards at the roofline. This and keeping the narrow door at the back of the wagon open gave some ventilation and, therefore, relief. Thankfully, Dracus was a compliant patient and complained little. Nevertheless, it was obvious that the man's wound and the loss of blood had taken their toll.

"You look miserably uncomfortable," a familiar voice said in halting Aramaic from the opening to the rear of the wagon.

Matthias turned abruptly and said, "You mean him," nodding at Dracus.

"No, *you*," Lady Asata said while astride her horse. "Do you ever get a break?"

Matthias just shrugged.

"Why don't you come with me for a while?" she asked. "It will do you good."

Matthias looked down at Dracus and shook his head.

The patient, however, heard the exchange and tried to raise his right hand. "Go," Dracus indicated by waving his hand. He then pointed at the slaves who crouched near his feet as he folded his hands under his head as if attempting to sleep.

"See, he's telling you he wants to rest. So you have no excuse," Lady Asata responded. "Come, get on the back of my horse."

Matthias hesitated.

Dracus again waved his friend on.

"You sure?" Matthias asked again.

Dracus raised his head with some difficulty and nodded as the two slaves fanned flies away from his bandaged side.

Matthias pushed himself up and hesitantly started toward the rear of the wagon.

"Come. And be quick," Lady Asata instructed. "Maneuver yourself onto my horse and hold on. We'll ride for the front of the column."

Matthias turned one last time but saw no contradiction from Dracus. Therefore, he did as Lady Asata instructed and awkwardly grabbed the girl around the waist with both arms. For her part, Lady Asata wasted no time and reined the horse around the wagon and then kicked it in its flanks to hurry past other slow but steadily moving animals. Matthias noticed that the dunes which surrounded them had become more gravel than sand with even an occasional outcropping of low growing vegetation.

"I don't see him," Lady Asata said to no one in particular when reaching the front of the caravan.

Then, stopping one of the lead riders, Lady Asata asked the whereabouts of Prince Teritegas and was pointed to the southwest. However, she first assured herself that she had her bow and quiver of arrows before riding off. Matthias could do nothing but trust the girl's judgment and hold tight.

It was not long before they approached three dark silhouettes standing tethered to some dead brush.

"There!" Lady Asata said, pointing at the horses. "They belong to Teritegas."

She rode up to the animals, patted Matthias on his hands to let him know to let loose, and dismounted. Matthias did the same. Lady Asata then crouched low and began to ascend a dune where, once at the top, she spotted three figures squatting in a depression behind several bushes that concealed a small watering hole at its center. One of the figures turned and signaled to stop. It was Prince Teritegas, holding a spear in his right hand.

Lady Asata, however, had other ideas. Continuing to crouch low, she crept slowly but steadily toward the prince, holding a bow in one hand, with her quiver of arrows slung over her left shoulder. Matthias reluctantly followed.

"I thought I told you…" Prince Teritegas started to say under his breath.

Lady Asata just held up her bow.

"We're here now," she said very matter-of-factly. "What's so important?"

"A lion! Just the other side of that brush. At the water's edge," Prince Teritegas whispered.

"Oh?" Asata responded, looking both surprised and pleased.

Prince Teritegas, however, was not interested in polite conversation and started to move carefully out of the cover toward the water hole, raising his spear above his shoulders. Lady Asata was not about to be left behind and tracked in his footsteps, with Matthias several paces behind.

Suddenly, as the prince raised his spear ready for the kill, one of two other men who led the charge suddenly stood up and waved vigorously. This same individual shook his head, attempting to signal, "No!"

"What the…" Prince Teritegas said, watching his prey escape over the dunes.

The two lead men returned quickly and stood at attention before the prince. One was in full explanation. Matthias understood nothing of their conversation; however, it seemed to placate Teritegas. Lady Asata turned to explain as best as she could.

"It seems that the lion is full of milk," she said as she touched one of her own breasts. "That means she must have cubs. We do not kill a nursing lion." Lady Asata was obviously disappointed for her friend.

The latter walked to where they stood. His look was one of letdown but in agreement with the decision to spare the lion. He said nothing as he patted Asata on her arm and walked past and up the dunes toward his tethered horse. Lady Asata did the same, as did Matthias and the two slaves.

The ride back to camp was both uneventful and quiet.

Matthias felt a sense of finality as the caravan approached a line of low dunes two days after his encounter with Prince Teritegas. He had returned to their wagon with no greater expectation than more of the same—hot days to complement an uncomfortably jarring ride. However, early afternoon on the second day out, things seemed to change. The landscape evidenced some low growing vegetation with an occasional breeze that blew from the northeast. And on her second daily visit to the wagon, Lady Asata said they were nearing the city of Meroe. Matthias paid little heed, as he was accustomed to a journey that seemed to have no end. Nevertheless, the excitement quickened among the herders and slaves as the caravan navigated the nearer of several sand barriers.

Matthias moved to the rear of the wagon. Then he saw it: a line of blue that snaked its way through the desert bluffs toward a green oasis directly in opposition to their path forward—the Nile River!

"How is our friend?" The question came from Lady Asata who had ridden to the rear of the column to check on Dracus.

Matthias turned quickly. Dracus was sitting with his back braced against the backboards, smiling at both although evidencing some discomfort.

"Improving," Matthias replied.

"Then why don't you step out of the wagon and get a better look at your new home?"

Matthias was intrigued by the comment, turned to Dracus, and finally succumbed to the suggestion. He landed hard on the grainy sand and tumbled twice before able to upright himself. Then, turning slowly, his attention was drawn to the horizon.

Rising about one-half mile to the east of the Nile was a walled city, which appeared to float above the river with expansive green fields and a forest radiating both to the north and south. Other enclosures with multistoried buildings and Egyptian-styled temples predominated while boats of all shapes and sizes moved effortlessly along the river's edge. Toylike figures and animal-drawn carts entered and exited from several gates that breached the city's walls as gray-black smoke billowed from an unseen origin that added to the perception of a community hovering among the clouds.

The caravan stopped at the river's edge almost opposite the central gate of the city to await transport to the eastern bank.

"Impressed?" Lady Asata asked, having ridden up from behind. "The Romans call it 'the island of Meroe,' as it is surrounded by rivers on all sides. I live in that complex over there." She pointed to a large walled enclosure north central within the city. "I imagine it will also be your home for the time being. The Candace lives there too. She will definitely want to spend some time with you."

Matthias understood most of what the girl said; although some words were lost in the translation. However, the word "home" was very clear, and he turned again to study the walled city and its environs. Journey's end! Never had he felt so out of place. What were Peter and his peers thinking!

PART THREE

Meroe

CHAPTER TWENTY

Palace Complex, City of Meroe, Kingdom of Kush

Matthias paced anxiously in front of an open balcony that faced west within the palace complex at Meroe. Actually, since their arrival four days previous, Matthias was unsure of his exact whereabouts within the compound since he had been restricted to his immediate environment and its access to a walled garden and what he was told was an adjunct to the palace. The Ethiopian had visited once with the stated purpose to check on Dracus; however, Lady Asata was nowhere to be seen, although her slaves continued to minister to his friend who was improving daily. Matthias was convinced that after all his efforts, the mission was doomed to fail.

While contemplating his dilemma, the door to his room opened, and a tall, slender man dressed in a long multicolored robe with graying hair and a mottled gray beard entered, speaking fluent Aramaic, and directed that he, Matthias, should follow.

"Who are you?" Matthias asked incredulously while standing his ground.

"That will be explained," the man replied. "Just come with me."

Matthias looked at Dracus who attempted to slide his legs off a bed.

"No, just you," the intruder said.

Matthias was in no position to object, so he exited the room that opened into a long nondescript hallway, which ended at a stairway to the first floor. Once on the lower level, the two men walked through a columned hall painted predominantly red and black to a room distinguished by two tall wooden doors inscribed with intricate carvings of mythological Egyptian gods. Two men in white kilts stood guard on either side of the doorway.

The stranger knocked once and then pushed hard on one of the two large doors as both entered another large room painted white with a marble floor and six brightly painted lion-figured columns set in opposition to each other. Three barred windows opened to the outside while another large wooden door gave access from the far end of the room. Between each column on the wall nearest to the hallway were elaborately carved panels terminating with a linen curtain to close off the space. A large mahogany table with three chairs stood at the far end of the room with several scrolls neatly stacked on top of the table. A wicker fan hung immediately above the table as a small boy, not more than ten years of age, dressed in a loincloth with white cap, pulled slowly on a rope attached to a fan in order to circulate air. Master of it all was a short, bald, dark-skinned male standing behind the table, dressed in a long, pleated white robe tied at the waist with a golden belt and ringlets of gold around both arms and forehead.

"Come," the man signaled as Matthias entered with the stranger following.

Both did as summoned and walked the length of the room to two chairs centered in front of the large table. Matthias only saw the man and the boy; however, he felt the presence of another perhaps concealed behind the wooden panels.

The stranger spoke briefly to the standing dark-skinned male, which was answered by a curt response. After which the stranger turned to Matthias and instructed that he be seated.

"This is Lord Harsiotef, the vizier of Kush. I am Ibrahim and will interpret for his lordship."

Matthias nodded although surprised by his escort's Jewish name.

"I hope you have found your accommodations comfortable," the vizier began. "I am sure you have many questions you wish to ask. And all will be answered in time. However, what most intrigues us is why you have come. I understand from my brother that you are some sort of prophet of your god. What interests you in the land of Kush?"

Matthias was momentarily taken aback by the directness of the question.

"I do not believe that I am a prophet of any god," Matthias answered haltingly. "I come to the land of Kush at the direction of those superior to me. I only hope to tell those who are interested of the life and mission of my Master."

"Could you not do the same in the land of the Jew?" Lord Harsiotef asked, with Ibrahim translating. "As you can see," he said, and he swung his open hand around and pointed at the six lion-headed columns, "we have a bounty of gods already."

"Several of my brothers were chosen for that task. Others were sent to the farthest boundaries of Rome. My mission is to Kush."

"And just what is that mission?"

"To tell the message of my Master, that of eternal life."

"By believing in him," Harsiotef added.

Matthias was silent for a moment; he then hesitantly responded, "Yes," and then as quickly added, "but my Master does not challenge any who are in authority. His domain is of a different world. I heard his message of tolerance and witnessed what others would call miracles."

The vizier stared intently into the eyes of the young man, which Matthias returned in kind. He also felt the strain of unseen eyes watching the exchange.

"And for this he was crucified by the Romans…and the Jews," the vizier finally added.

"Yes."

"However, you believe he is not dead but lives."

"Yes," Matthias answered again.

The vizier stood.

"Well," he began, "I am sure you have an interesting story to tell. The Egyptians preach of an afterlife too, you know."

Matthias said nothing.

"Oh, I almost forgot," the short, bald man said and waved both men to stand. "This here is Ibrahim, a Jew from your land. He now lives among us and is useful to our queen as an interpreter. He may also be useful to you from time to time."

The three stared silently at each other for a long moment.

"And you want to preach this message of 'tolerance' to our people."

Matthias nodded.

"We will see. I have to discuss it with the Candace. Until then, you will have to restrict your activities. I am sure we will talk again."

The man stepped around his desk as he started toward the large hallway doors as Matthias and the interpreter left the room. The vizier then walked slowly back to his table.

"Interesting," a deep-throated female said from the concealed end of the wooden panels.

There finally emerged a dark-skinned, grossly obese figure dressed in a multicolored, fringed robe that reached her ankles. An elaborately knotted golden belt tied the garment around her rotund waist while a large jeweled pectoral of a vulture hung across her breasts. Her fingers were decorated with several large rings and her head circled by a golden band with two cobra heads centered at the front.

"Ma'am," the vizier replied. "My brother says that he listened to these stories while in Judea and was convinced of their truth. However, we don't need zealots stirring things here, not saying that he would. He bears watching. We cannot forget that the Romans sacrificed this man's leader as a troublemaker."

The Candace did not respond immediately. Her thoughts were elsewhere.

Finally, she said, "I also found him to be interesting. I have spoken to your brother, and it seems that he credits this young man with several unexplained events on the journey back to Kush." Then, after some reflection, she added, "However, I agree that we do not need to upset our own. The priests are still smarting from their loss of power to my predecessors, and I cannot have a complete stranger going off unchallenged, preaching the attributes of another god. Like you say, this Matthias bears watching. Do you know who might be up to the task?"

The vizier thought for a moment, and then a slight smile cracked his lips.

"I might have an idea in that regard, ma'am," he said. "Let me work on it."

The Candace nodded and then turned to leave through the back door followed by an entourage of three slaves.

"Oh," she interjected before turning into the hall. "I have given permission for the tribal prince who accompanied your brother to leave Meroe for his homeland. We have enough problems with our eastern neighbors without adding another."

"Agreed," the vizier responded.

He then returned to his desk and stared at the chair where Matthias had sat. Although unintentionally, the young apostle had garnered more attention than he could ever have intended.

Lady Asata was angry with herself for agreeing to her father's proposal: simply put, she was to spy on the man, Matthias, by being a constant companion. Not that she had much choice, as her father said it was at the direction of the Candace, and to oppose the queen mother was not an option. Therefore, she reluctantly walked into the garden that fronted the rooms where Matthias was lodged, hoping that he had received her message to meet this morning. She was not disappointed.

"Hello," she said with a pleasant smile while tapping a waiting Matthias on his left shoulder.

The interpreter, Ibrahim, stood off to one side.

"I'm glad you came," she continued. "You have been confined far too long."

Matthias could not agree more.

"So why don't you put aside whatever you are doing and let me show you Meroe. I doubt if your friend would object just this once."

It took Matthias only a moment to think over the invitation before accepting.

"Good. I will see you back here in about one-half hour. I'm going to get our transportation. And be prepared to walk." Lady

Asata smiled as she said the latter and then turned back into the palace.

    Mathias also smiled to himself. Walking for long periods of time was second nature to him. Still, he was intrigued by this girl and her apparent interest in *him*. It was not an emotion to which he was accustomed.

CHAPTER TWENTY-ONE

Lady Asata was good to her word and, within a very short period of time, reappeared just outside Matthias's apartment with a chariot fronted by a lion-crested shield and drawn by two matched horses. A young man, probably not more than fourteen or fifteen years old, stood at her side presumably to care for the chariot when Asata was otherwise occupied. Lady Asata was also pleased that the Candace had asked the interpreter to accompany them, no doubt as another spy, which suited her perfectly.

"Come," Asata instructed as she gestured with both hands. "We are losing precious time. There is much I want you to see."

Matthias and Ibrahim did not argue but stepped up onto the chariot and held tight to a copper rail that topped the vehicle's front shield.

"First, I will take you down the main thoroughfare, which leads to the busier parts of our city. Ibrahim will interpret as we go."

She then lightly cracked a whip on the hindquarter of one of the two horses, and they started moving toward a large open gate. Once beyond the gate, a different world emerged.

Gone was the relative serenity of the palace replaced by the vibrant sounds of a busy city. Immediately to both their right and left was a large bricked avenue, which cut through the heart of the palace district anchored by a circular park and a tall obelisk with three smaller streets intersecting at the circle. Lady Asata maneuvered her chariot through the crowds and partially around the circle until she was headed east, down a wide avenue past large, multistoried buildings toward the next obstacle, which appeared to be another temple similar to those Matthias had witnessed at Thebes.

"These are the homes of our more-prosperous merchants," Lady Asata explained through the interpreter as they moved slowly toward the temple. "It does not hurt to be near the center of it all. And we are heading there," she said as she pointed to a large, walled building inscribed with Egyptian-styled figures, which lie straight ahead and appeared to be surrounded by several open plazas.

As she approached, Lady Asata slowed so that her guest could be suitably impressed.

"The temple of Amun," she said with some pride. "I am one of its daughters," which she added while looking directly at Matthias as if to challenge his beliefs.

Then she suddenly stopped and stepped down from the chariot as she bowed her head toward a cortege of white-robed men, some carrying spears and others small drums, as they emerged from a side gate to the temple complex. A muffled sound came from inside the one curtained conveyance as the entourage stopped, the curtain parted, and a hand extended, signaling Lady Asata to step forward. The girl did as commanded and knelt at the slightly opened curtain while two hands reached out and cupped the top of Lady Asata's head. After some muffled words, an abrupt signal was given, and the parade of robed men continued west, down the congested roadway.

At first Matthias was mystified.

"The High Priest on his way to the palace," Ibrahim whispered in Matthias's ear. "On his way to visit the Candace. A power in his own right and one to be avoided."

The young disciple looked over his shoulder at the interpreter and wondered at the warning. Then Lady Asata climbed back onto the chariot and started moving slowly again through the crowds toward an eastern gate of the city. Matthias also noticed that the crowds which circled the temple had grown with vendors selling merchandise to any who would buy. The smells of fresh produce and spices permeated everything.

"This is Meroe's main market. Many come here from all parts of the kingdom to sell their wares and produce," the girl explained.

"And further down that road?" Matthias asked, nodding past the temple to the south and down an intersection congested with more people. "What goes on down there?" he asked.

"The same," Lady Asata answered. "I have other places to show you, however, that are much closer." And again she nudged the two horses with a gentle flick of her whip.

Once past the market, the roadway narrowed with the buildings less impressive than those fronting the avenue just east of the palace. Matthias also observed that several men in pairs with swords at their sides mingled among the crowd. Many of the buildings were occupied by individuals sitting at tables that extended into the roadway, working at what looked to be various golden objects and other precious artifacts of different shapes and sizes.

"This is where most of our jewelry is made," she said over the din of the congested roadway. "It is traded to all parts even to Rome."

While she spoke, Lady Asata kept navigating through the narrow thoroughfare, passing several stalled carts; although it could not be overestimated what the lion-figured shield affixed to the front of the chariot did for her efforts.

"Our next stop is just ahead," she said, and the chariot came to a stop only two blocks farther east in front of a three-storied shop with a large barred window painted red.

"We need to go inside," Lady Asata instructed as she handed the reins of the two horses to her young companion and pushed her way to the interior of the shop. Matthias and Ibrahim did likewise.

"I doubt if even Rome has this," she said as she held up a length of shimmering green cloth that was pulled from a table with many similar but different-colored bolts of fabric. "Feel it!" Lady Asata demanded as she held out the brightly colored material.

The slightly embarrassed young man did as requested and was instantly amazed by the smooth texture. He smiled back at Asata just as a strange-looking man stepped from behind a curtain and approached his admiring visitors.

The shopkeeper bowed slightly as he held both hands together and asked if he could be of assistance. Matthias had never seen any person quite like this man who had a yellow tint to his skin and slanted eyes. His embroidered scarlet robe fell to the floor with long open sleeves, which were used to conceal both hands and arms; he wore a circular red cap which highlighted his white hair and stringy white beard.

Lady Asata returned the bow.

"Your shop is a marvel," she said as she continued to finger the foreign material. "Perhaps I'll come later to buy. Right now, I want to show my friend something he has never seen," Lady Asata said and looked over her shoulder at Matthias who was carefully eyeing everything.

The shopkeeper backed up a few paces as he was joined by a much younger individual, probably his son, who stood at the older man's side and watched. Finally, the older male spoke and began to explain how the cloth was made by a secret process from the excretions of a caterpillar. Matthias listened politely as Ibrahim interpreted.

"And it comes from a land I am sure you know nothing about," the interpreter, Ibrahim, added. "Far from here but as big and as powerful as Rome. Caravans come from many different lands to buy at our markets and avoid the Roman tax."

Satisfied that she had duly impressed her guest, Lady Asata pointed to the doorway as she walked back into the crowded street and climbed onto the chariot.

"There are a few more stops I wish to make," she said, taking the reins from her young slave.

Assuming that both Matthias and Ibrahim had followed, Lady Asata started down the now-narrow avenue toward what was obviously another gate in a wall that circumscribed Meroe. Then, without warning, Lady Asata cut the chariot to her right and down another narrow roadway that crossed another thoroughfare toward the southeast quadrant of the city that belched columns of gray-black smoke from multiple smokestacks.

"The ironworks of Meroe," she explained as they approached the first mudbrick building from which slaves were busy moving ore to hot kilns as others piled ingots of newly cast iron into neat stacks against an outside wall. The smell was perhaps not unlike that of a smoldering volcano with slag from the kilns creating unlikely mountains behind each shop.

"This is what makes Meroe rich," Lady Asata shouted to make herself heard above the workings of the iron factories. "Even the Romans buy our iron," she said with obvious pride.

Lady Asata then drove quickly past the site and turned south toward another gate, which opened to a narrow bridge that crossed a causeway filled with water diverted from the Nile to feed the iron works.

"The last place that I am going to show you is one of my favorites," she said and continued south along a dirt road that cut through green fields as they fanned out toward a distant forest. Just outside the gate, carts and camels were corralled, waiting to be loaded with the precious ore, while ragtag workers and women with small children congregated in a haphazard camp just beyond the wall. To the north, three distinct rows of pyramid-shaped buildings rose from the desert.

"What are those?" Matthias asked, pointing at the strange structures.

The interpreter tugged at the arm of Lady Asata who slowed the chariot enough to explain that the structures were tombs of both wealthy inhabitants and deceased rulers of Kush.

"We will visit those another day," she said without stopping. "Right now, I am headed for the river."

She flicked the hind ends of both horses to speed their ride down the narrow roadway congested with carts hauling logs to be used by the iron factories.

Matthias smiled to thank the girl for her insights. However, he could not take his eyes from the congestion of humanity that used this sector of the city and its wall to build their makeshift shelters in an effort to protect themselves from both the oppressive heat of the day and the chill of the night. He wanted to learn more but thought better than to ask.

Nearing the edge of the forest, Lady Asata turned west toward the Nile and an embankment that harbored several large boats.

"We will stop here," Asata said. "It's only a short walk,"

She again handed the reins to her slave while she started for the encampment located at the edge of the river. Matthias and Ibrahim again followed dutifully.

CHAPTER TWENTY-TWO

Near the river but far enough inland to allow carts to pass, several tall wooden stockades rose skyward from an open field. Strange bellowing sounds and loud trumpeting could be heard from each enclosure, which Lady Asata could tell by Matthias's puzzled look that he had no inkling of what lay ahead. Then a large cage balanced on a two-wheel cart pulled around one of the enclosures and almost knocked them out of the narrow roadway as three lions roared their disapproval.

Watching the wagon move toward the docks, Lady Asata gestured by raising her right hand in a fist.

"Idiot!" she said in her native tongue, which Ibrahim did not have to interpret.

"Disregard that crazy man. This is what I want you to see," she said as several other wagons with caged animals drove past. "Here is where the wild beasts of many kingdoms come before being sent to Rome or other lands beyond where the sun rises. Come, let me show you one of the wonders of Kush."

Lady Asata waited only for the next moving vehicle to pass before hurrying across the roadway toward one of the enclosures. When Matthias and Ibrahim approached, she was standing at the top of a crudely built scaffold that overlooked one of the stockades and gestured for Matthias to come and stand beside her.

"Have you ever seen such magnificent creatures?" she asked, watching three large rhinoceroses paw at a log barrier that separated them from freedom. Suddenly one of the three butted its head against the log wall, which shook the platform.

"Not a happy fellow," Matthias said, grabbing a split rail for balance. "What are they called?" he asked. "I have never seen one before."

"Rhinoceros," she answered. "They are particularly valued for their horns."

After a few minutes of watching the rhinoceroses circle the enclosure, Lady Asata started down a makeshift stairway and walk quickly to the next even-larger stockade.

"Come," she said, gesturing with her hand. "These are found not far from here."

Climbing another crude scaffold, Matthias and Ibrahim stared over Lady Asata's shoulder and wondered at five elephants huddled together at the center of an enclosure where a large pile of branches with green leaves had been stacked. One of the elephants was examining the offering with its trunk.

"Have you seen these before?" Lady Asata asked, turning to Matthias. "Several kingdoms are particularly fond of them and use them in battle."

Matthias smiled politely. *What a waste,* he thought to himself. Then, as if to underscore his private thoughts, Lady Asata turned and pointed to a canopied enclosure that abutted a wide road that ran parallel to the stockades stacked high with elephant tusks and animal skins. Several men in various styles of dress circulated among the neatly piled trophies.

"People from many different kingdoms come to Meroe just for that," she explained.

Matthias's attention had turned elsewhere, however, as he studied two figures standing on top of a scaffolding located two stockades west of the elephants' enclosure. Each appeared to be throwing something over a log wall; then suddenly one of the figures lost his balance and fell forward. A moment of silence passed. After which the second figure started down the scaffolding all the while frantically yelling and gesturing with both hands and arms.

"He's saying that his brother has fallen in with the lions!" Ibrahim interpreted. "He's calling for help!"

Two men responded immediately and began to run toward the panicked cries while Lady Asata, Matthias, and Ibrahim kept their place on the platform, straining to understand what was happening. They could see very little from their vantage point, so they, too, moved off the scaffold and toward a crowd that had begun to assemble in front of the enclosure where the lions were penned.

"You've got to help!" a young man pleaded while standing at a gate that opened into the stockade. "I think my brother has broken either an arm or a leg! He can't move!"

Although five or six men listened, no one reacted.

"Please help!" the young man yelled again to any who would listen. "Please!"

Matthias stood behind those who circled the frightened youngster, and when it was obvious that no one was going to step forward, Matthias maneuvered around the crowd and headed for the stockade gate.

"Where are you going?" Lady Asata asked, more as a challenge than as a question.

"If no one will help, then we have to," Matthias said through Ibrahim as he reached for a wooden crossbar and threw it to the ground. The gate partially opened.

"Well, you can't do it alone," Lady Asata said as she reluctantly reached for a short sword that was buckled to her waist.

Others just continued to watch while Ibrahim and the panicked boy followed Lady Asata into the enclosure.

"Where is he?" Lady Asata asked.

"Over there!" the young man answered and pointed to a still figure just below the scaffolding.

A twisted bag containing two or three slabs of raw meat was slung around the boy's arm as four lions began sniffing the air as they began to hesitantly approach from the opposite side of the stockade. Matthias was the first to reach the stricken youth.

"It looks like he has broken a leg and maybe an arm. I need your help!" Matthias hollered.

"Great!" Lady Asata muttered under her breath as she moved toward Matthias while trying to stay focused on the encroaching lions. She maneuvered her sword in front of her as she stepped around Matthias who was attempting to disentangle the bag of meat from the boy's shoulder.

"Here," Matthias finally instructed, with Ibrahim translating as quickly as the words were spoken, "take this and throw it as far as you can that way," and he pointed to the opposite side of stockade. "Maybe we'll get lucky, and the lions will chase the food and not us."

Lady Asata did not need an interpreter to understand what Matthias was saying, grabbed the pouch and flung it as far as she could across the open space. The lions let out a roar and then turned their attention to the meat.

"Let's get out of here!" Lady Asata hollered while assuming a defensive crouch with her sword held in front of her.

"Tell him," Matthias said to Ibrahim, "that this might hurt, but I'm going to lift from his right side and try to carry him. You and the boy follow the girl." Then, without waiting for objections, Matthias lifted the injured youth who began to struggle. However, Matthias tightened his grip and ran as fast as he could for the open gate. Lady Asata followed, walking backward, still in her defensive crouch, as did Ibrahim and the boy's brother. The lions noticed the movement and started moving cautiously in their direction as loud roars resonated within the stockade. Ibrahim finally closed the gate behind them, securing it with a wooden crossbar.

"Yes!" Matthias said defiantly as he laid the injured youth on the dirt roadway. The uninjured boy attempted to maneuver himself beside Matthias as he tried to comfort the other by wiping his brother's forehead with a dirty rag worn as a turban around his head. Lady Asata looked down at the three and breathed heavily.

"What's going on here!" a gruff, new voice asked from the sideline. "Has someone been bothering my lions?"

Matthias paid the man no heed as he continued to examine the injured youth. However, Lady Asata sheathed her weapon and walked over to the disgruntled spectator.

"No," she said firmly to a stout, balding man who stepped forward and stood face-to-face with the girl. "By good fortune, a life has been spared. Does that bother you for some reason?" she asked.

"And who might you be?" the man asked. "This is my business, and I tolerate no interference by anyone."

The man took a step closer to Lady Asata.

"Then I would be more careful about how I treat my workers," Lady Asata said without flinching.

At that same moment, she noticed that Matthias had maneuvered the injured boy onto his right side while attempting to fix splints to both the left arm and leg. She was puzzled as she watched Matthias mutter something into the youth's ear as the boy moaned, and his body shook.

Turning her attention back to the balding man, she added, "Perhaps I should introduce myself. I am Lady Asata," and she pointed to the lion emblem on her right armlet. "My father is Lord Harsiotef. Do we have issues that need to be discussed?" Her challenge was unmistakable.

The man said nothing but took a step backward and then lowered his head.

"Lady Asata," he said obsequiously.

"Good," she replied. "We will be leaving as soon as the splints are in place. Matthias…"

Matthias looked up as he attempted to raise the injured youth helped by the boy's brother.

"We are ready. Do we have some way to get him back to the city?" Matthias asked. "The boy cannot stand in the chariot." Ibrahim interpreted loud enough for another in the crowd to step forward and offer the use of one of his carts.

"Thank you," Lady Asata said to the man who bowed slightly. "Let's go then. I'll take the chariot and meet you at the city gate. Ibrahim, you go with Matthias."

"Yes, ma'am," Ibrahim replied.

"You'll have to handle the cart," Matthias said to the interpreter as the youth was maneuvered into the bed of the two-wheeled vehicle.

Matthias felt his arm tugged at the elbow as he was pulled aside by Lady Asata, who asked, "What was all that muttering you were doing while fixing a splint to the boy's arm and leg? He seemed to react when you did it."

Matthias started to answer and then shook his head, saying, "Nothing. Just a prayer for his recovery."

Lady Asata nodded knowingly as her chariot pulled alongside and said, "I suspected it was something like that. Whatever it was, it worked. Now let's get back to Meroe." She looked up at the sky, which had begun to cloud over. "It looks like rain."

Ibrahim obligingly snapped the reins against the backside of a donkey as the cart pulled forward and Lady Asata's chariot did likewise.

It had been a long and intense day.

Lord Harsiotef sat at his table in his grand room and stared blankly toward the open window. His daughter had just left after recounting her experiences of the day and her encounters with the young prophet. He was not quite sure what to make of it all. Certainly, the boy had more backbone than first suspected. Suddenly a door opened, and a large shadow entered the room framed by light from the hallway: the Candace.

The woman walked deliberately to one of two chairs in front of the vizier's desk, struggled to sit down, and once seated, proceeded to question her chief minister.

"What troubles you?" she asked. "I can read it on your face."

"Nothing, really, ma'am," the vizier answered. "Asata was just here and gave a full account of her day with our young friend."

"Oh? And how did that go?" the Candace asked.

"It seems rather predictable. However, there was one incident at the animal stockades that bears some note. A worker—a boy, actually—fell in with the lions, and our young prophet took it upon himself to play the role of hero. He and Asata snatched the injured youth from the lions and tended to his wounds."

"That does not surprise me," the Candace said. "Zealots can be fearless though foolish."

"I'm not so sure he is a 'zealot,'" the vizier answered. "However, that is not what bothers me."

"Explain."

"While this Matthias was tending to the injured young man, he would whisper something to himself, and the boy's body would shake in response. Then the boy would relax, and Matthias would continue with his efforts."

"Magic?" the Candace asked.

"Perhaps. Asata did not think so. However, I am not so sure."

"This is precisely what I do not want," the Candace replied. "I cannot upset our local priests by another claiming to speak for a higher god. Remember, it has not been that long since the priests of Amun were challenging my authority, even displacing some of my predecessors! We do not need another god in the pantheon of Kush!"

The vizier sat up straight and looked directly at his ruler.

"What do we do then, ma'am? Take this Matthias prisoner?" he asked.

The Candace pushed awkwardly on the arms of her chair as she started to rise.

"No, not yet, at least. Keep doing what you are doing. And tell Asata to be especially watchful. Maybe I will speak with the young man myself."

"As you wish," the vizier responded.

"And get some rest," the Candace added as she turned into the hallway. "The problem, if there is one, will not be solved tonight."

Lord Harsiotef stood from his table and walked the short distance to the door and closed it. He then strode across the room to an open window. It was beginning to rain, and its fresh, sweet smell was a welcome balm, perhaps even a good omen.

CHAPTER TWENTY-THREE

Southeast Gate, City of Meroe

Matthias approached the open city gate with some apprehension. Other than his outing with Lady Asata, he still chaffed with his restriction to the interior and immediate environs of the palace. However, he could not escape the pull of his mission and the thought of the community that had sprung up haphazardly along the southeastern wall of the city where, just hours before, they had taken the injured boy and his brother. Dracus and Ibrahim stood with him at the gate that was a boundary to the ramshackle village which, for Dracus, was his first attempt to leave his sickbed as guards patrolled access at the gate presumably to watch those who entered or left Meroe.

The three walked quickly past the sentries, not expecting trouble; however, Matthias did not wish to attract unnecessary attention either. Once beyond the gate, he and his two companions crossed a bridge that spanned a causeway and then turned north as they walked down an irregular road that paralleled a canal, which traversed a congestion of crudely built huts and lean-tos that served as housing for an odd mix of inhabitants. Small children ran every which way that made navigating the crowded thoroughfare difficult, as did smoke from the city's ironworks that occasionally belched an envelope of noxious fog. However, Matthias remained focused and led his small entourage down the narrow, winding passageways to the hut of the injured boy and his family.

"I believe that's the one," Ibrahim said as he pointed to a shack made of wooden slats located near the end of the cluttered, makeshift roads. "I still don't think this is a good idea."

Matthias continued as if he did not hear the man and approached the ramshackle hut with an air of confidence. Two small children ran out a door and blocked further progress.

"Are you here to see Brother?" one child asked through Ibrahim.

"Yes," Matthias answered.

"Wait." Both children then turned and ran inside a curtained doorway.

Moments later, the brother of the injured boy appeared and confronted his visitors.

"Welcome," the boy said, with Ibrahim interpreting, "I am Attla. You come to see Adda. He is much improved. Come," and the boy held a frayed rug to one side so Matthias and his companions could enter.

Once inside, Matthias found the hut to be very simply furnished, with bedding stacked neatly against one wall and everyday items such as pots and pans against another. An opening in the roof let out smoke from a small fire used to cook meals.

The injured boy was lying flat on his back with his splinted arm and leg positioned tightly to his side; seven candles that traced the shape of his body burned on a dirt floor. An elderly woman wearing a brightly patterned turban and holding a small bowl of dark liquid in her hands was seated cross-legged at the boy's head while another woman, more middle-aged, sat to her right. The two children who first greeted Matthias were now kneeling at the injured boy's feet, looking up at Matthias and smiling.

Attla introduced those who surrounded his brother, "This is my mother," and he pointed to the woman without the bowl, "and the other is her friend. She is here to administer the cure."

For the first time Matthias noticed how similar the two boys were in appearance. And he could smell the odor of incense while noticing a small palm frond cradled in the older woman's lap with a candle and a large bowl of dark liquid held over the injured boy's head. Matthias looked on silently.

"My friend brought clean bandages to rebind the wounds," Matthias finally said, nodding at Dracus.

Ibrahim interpreted while the family listened attentively as the injured youth groaned weakly.

"Do you think it necessary to change the bandages?" the brother, Attla, asked.

"I do," Matthias answered.

Attla looked to his mother, who said something unintelligible to the other woman. The latter immediately put down her bowl and candle as she stood, grimaced, and said something obviously unpleasant to the mother.

The boy's mother also stood and responded in kind. She then turned to Attla and gestured at both Matthias and Dracus.

Ibrahim interpreted that the woman had given her permission to change bandages. He also interpreted the woman asking, "Where does your companion draw his powers? The old woman's power comes from the forest. What of your god?"

Matthias shook his head slightly as he waved Dracus to the prone young boy.

"I follow one who performed many miracles and spoke of only one god. It is this god that we praise. Whatever powers Darcus and I possess come from him."

As Matthias spoke, Dracus bent next to the injured boy and begun to carefully unwrap the soiled ties around the splints as the youth groaned and moved from side to side. Dracus worked very quickly, and the wounds were finally exposed. The man then signaled with one of the clean rags taken from his pouch, which Matthias took to mean that Dracus wanted water in order to cleanse the injuries, and told the same to Ibrahim. This was interpreted to the mother, who had Attla bring a large clay jar from the opposite side of the hut and place it next to Dracus. The latter immediately poured water onto a clean cloth and began to wipe the wounds on both the arm and leg. Matthias also gently placed a hand on each and muttered something inaudible to which the boy first shook and then settled back as if in a restful sleep. Dracus followed by wrapping the injuries in clean bandages and reattaching the splints. All this was done under the suspicious eyes of the older woman who still held a palm frond at her side.

"His condition should improve. Right now, he must rest," Matthias said as he stood and faced the mother. "We will check again later…with your permission."

The mother nodded her assent. The other older woman just continued to stand to one side and watch, never letting her focus change from either Matthias or Dracus. Finally, the boy, Attla, held the curtained door open, suggesting that it was time to leave.

Matthias, Dracus, and Ibrahim stepped quickly outside, which was still congested with local citizenry going about their daily lives. After again promising to return, Matthias looked at Dracus, raised his right hand, and swept it in a half-circle around himself.

"I think we have discovered why we were sent to this land," Matthias said. "This is where we will establish our mission."

He studied the landscape of huts and lean-tos with an intensity that Dracus had rarely seen.

Ibrahim broke the spell.

"I think we should return to the palace. It was not a good idea to leave in the first place. They will be looking for us," he said.

Matthias just shrugged and started slowly toward the city gate, as did Dracus. Ibrahim's words could not compete with what Matthias now understood to be his fate; all of which was observed and scrutinized by an old woman who stood in silence, still holding a decaying frond.

Matthias had to endure the unrelenting chastisement of Lady Asata for having ventured outside the palace without her. Fortunately, two of the three days that followed were washed out by an inundation of rain, and Matthias could not venture far from his restricted space anyway. However, the third day held the prospect of good weather, which tested Matthias's resolve: he desperately wanted to revisit the injured boy; yet he had promised Lady Asata that he would do nothing without informing her first. It was almost as if the girl could read his mind and wanted to unravel his plans. Regardless, she finally relented and agreed to at least talk to her father about a visit, but only on certain conditions.

"First," she said, "you must agree to keep me with you at all times. Second, no preaching about your god. And finally, the visit must be kept short, and we return to the palace as soon as possible."

Matthias did not see that he had any alternative but to agree, so he did. His thought was that any contact with the community beyond the gate was beneficial; besides, he needed Lady Asata to interpret. Therefore, it was he, Lady Asata, and Dracus who crowded onto Asata's chariot midday the fourth day back at the palace and rode toward the southeast wall of the city. The weather was clear, and there was little evidence of the hard rains of the days previous other than standing water, which Asata splashed through without concern for pedestrians using the same cobbled roadway. Once outside the gate, she turned north and hugged the bank of the canal until stopped by Matthias again, unconcerned for pedestrian traffic.

"Here?" Lady Asata said, looking slightly surprised. "Let's get this over with," she said and stepped off her chariot, tied the reins of the two horses to an overhang from the roof of the hut, and looked for Matthias to lead the way.

Attla walked out the curtained doorway to greet them.

"Welcome, my brother's healer! Please come inside."

Matthias complied, as did the others. Once inside Matthias could see that the injured youth was much improved. Adda was sitting on a stool with his broken leg extended and his broken arm hanging stationary at his side while hugging a wooden crutch made from a tree branch. The most encouraging sign was that, on seeing Matthias, the boy pushed himself up and broke out in a smile.

"As you can see, I am much improved," the boy said. "I can even walk."

He steadied himself with his cane as he hobbled awkwardly around the limited space inside the hut.

"That is wonderful," Matthias responded. At this same time, the boy's mother maneuvered herself between both and held up a bowl of a sweet-smelling, pasty-looking food. While doing so, she asked Matthias a question, which Lady Asata interpreted.

"She wants to know how your god can work his healing so fast?" Lady Asata translated while Matthias tried to comprehend.

"That is a miracle which only he knows," Matthias finally responded. "He is not only a loving god but a powerful one."

Lady Asata frowned as she translated while at the same time glaring at Matthias. The boy's mother gave an accepting nod.

"Let Dracus look at your leg," Matthias suggested. "Just to make sure the bandages are doing their job."

At that moment, the curtained doorway opened, and Attla reappeared with five women holding small children, three of which were babies.

"Could you use your powers to help these women and their children?" Attla asked. "They are very sick, and the women have nowhere else to go."

Matthias was speechless; however, Lady Asata was not.

"Matthias, you promised," she said. "You found what you came to see. Now let's return to the palace."

Matthias signaled Dracus to come stand beside him.

"Let my friend examine the children. I will say a blessing. Then we will go."

Not waiting for Lady Asata to object, Matthias had the first woman and her baby step up to Dracus, who pulled aside a blanket that enshrouded the child, felt the baby's forehead, and tested its breathing. He then reached into his pouch and pulled out an herb of small leaves which, through the translation of Lady Asata, he instructed the mother to boil and feed to her baby. Matthias then concluded the examination by placing his hand on the top of the child's head while saying an inaudible prayer. This was repeated until every child was seen.

"Now let's go!" she insisted. "The palace will be missing us."

Without waiting for excuses, she turned and started out the door, with Matthias and Dracus only steps behind.

"Thank you again," Attla and Adda said in unison as the curtain at the doorway remained open, and the women with their small children crowded the space. "You will visit again, won't you?" Attla asked.

Matthias did not want to aggravate the situation, so he answered with only a half-smile and waved. He then stepped onto the chariot as it began its tortuous course through the crowds back to the palace. As he watched the spectators move away from their moving vehicle, he thought he spotted a familiar face, an old woman wearing a brightly colored turban, and then the figure was gone.

Matthias gave it no further mind. He had accomplished what he had set out to do: the seeds of his mission were sown.

CHAPTER TWENTY-FOUR

The return to the palace was full of anticipation. Lady Asata had disappeared almost from the time of their arrival, replaced by a contingent of two sword-wielding guards who reluctantly permitted a short detour to their room before escorting both Matthias and Dracus to the smaller of two palace throne rooms. That was late morning. It was now approaching midafternoon, and still no explanation for the shunting about the compound with an escort.

The room they occupied had ten columns, five built out from two opposite walls with a raised dais positioned at one end. Two chairs, one larger than the other, each decorated with multicolored hieroglyphs, were centered on the dais with a white-fringed canopy extending over the whole. A third stool was placed to the left of the smaller chair. Large copper stands with saucer tops and a flame burning in the middle of each stood in front of the columns while three doors granted entry, two from the rear and the other to the left of the dais. Surprisingly, there was little color other than monochromatic yellow-gray walls and a sandy tiled floor. Unique to the room was a bust of Caesar Augustus buried faceup at the entrance, forcing most to step on the image before entering.

Having endured the forced march through the palace, Matthias sat crossed-legged next to Dracus against one of the walls with guards on each side, waiting for events to unfold. Matthias could only imagine the worse.

Finally, without fanfare, the rear door to the room opened, and several men wearing white kilts entered and stood to one side between columns near the dais. They were followed by three men with shaved heads dressed in loincloths, carrying large boxes, each of whom positioned themselves to the right of the dais where they opened the boxes and took out what looked to be tablets and styluses. This must have been a signal to the guards, for they each kicked Matthias and Dracus in the leg, pulled them to their feet, and pushed both between two columns near the dais.

Then the two large doors that gave entry from the hallway suddenly opened as at least three dozen men and a smattering of women, some dressed in traditional Egyptian manner, hurried into the room and stood as close as possible to the dais, each engaged in a hushed conversation. Matthias even spotted two or three individuals dressed in the Roman fashion. He also thought he spied an old woman wearing a multicolored turban bobbing among the spectators.

Two guards next opened the rear door again, and the room fell silent. The vizier, dressed in a long red-and-black robe fringed with golden tassels, entered holding a long black rod, which he tapped three times on the tile floor and then shouted something Matthias did not understand. Obviously, whatever it was cued the next in the procession as five men and two women entered, two of whom Matthias recognized immediately: the man he knew as the Ethiopian and Lady Asata! They each took a position behind the scribes while another large man with a shaved head, yet more regally dressed in a white kilt with a leopard skin draped around his shoulders, walked and stood in front of the stool on the dais.

The vizier stepped forward and again tapped the floor with his rod. He shouted something, and all in the room lowered their heads as two young men entered and stood on either side of the elevated chairs, one of whom was Prince Teritegas. Matthias did not recognize the other.

"It is best you bow," a man whispered in Matthias's ear. It was Ibrahim who had slipped in unnoticed and stood to Matthias's right. "The one you know," he whispered. "The other is Prince Amanikhabale, the oldest son of the Candace. Say nothing no matter what happens," Ibrahim warned.

Matthias started to speak, which Ibrahim stopped with a grimace and a tight grip on his shoulder.

"Nothing!" he reiterated. "Say absolutely nothing! I will explain if I can."

Matthias turned slowly toward the dais only to watch the spectacle continue as two others entered the room, one a male dressed in an elaborate red, white, and black robe with a large jeweled pectoral hanging from his neck, rings on almost every finger, and a white conical crown on his head. He was followed by a very obese woman dressed in a golden robe tied at the waist with an elaborately knotted belt and bejeweled with a large pectoral and rings; she was crowned by a golden band displaying several large jewels with two cobra heads centered on her forehead. Both carried what looked to be a scepter with an open loop at one end. The male took a seat in the smaller chair while the female sat in the larger. Once seated, the vizier turned to those assembled and knocked his black rod twice while again uttering something which Matthias did not comprehend.

This prompted two guards at the back of the room to escort three men in long robes and turbans to the dais, followed by four slaves balancing a large green-and-gold box on two long poles supported by their shoulders. Once at the dais, the escort stopped, bowed slightly as the slaves carried the box up to the seated figures where it was opened as one of the turbaned men stepped forward to display the contents: jeweled cups, rings and other assorted golden objects.

"Tribute from Persia. The three men are its ambassadors," Ibrahim whispered. "They need Meroe's goodwill for safe passage to the lands west and north of here."

The vizier again hit the floor with his rod and shouted.

Almost instantly two additional guards entered, escorting two men dressed in bright yellow-and-green robes with large mythological creatures embroidered on each. The two were followed by slaves who carried bolts of shimmering cloth, which were presented at the foot of the dais.

"Ambassadors from the land where the sun rises," Ibrahim explained. "Their gift is greatly prized."

As he spoke, the man dressed in bright yellow picked up a bolt of red cloth and held it out to the obese woman who felt it, smiled, and then sat back as the bolt was placed with others.

The vizier again tapped his rod, and the guards who surrounded Matthias and Dracus came to life as they hit their charges in the calf of their legs with the butt end of their spears and started for the dais. Matthias was momentarily stunned. Once at the dais, the vizier looked up at the enthroned man and woman, said something unintelligible, then turned to Matthias.

"He has introduced you to the Candace and her consort," Ibrahim explained. "It is protocol that you bow." Matthias and Dracus complied.

"A prophet!" the prince unknown to Matthias responded. "We are indeed honored."

The speaker took a few steps closer to the large man seated on the stool in front of the consort as his eyes focused on Matthias who held the stare. Ibrahim continued to interpret as his grip tightened on Matthias's shoulder to indicate caution.

"Actually, I understand there is more! Is this not the man who jumped into the den of lions and rescued an injured attendant? It is a double honor indeed!"

Matthias's silent stare continued. What registered was a slender man of medium height who was used to unquestioned authority. There was an immediate dislike, which Matthias felt confident was mutual.

Another finally interrupted the prince's interrogation as the man known to Matthias as the Ethiopian stepped up to the dais, stood to one side of the armed escort, and addressed the Candace.

"I traveled from Jerusalem with this man," the Ethiopian said, "and I found his actions to be honorable. If he is a prophet, then perhaps we should listen."

The Candace gave no response. However, the heavyset man wearing a leopard skin signaled that the prince should bend toward him, for which the man was rewarded with something whispered in his ear.

"I understand your position, my Lord Treasurer," Prince Amanikhabale began. "And I also understand that this prophet can heal with just a touch of his hand. Am I not right? It is reported that he did so as recently as this morning!"

"That I know nothing about," the Ethiopian replied. "Does it matter how the gods may favor him? This man's efforts only benefit us all."

"I wonder. Do they really?" the prince retorted as he looked down at the man seated on the stool. "We know where the loyalties of Amun lie. However, what of this man's god and those who follow him? Are they loyal to the Candace and to Meroe? What do we really know of this one who calls himself Matthias?"

The young disciple again felt Ibrahim's grip tighten.

"Enough!" a gruff female bellowed from the back of the dais. "This man is my guest and will not be treated this way! Stand aside, Amanikhabale, and let this child come to me. Come!" and the Candace signaled with her scepter that Matthias should stand in front of her.

"Are you, indeed, a prophet?" she asked, bending forward. "How young! I see no fire in your eyes. Perhaps Prince Amanikhabale mistakes you for having the power he wishes to possess: insight to his own future." Then, turning her attention to her son who faced his mother with a deep scowl, she added, "And unless he changes his attitude, I would not say it is too promising."

An abbreviated but noticeable gasp emanated from the spectators while the Candace leaned back in her chair with a half-smile.

"You may return to your escort," the woman said, dismissing Matthias. "We will speak more of this later. However, today is not meant to be one of gloom. We rejoice that our youngest son is to marry!"

She signaled that the man standing silently to her right should step forward.

"In a month Prince Teritegas is to marry Lady Nasaisa of Nepata. At such time, we will all rejoice in this union!" she said and took the left hand of her youngest child and gently squeezed. "Now I wish to speak with my ministers." Then, without waiting for further protocol, the Candace rose and quickly left the hall through the side door.

Matthias watched the conclusion of the spectacle with more than detached interest. He particularly noted the clinched fists and skewered faces of both the older prince and the man with a leopard-skin cape. Obviously, mother's bite could still sting.

"I think that went rather well," a very satisfied woman sitting awkwardly in a side chair said to her vizier in the privacy of the man's office located not far from the throne room. "My eldest son did not look too happy. However, that was to be expected. I also doubt that the high priest was pleased. If you think on it, the joining of my family with the girl's, who has a heritage from the dynasty of pharaohs, is providential. My youngest may yet be my heir."

A crack of thunder punctuated the room.

"It is to be hoped that will be the outcome, my lady," the vizier responded, somewhat startled by the unexpected noise. "However, we must proceed with caution. Both your son and the high priest are not to be underestimated, especially as the prize are the two golden cobras that circle your head."

"Then we must try harder," the Candace said. "My oldest is completely under the control of the high priest. Did you notice how he acted today?"

"It was hard not to," the vizier responded. "And why attack the young Jew so vigorously? He can mean nothing to them."

"But he does," the Candace replied. "Allegiance to any faction but their own is a threat. It is their history. Remember the turmoil caused by the homage paid to Aten and not to Amun. Even I am a threat, although they dare do nothing about it. However, let my oldest come to power, and the high priest and others like him will rule once more."

"Then we must not allow this strange, young man from Judea to disturb the status quo. I will speak with my daughter again about keeping a watchful eye on him. Although, to date, his activities seem harmless enough."

"Perhaps," the Candace replied. "I must admit that I am intrigued by this claim that he is a prophet. However, you are right to keep him under scrutiny if only because my son and the high priest have taken such an uncommon interest in him. Just keep me informed."

"Of course," the vizier said as he nodded, and another bolt of lightning illuminated the night sky. "And the wedding will only solidify Prince Teritegas's claim as the rightful heir. This is a battle we cannot afford to lose."

The Candace stood to leave, however, not before turning and speaking again to her vizier.

"No, we cannot," she said resolutely. "No, we cannot."

Matthias stood in front of one of two windows in his bleak room and watched without seeing the bank of dark clouds move over the city. His mind was elsewhere. He did not understand the animosity of either the royal prince or the high priest. He had pondered all evening on the subject and could think of nothing, not even a slight that had passed between him and either man. Yet, for some reason, he was fiercely disliked by both.

"Are you ready for your lesson?" a familiar voice asked as the door to the room opened.

"Ibrahim," Matthias said as he came out of his deep thoughts. "I forgot that you were coming. Yes, let's get started."

The older man could see the troubled look in the eyes of his young student.

"Is there something I can help you with?" the older man asked.

"No," Matthias replied. "I need to work this out for myself."

The interpreter took a tablet and laid it on the sole table in the room as rain began to pummel an outside window casing.

"Then let's get started," he said. "Learning the local language will take time."

The two sat in chairs opposite each other as Ibrahim scratched several words on a tablet with his stylus. He pronounced each word and gave its definition; Ibrahim then expected Matthias to repeat what he had said. However, Matthias remained distracted and was silent.

"I know you are worried about what happened. However, Prince Amanikhabale was just playing with you. Have nothing to do with him or the high priest. I warned you about them. Just stay as far away from both as you can."

"I have tried," Matthias answered.

"Then you have nothing to worry about."

"I hope you are right."

"I am," Ibrahim said. "They have more important things to do than to concern themselves with you. However, I can see that it is a waste of time to continue our studies tonight. We will start again tomorrow."

"I think that is for the best," Matthias agreed.

Ibrahim needed no further encouragement and walked to the door. He turned as if to say something, thought better of it, then exited. Matthias watched absentmindedly as he turned to the open window where rain continued to blow across the city and wondered how long he would remain a prisoner to the politics of this strange land.

CHAPTER TWENTY-FIVE

Three days of rain kept most everyone indoors until the seasonal flood subsided. Although the main thoroughfares and plazas of Meroe were bricked and well drained, the side streets and alleyways were not so well maintained. Therefore, like most, Matthias waited out the inundation and a return to normalcy. His goal was simple: continue to build the mission. Consequently, Lady Asata's unexpected assent that they return to the huts outside the city wall was greeted with enthusiasm.

As usual the three of them—Asata, Matthias, and Dracus—charged through the neighborhoods and splashed along the crude roadway that ran parallel to the channel that fed water to the iron works. Once arrived at Adda's hut, they were greeted by the young boy now walking almost effortlessly with the aid of a cane who explained that his brother had returned to the animal pens, hoping he still had a job. Matthias suspected otherwise but said nothing; the family had endured enough.

Surprisingly, Adda oriented the conversation to Matthias's involvement with the Master, especially stories of healing the sick and lame. Adda wanted to know, should he not now be considered one of the chosen as he was blessed by his prophet? Matthias sat the boy down and, using Lady Asata as an interpreter, tried to explain that everyone was "special" in the eyes of God; you just had to believe to see the truth. He continued by relating several of the healings he had witnessed and again gave an account of the crucifixion and the empty tomb.

It was obvious that Matthias's stories made Lady Asata uncomfortable as she was hesitant in her translation and at one point asked, "Why do you tell him such things?"

"Because it is what I experienced," Matthias answered bluntly.

As they spoke, others entered the cramped space and listened to Matthias as interpreted by Asata. It was a mixed lot of women and small children with a smattering of older men.

"How long were you with this god?" one asked.

"Almost from the beginning," Matthias responded.

"But he was also a man? Like us?"

"Yes."

"So why did he not prevent his own death?" one of the males asked from the rear of the hut.

"But he did not die!" Matthias explained with passion rising in his voice. "I know it is hard to believe. However, I was there and saw the empty tomb. He suffered for us, yes, and then promised that those who believed would one day join him in paradise. We just have to heed his words and follow his way."

A woman kneeling in the front of the others reached forward and touched the hem of Matthias's robe.

"That may be, but it was you who healed my child," she said. "If you believe in this one god and can perform such wonders because of that, then I can believe too."

A murmur among those crowding around Matthias punctuated the woman's words.

Matthias was surprised how easy it all came. It was as if he was venting everything he had silenced since leaving Judea. Lady Asata was not as comfortable, however, and continued to stumble in her translation partly out of amazement at the stories coming from Matthias's mouth.

"We need to go," she finally insisted. "I did not expect this to turn into a worship experience."

Matthias looked up at the girl but found no solace.

As he stood a tall, gaunt woman with a withered face and long fingers stepped forward with two children, one a young girl, perhaps three or four years old, and the other a boy barely a toddler. Both children mirrored the woman with large, sad eyes and emaciated frames. The woman started to speak, but Lady Asata held up a hand to stop her; she did not understand the dialect. Finally, Adda pushed himself up from the floor and stood next to the woman who continued her talk. Once finished, Adda translated back to Lady Asata, who when finished turned to Matthias, visibly shaken.

"She says that she, her brother, and his wife came to Meroe from far away," Lady Asata repeated. "The brother went to work at the iron works and died. His wife also died of disease. Now she is left with his two children which she cannot support," Lady Asata continued. "She is going to return to her home village and wishes to leave the children with you! Having heard what you said, she knows they will be safe and well cared for."

Lady Asata shook her head.

"So what are you going to do?" she asked almost as a challenge.

Matthias was silent for a moment as his eyes darted first to Asata then to the woman and finally back to Asata.

"I don't know what to do," he stuttered. "We certainly cannot take these children. It is out of the question! Surely there are others who can care for them."

Lady Asata translated as she faced the despondent woman. The latter took a half-step forward and raised her head as tears welled in each eye.

"Please!" she implored Matthias. "Take the children! They will not survive a return to my village. Please!"

She held out her hand as the young girl leaned into her legs for security.

Matthias was conflicted, and the emotion showed.

Lady Asata just shook her head. Finally, Adda offered a solution.

"I know two old women who take in orphans," he said. "They have a hut near the other side of our village. I will take you there."

"That's a good idea," Lady Asata replied almost immediately. "Let's do it. The children and the woman are to remain here until we return. Explain that to her."

Adda did as requested.

No one questioned Asata as she led the way out of the hut to her chariot for the short ride to the limits of the ramshackle community. Matthias was open to almost any idea.

The chariot zigzagged around huts and blanketed lean-tos until finally reaching a crudely improvised structure that barely held a roof upright, with small children playing in a rutted footpath that ran parallel to the shack. A woman holding an infant in her arms stepped from behind a half-enclosed wall and stared up at those in the chariot. Adda directed a few pointed words at the woman who nodded and then stepped inside the crumbling structure. Lady Asata indicated that they were to follow. Once inside, other children of varying ages scrambled about on a dirt floor, either playing or crying for attention.

"This is the place for children who have no home," Adda said matter-of-factly. "There are women who care for them until taken by others."

"What others?" Matthias asked almost defensively.

"Those who need workers for the fields or at the iron factors. Some even go with the caravans," Adda explained. "We all try to provide, but it is very difficult. The old women do their best."

While they talked, Lady Asata walked briskly around the circumference of the hut, holding a cloth over her mouth as she dodged children with each step. At one point, she stopped and looked down at a jumbled pile of soiled blankets and clothing.

"Is that where they sleep?" she asked.

No one answered.

When Lady Asata finished navigating the cluttered space, she looked at no one but stepped immediately outside. Matthias noticed the drawn look on the woman's face and the quickness of her stride. Therefore, he opted to let Lady Asata explain her actions when she thought it appropriate.

After climbing onto the chariot and when joined by the others, she looked directly at Matthias and pointed her finger.

"Under no circumstance will those two children come to live in such filth!" she said in Aramaic as good as it was possible for her to manage. "We will take them with us to the palace, and I will speak with my father. The present situation is impossible!"

She then spurred the two horses down the barely discernable roadway scattering pedestrians without caution.

Matthias kept his silence. In that instant he realized that the mission had gained an important ally!

CHAPTER TWENTY-SIX

Lady Asata watched her father as he paced in front of two whitewashed columns capped with golden lion heads, which decorated the interior of his private quarters. It was not often that she and her father were at odds; however, on this occasion, there was a complete difference of opinion.

"You absolutely must not take on this responsibility!" Lord Harsiotef barked at his daughter. "The palace is no place for rearing two orphans of such dubious background. I blame myself for not paying more attention to your future. However, this will change, I promise you! It is the Jew who has led you down this path, isn't it?"

Lady Asata was momentarily taken aback by the rebuke.

"You forget that I am also an orphan taken in by a kindly man and his wife. And that did not turn out so badly." There were tears in both eyes when she finished her thought.

Lord Harsiotef embraced his daughter.

"There is one important difference," the father explained. "I was protected by the Candace. Your friend is not. And what do we really know about him? Are either of you in a position to rear children?"

Asata was not to be dissuaded.

"Matthias is not the issue here!" she insisted. "However, I can tell you from observing him over the past several weeks that he is as uncomplicated a man as can be found. And if we don't take the children into our custody," she asked, "what is to become of them? You should have seen that disgusting environment! I could not live with myself, knowing that is to be their fate. Father, I have to do something!"

"The best I can do is put it to the Candace," Lord Harsiotef said, backing away from his daughter and again standing aloof between two pillars. "I cannot predict how she will react."

Asata knew it was fruitless to argue and bowed slightly in obedience. Even more distressing, Asata had grave doubts on the likelihood that she would achieve any type of success on the subject of either child now.

Matthias could only imagine what was transpiring between Lady Asata and her father as he sat stoically in one of two chairs in his room, staring at two frightened children with their eyes wide open and their backs pressed against a wall as Dracus and one of Lady Asata's slaves hovered nearby. He was still struck by Asata's revelation that she, too, was an orphan abandoned to a caravan and later adopted by the vizier and his wife. Still, he had to ask himself, was this all a happenstance or somehow part of the Master's greater plan? He knew nothing about fatherhood; indeed, he barely provided for his own needs.

Suddenly there was a loud knock on the door as it swung open, and Lady Asata walked immediately to the children.

"Father said he would take the matter up with the Candace," she said. "He made no promise." She had decided not to explain her own misgivings.

"When will we know?" Matthias asked.

"That, too, is uncertain," she answered.

Matthias merely shook his head. There was little else to do but wait. Thankfully, the girl had not succumbed to the arguments of her father...yet.

The attention of all was again drawn to the doorway as a stranger dressed in a white pleated kilt and the headdress of the royal guard pushed his way into the room and pointed at Matthias.

"Come!" he demanded in a low voice.

Matthias understood this word, at least, and knew that the man would tolerate no argument. He looked at Lady Asata for a quick answer, found none, and therefore moved hesitantly toward the door. The guard motioned that he should move faster. Lady Asata followed. She could not imagine what required such urgency; however, her father's warning still resonated.

The three moved quickly down a hallway painted with images of various gods and heroic figures reposed in idyllic settings until they reached another extremity of the palace far removed from Matthias's quarters and considerably more ornate. The number of people surrounding them also substantially grew where, on nearing their destination, armed guards stood at nearly every doorway. Finally, when they reached a location where the hallways converged into a large alcove painted with two oversized golden chariots, their escort muttered something which apparently satisfied the sentries, and one of two mahogany doors opened.

"Prince Teritegas's quarters," Lady Asata said under her breath as both she and Matthias were escorted into the room.

Matthias said nothing but took careful note of their environment. Like most everything else in the palace, the walls were whitewashed with fluted pillars built away from the wall, creating the effect of a hallway. Floor-to-ceiling curtains hung at the eastern end of the room, which obviously led to an additional living space. At least a dozen men milled about, engaged in hushed conversations where every so often one of them would look apprehensively for signs of activity behind the curtain walls. A strong odor of incense infused the room.

The escort pulled aside one of the curtains and disappeared. He soon returned and waved both Matthias and Asata into the curtained area which was, indeed, another living area with several ornately decorated chairs and two tables set haphazardly against one wall and a large overstuffed bed pushed against another. A patio extended beyond a bank of more curtains where water from a canal splashed at the edge of the tiled floor. However, all attention was on the bed.

"Come this way!" a familiar voice insisted, although Matthias and Lady Asata hesitated. Ibrahim, therefore, waved as he repeated himself.

"They are here, ma'am," the interpreter said as he stepped to one side while Matthias and Lady Asata approached.

Those gathered at the bedside turned cautiously and looked to see of whom Ibrahim was referring. One individual in particular evidenced immediate interest.

The Candace twisted her bulky, blue robe to one side and stood.

"Come, my young prophet," she said in a subdued voice as she held out both arms. "As you can see my youngest has taken ill."

The Candace looked down at the bed and gently laid her hand on the forehead of a reclining Prince Teritegas, who was covered to his neck with a pale-yellow blanket. White smoke from two tall incense burners spiraled upward on either side of the prince while white robed priests murmured close by. Ibrahim came and stood close to interpret.

"So far, nothing has helped," and the Candace pointedly stared at the attending priests. "Perhaps you can do better." Her lips were pursed; however, Matthias could see the distress in her eyes.

"I will need my friend and his medicines," Matthias said after a moment of hesitation as he looked over his shoulder at Ibrahim. However, Lady Asata understood and barked an order to one of the slaves who stared back but did nothing.

"Go!" the Candace snapped. "You have your instruction. Bring this man Dracus to me!"

The startled slave ran toward the curtain shield.

"I will do what I can," Matthias said.

He noticed that the prince was being bled by the application of bloodsuckers and put his hand out to stop the practice. The priest hesitated until the Candace intervened.

"Do as you are told!" the woman snapped again. Then, looking at those who surrounded her son, she continued, "In fact, all of you, out! Now!" she ordered. "Your smoke and chants do nothing. Out!"

One of the priests who seemed to be overseeing the others stiffened, as if to question the woman. However, he, too, eventually bowed to her will and left the room.

The Candace came and stood next to Matthias and put a hand on his arm as if to reassure him that she was not as difficult as he had just witnessed.

"Please do your best," she pleaded. "Perhaps your god will see fit to spare my son." Tears came as she spoke.

Matthias looked down at the young prince and understood the woman's concern. The man was ashen white with sweat beading on his forehead, as every so often he would mutter something and shiver as if in delirium. Matthias felt the man's forehead, and it was warm.

"I need more blankets," Matthias said to no one in particular as Dracus was escorted into the room

"And we will need herbs to cure the fever," Matthias said as Dracus nodded and unshouldered his medicine bag. "And water. I need fresh water with clean rags as soon as possible."

Matthias then put both hands on the man's forehead as he closed his eyes and moved his lips in silence.

The Candace watched with hope. Just maybe all was not lost.

―⚬―

Matthias stood with Dracus and Lady Asata on the far side of the room while slaves changed bed linens. It had been two difficult days of touch and go as Prince Teritegas's fever first subsided and then reoccurred, at times more severe than others. However, his condition stabilized, and the man slowly improved so that now he was sitting and eating soft foods. He was even able to bark some inconsequential domestic orders. Matthias was greatly relieved, as was his mother.

"You have done well," the Candace said as she turned from the bed and approached the three tired figures standing next to the patio. "Your god has shown favor to my son."

Matthias started to say something but was stopped by a raised hand.

"My vizier informs me that you have two children under your care," the Candace said unexpectedly. "I do not see that the palace is a fit environment," she continued.

Matthias listened apprehensively.

"I have given this much thought and have decided that you should move out of the palace and find a place suitable for both you and the children," she continued. "I will even allow you to instruct others in the ways of your god. However, that is so long as what you preach does not conflict with the laws of my kingdom."

The Candace looked into the eyes of Matthias, expecting a response.

Matthias still hesitated. Lady Asata sensed the impasse and spoke up.

"He understands, my lady," she said with a broad smile. "He is just struggling with our language. Your offer is most generous."

"Good," the Candace replied, "then let it happen as soon as possible," and turned abruptly as she returned to her son's beside.

Lady Asata bowed slightly, as did Matthias while the woman walked away. If at that moment anyone had studied Matthias closely, they would have noticed tears in his eyes.

CHAPTER TWENTY-SEVEN

Matthias stood with legs spread and his hands on his hips as he surveyed a parcel of real estate near the city's southeastern gate for use as an orphanage. At his request, Lady Asata had accompanied him to help scrutinize the property as had Ibrahim. The two-storied, walled enclosure was located not far from the ironworks where every so often a gust of gray-black smoke would blow their way.

"This looks promising," Lady Asata said with Ibrahim interpreting.

Matthias agreed.

"Has my father spoken to you about finances?" Asata asked.

Matthias responded he had not.

"Apparently, my uncle, the one you know and met in Judea, wishes to contribute to your cause. Therefore, perhaps you can afford something like this. Besides, I understand that the owner was a merchant who has not returned to the city for years. The property has stood abandoned since that time. I suspect that its proximity to the ironworks might have something to do with the latter."

"That is all correct, my lady," Ibrahim replied. "I once partnered with the previous occupant, that is, until he got crossways with his government. I have heard nothing of him since that time. That is how I came to know of this place."

"Can we go on the property?" Matthias asked.

"Certainly," Ibrahim said as he pushed on a weathered wooden door that breached the wall of the compound, and with effort, it swung it open.

Lady Asata entered first followed by Matthias and then Ibrahim. They entered through a gate that breached a wall that surrounded the building. Once beyond the wall, it was obvious that the main structure and its environs needed considerable repair before anything would be considered habitable. To their right and away from the main road was a garden of trees and flowers, most overgrown with weeds that ran to one side of the main house. The latter looked solid; however, several of the shutters that protected the windows were damaged or had blown off completely. And several roof tiles lay broken on the ground.

"Shall we go inside?" Lady Asata suggested.

The interior of the main building was not much different than its exterior: well-constructed but needing repair.

"You would probably want to resurface everything," Lady Asata said, "and repair some of the floor tiles. However, there certainly is enough room for what you need," and she slowly examined each of the four rooms that made up the first floor.

"Yes, I agree," Matthias replied. "However, I wonder if there is not too much space. I don't know how I could afford all this." He looked to Ibrahim.

"Actually, I do not know what the cost would be," the man answered. "I suppose that, after so long a time, the property belongs to the state, and the state can do with it as it wishes."

"And there is my uncle," Lady Asata added as an afterthought. "Let's look at the rooms upstairs."

After examining four more rooms off a central second-floor hallway, they returned to the first level.

"Well, Matthias," Lady Asata asked, "what is it to be?"

The young disciple was deep in thought.

"It could work," he finally said. "The roof needs to be repaired. And the windows shuttered," he added. "All this will take time *and* considerable expense. When do you think I could talk to your uncle? I would like to show him the property."

"I am sure that is possible. I will speak to Father."

As the three continued to examine the complex, a sudden commotion grew on the other side of the wall. This was followed by multiple loud knocks on the gate, which finally swung open as two guards with spears entered the compound. They were followed by a more-familiar figure.

"Your father told me that I would find you here," Prince Teritegas said with a broad grin. His countenance was brimming with health, especially considering the past several weeks. "So have you found your orphanage?" he said to no one in particular as he walked quickly from one end of the main house to the other, examining the lot as critically as his inexperienced eyes would permit. He then turned suddenly to Matthias.

"Probably," Lady Asata answered, suspecting Matthias's discomfort. "Do you have any idea who we would contact about purchase? This site has been abandoned so long I wonder if anyone would know."

Prince Teritegas thought for a moment.

"No, I really do not know. The priests of Amun used to control this part of the city, that is, until they were chased out. However, don't let that concern you. In fact, this is one of the reasons I have come," he said with a hint of mystery.

He had everyone's attention.

"My wedding day approaches," he said, smiling. "If you listen carefully, you can hear the workmen pounding away at the platforms and regalia for the grand event."

There was silence as all listened to low staccato sounds in the distance.

Then, turning to Matthias, he said, "My young prophet, I am indebted to you for my life." Matthias started to say something but was warned off by a wave of the prince's hand. "No, I know this," Prince Teritegas continued. "If I had let the others continue with their ministrations, I would probably not be here today. So I wish to gift you this property as repayment for what I am indebted."

"Do you think this is possible?" Lady Asata asked without waiting for Matthias to reply.

"I will speak to Mother about it when I get back to the palace," he answered matter-of-factly.

Matthias was speechless.

"The other reason I came," he continued, "is that I want to ask you, my young prophet, to do me the honor of blessing my marriage. I suppose that I have to put up with the others too. However, considering everything, your blessing would be very special to me."

Ibrahim translated almost as fast as the words were spoken and let out an involuntary gasp at the request. He probably reacted as the others felt.

Matthias just stared at the prince, stunned. He finally nodded his head.

"Good!" Prince Teritegas said as he slapped Matthias on the shoulder and turned to walk out of the enclave. "I have much to do, like arrange for a tribute of cattle I must pay to my future father-in-law. I can just see him trying to corral the lot. It will be worth all my effort just for that! And I will talk to mother." He then disappeared behind the wall followed by his armed escort.

"Unbelievable!" Ibrahim whispered under his breath as soon as the prince had left.

"Do you comprehend the significance of this honor?" Lady Asata asked Matthias. "You are not only under his protection. He is elevating your god to be an equal with the others of Kush. After this, I may even come to believe!" she said in astonishment.

Matthias heard the accolades and the promised preferment; however, he was muted by his memories of the past. The Master was proclaimed as the "chosen one" by the people only days before he was crucified. Was this to be his fate? His mind could not help but fix on this confluence of events.

"Matthias..." Lady Asata said, placing a hand gently on his arm. "You do understand what has happened here?"

Matthias finally refocused on the present and the others who stood staring at him incredulously.

"Yes," he said, smiling. "Of course, I understand. It is everything we want."

"Good," Lady Asata replied. "For a moment I thought we had lost you. And if I know the prince, he will be as good as his word, and we will have our answer by midafternoon. Although I suspect that will be a mere formality. Work can begin this week!"

She turned again toward the main house.

Matthias nodded yet wondered if either of his companions understood how a much greater power was actually leading the way.

CHAPTER TWENTY-EIGHT

Main Courtyard of the Palace, City of Meroe

Crowds had begun to assemble early in front of the large temporary stage built at the entrance to the palace as it opened to the main thoroughfare of the city. Open air tents and canopies were staked haphazardly nearby. It was a day of celebration, the marriage of the Candace's youngest son to the daughter of one of the most prominent families of the kingdom, and those in attendance wanted to make the most of it. Therefore, men and women dressed in their most colorful robes and headdress danced and chanted to the rhythm of unseen drums while children gathered in small groups to mimic their parents. Scattered among the crowd were the temporary stalls of merchants selling mementos and other charms and trinkets. It was a day to be festive, and anyone who witnessed the event could not help but be caught up in the jubilant celebration.

Matthias was an unlikely observer of the day's events as he took his place among the guests seated on a large platform to the right of the Candace and other participants in the wedding party. The previous two weeks had passed as if only hours in duration.

As anticipated, the prince was good to his promise and spoke to his mother, the Candace, who almost immediately sent word that the property was Matthias's by gift. It was then slow going at first with only him, Dracus, and one of Lady Asata's slaves working to refurbish the compound. However, about three days into the project, the brothers Attla and Adda offered their services; and soon after, and probably at Lady Asata's instigation, five slaves from Prince Teritegas's household were assigned to the mission. Thereafter and working virtually night and day, the main structure was made at least habitable so that he, Dracus, and his two wards could reside in one of the upper rooms of the main house. Matthias would have preferred to have continued his labors without interruption. However, he was too indebted to the prince to avoid the wedding and, therefore, watched with respectful attention as the ceremony slowly began to unfold.

It actually was not until late morning when everything finally quieted on the platform as six men in multicolored kilts, each carrying a large ram's horn, trumpeted the arrival of the Candace and other members of the royal family. They immediately took their places at the center of the dais, with the Candace enthroned in a very ornate chair and her consort seated to her left and Prince Amanikhable standing next to him. Next, other officials of the kingdom, including the vizier, Lady Asata, and the one Matthias knew as the Ethiopian, took their assigned places.

The six trumpeters sounded again, and a procession of white-robed priests, some wearing leopard-skin capes, slowly entered the main gate of the complex led by incense bearers, which was followed by a large canopied sedan chair, out of which emerged the high priest who took his place on the stage immediately to the left of the royal consort. Another priest wearing a long white robe with a lion skin tied at his shoulders and a blue skull cap took his seat immediately to the left of the high priest. A moment of silence passed as all waited in anticipation of what came next.

It was not long before the trumpeters again blew their horns, which was echoed by the cadence of rhythmic drums. The drumming grew louder and the crowd more exhilarated as men disguised as lions wearing grass skirts and haloed by simulated lion manes danced into the plaza pursued by others wielding spears and highly decorated shields. At their heels came women in long multicolored robes, some bare-breasted but all collared with large golden necklaces, chanting to the sound of other drummers who walked alongside, beating out a staccato rhythm. The parade came to a halt in front of the platform and paused as those standing in the plaza pressed for access as trumpets sounded and the staccato beat of the drums resumed.

All eyes then turned to the main gate as four elephants entered the compound with colorful designs painted on their faces and golden orbs fixed to the tip of a tusk, each led by turbaned attendants in battle dress. As they passed the dais and the drums grew louder, a contingent of armed soldiers in full regalia entered the plaza, some with shields and spears and others with swords strapped to their sides, followed by a phalanx of charioteers—all of whom came to a stop and then maneuvered themselves into a passageway from the gate to the wedding platform.

Suddenly the drums stopped, and all eyes again turned to the main entrance, where the glint of a golden chariot pulled by two matching black stallions moved slowly toward the celebrants, with Prince Teritegas holding the reins with one hand and waving to the joyful crowd with the other. His green-and-gold embroidered tunic competed with his ornately decorated chariot for attention, as did his lapis-blue crown.

The prince came to a stop at a stairwell that led up to the royal dais where he approached his mother, bowed slightly, and then took his place to her right. All eyes next turned again toward the main gate as the drums resumed a low, rhythmic beat.

Another group of celebrants appeared, this time women in long, diaphanous dresses who surrounded four bearers carrying a sedan couch shielded by a gold-and-white curtain. Once at the platform, the four bearers lowered the couch as women formed a pathway to a flowered stairway, and the man who Matthias had come to know as the rich merchant rose from his chair and walked to the top of the temporary stairs.

The women who had earlier chanted behind the lion dancers now began a new song as the curtain to the sedan couch was raised, and the bride, Lady Nasaisa, appeared in an azure-blue robe trimmed in gold with a veil of the same color that hung loosely from her head to her waist. Multiple rings, bracelets, and golden necklaces—some with precious stones—were displayed on her hands, arms, and neck. The crowd roared its approval as Lady Nasaisa was escorted to the top of the platform by two of the white-robed women, where she was met by her father who took his daughter by the hand and led her to Prince Teritegas.

There her escorts pulled back Lady Nasaisa's veil, which revealed a diamond headpiece accented with blue sapphires and pearls with matching strands of the same jewels dangling from each ear, a fitting bride for the future king of Kush. Prince Teritegas reacted with a broad smile as both bowed once to the Candace and then turned to the center of the stage as the high priest of Amun and his attendants maneuvered themselves in front of the couple.

Dipping the tips of his fingers into a bowl held by one of his attendants, the high priest splashed the prince and his bride with a red liquid while intoning a prayer as he raised his hands skyward. Next, the priest dressed with a lion cape stepped forward and placed his hands on the foreheads of the royal pair as he also recited a prayer. The proceeding then stalled. Finally, Prince Teritegas, understanding the reason for the delay, took his bride by the hand and led her to where Matthias stood as both looked at the young disciple expectantly.

"They want your blessing," Ibrahim whispered in Matthias's ear. "Like that given by the other priests."

Matthias froze. He did not know what he should do; however, inaction was not an option.

Almost instinctively he removed his corded belt, took two steps toward the couple, and loosely wound an end around each of their hands.

"What God had joined together let no man put aside," he said very haltingly.

He then placed a hand on each forehead, gave a blessing for happiness in the Meoritic tongue, and then stepped back. Prince Teritegas smiled.

The couple returned to the center of the platform, where the Candace and her consort came forward and stood beside the prince and his bride. Drums began to beat again as the crowd roared and loud songs filled the plaza. The ceremony was over.

Matthias was transfixed by it all.

"You did well," Ibrahim whispered. "Did you notice the look the high priest gave you?" he asked.

Matthias shook his head that he had not.

"When the prince and his bride came to *you* and not you to them, the high priest could barely contain himself and was only held back by a wave from Prince Amanikhabale. The wedding was worth it if just for that moment."

Matthias had no response. He did not want to make an enemy of the man and others like him. The years spent with the Master had taught him that perceived opposition to those who governed should not be taken lightly. On the other hand, he did not have the power to change what was. At least the Prince and Lady Nasaisa were exuberantly happy, and for the moment, that would have to be enough.

PART FOUR

Shadows

Eighteen months later

CHAPTER TWENTY-NINE

Christian Compound, Meroe

Matthias stood just outside the rear entrance to the main house of his mission complex, straddling a narrow walkway built by both him and Dracus from discarded stones taken from a wall that separated the main property from an adjacent mudbrick building. What he saw filled him with both wonder and pride—and for good reason. What once was a rundown parcel of property was now a thriving center of charity housed in two two-storied buildings with a population of thirty orphaned children and more than two dozen single females with an additional commitment to feed those in need from a newly constructed kitchen. He had worked hard for his accomplishments; however, so had others.

Lady Asata gave her time freely whenever she could, especially during construction of the children's sanctuary. And, as usual, Dracus volunteered throughout every phase of the project, making himself virtually indispensable while Lord Teritegas continued to volunteer his slaves. The twins, Attla and Adda, also worked indefatigably and so closely with everyone they asked to be baptized and were now live-in house parents and loyal attendees at a midafternoon prayer service. In fact, the brothers convinced three of the women to join their ranks, which significantly helped the effort.

The priests of Amun visited twice and inspected each facility, even attempting to tax the mission for being subject to their control. However, a few well-chosen words from the palace, and the priests made a hasty retraction of their demand. Occasionally women with orphaned children would be stopped at the city gates. However, Prince Teritegas resolved this issue by having someone known to the guards, usually Adda or Attla, meet and accompany the women to the compound, or the women themselves would display an official warrant that allowed entry. By any measure, the mission was a far greater success than Matthias could have anticipated, and that is why this day was so special: a visit by the Candace herself!

Perhaps because of this, rarely had he seen Lady Asata so disconcerted. Matthias could not recollect any element of the mission she had not checked and then rechecked to ensure that all was up to her standards. Even the children were cautioned to be on their best behavior, which occasioned Matthias to take the woman aside and remind her that they were just that, children, and could not help but show their enthusiasm. At first, Lady Asata would back down. However, within hours she would be at it again, and Matthias would have to remind her to see the world through the eyes of a child. What he did not correct, however, was the woman's insistence on good workmanship with attention to detail. An example was the garden where he now stood, which had blossomed into its full glory mostly due to Lady Asata's oversight.

"Are you coming?" Asata asked, startling Matthias out of his daydream.

"In a moment," he responded. "They aren't here yet, are they?"

"No. But it won't be long. We need to be ready," the pretty girl replied.

"It will be all right, Asata. Trust me."

"Have it your way then," she said playfully as she turned and went inside the main building.

Matthias took one last look around him, which only served to confirm what was on everyone's mind: a visit by the Candace was not to be ignored.

The western gate to the mission suddenly swung open as two kilted guards with swords drawn entered and stood just inside the wall at rigid attention. Lady Asata and Matthias stood not far away, side by side, at the head of a line of children and adults outlining a pathway to the main house.

Finally, the man Matthias knew as the Ethiopian entered the compound followed by Lady Asata's father. A few moments later, two slave girls in yellow garments came through the gate, stopping just inside the wall as they both turned back to face the entrance. All stood quietly in anticipation of what was to follow when the Candace herself dressed in a long blue-green robe accessorized with multiple golden bracelets and necklaces entered the compound and strode purposefully toward Asata and Matthias as the two slaves maneuvered themselves behind their sovereign. The Jew, Ibrahim, stood just to the right of his queen.

A young girl, the same child abandoned to Matthias, nervously stepped forward and handed the monarch a bouquet of flowers.

"Thank you. They are very pretty," the Candace said as she handed the bouquet to one of her slaves. She then turned her attention to Lady Asata and Matthias.

"Show me what is here," the woman insisted. "I have heard much about your mission."

"Yes, ma'am," Matthias responded. "This way, please."

He held out his hand toward the front doorway of the main house.

After about a twenty-minute inspection of the property and some interaction with the children, the entourage ended up in the large garden between the two main buildings. Matthias noticed that a guard in full battle dress had pulled Lady Asata's father aside; after which Lord Harsiotef suddenly took a step backway and held a hand up to his mouth as he turned to face his queen but did not move.

"I am impressed," the Candace said to Matthias with a smile. "You have done well. Perhaps we can talk of extending your mission to other cities."

Asata's father finally rejoined the reviewing party. Obviously, something was very wrong as tears welled in both eyes. He bowed slightly to his sovereign and suggested that they stand aside for a moment. Apparently, the Candace was as confused as everyone, for she walked hesitantly behind her vizier.

There suddenly was an audible gasp from the queen as she sat awkwardly on a stone bench braced against a lemon tree that shaded a garden of jasmine and gardenias.

"I must return to the palace!" the woman stuttered as she began to move quickly toward the open gate.

Lord Harsiotef merely nodded and followed.

"Father…" Lady Asata said hesitantly.

"Not now, daughter," the vizier responded. "Price Teritegas has been killed!"

"What!" Asata said, not believing what she had heard.

Her father waved his daughter off as he left the compound. Within minutes the grounds had returned to near normalcy with the children beginning to scatter in the outside yard to play.

"I need to go too," Lady Asata said. "I don't understand why my father said what he did. Somehow I'll let you know what has happened."

The woman then disappeared, which left Matthias standing alone, mute and confused. He would wait. There had to be more to the vizier's declaration than first understood.

Matthias puttered around the garden and the first floor of the main house, watching the children eat and play while awaiting news from the palace. Even afternoon prayers came and went with no word, which gave Matthias more cause for concern. Finally, one of Lady Asata's slaves returned and immediately sought out Matthias.

"And what does our Lady have to say?" he asked.

"Prince Teritegas was killed in battle, sir," the slave replied with head bowed and hands clasped in front of her face. "The battle was a victory for our kingdom, but the prince is lost."

Matthias did not know how to react. The consequences of Prince Teritegas's death were too overwhelming to begin to comprehend.

"And what of Lady Asata?"

"She is with the Candace," the slave responded. "Our queen is very ill and has taken to her bed. Lady Asata is with her."

"As she should," Matthias muttered to himself. "Thank you for bring me this much information. You may return to the palace."

The slave left and was replaced by Dracus.

"What we have heard is true, my friend," Matthias said, staring at his longtime companion with an uncharacteristic, sorrowful expression. "Prince Teritegas was killed in battle. And Lady Asata remains with the Candace. Whether this changes anything I cannot begin to speculate. We will just have to wait and see how events play themselves out."

Dracus nodded and put a hand on his mentor's shoulder. Both sensed that a cold, dark shadow had been cast over their world.

CHAPTER THIRTY

Palace Complex, Meroe

The contrast of urgency proclaimed by the palace guards to the sullen atmosphere projected by those inhabiting the Candace's chambers struck Matthias immediately. He was told to stop whatever he was doing and to accompany the six-man escort to the palace, where the reason for his summons would be explained. Once there he was told to wait in an anteroom adjacent to the Candace's living quarters, which he did while observing several very somber officials enter and leave without comment. This was not a happy place. In fact, the past two weeks since it was announced that Prince Teritegas had been killed were anything but joyous.

At first, there was little difference in their daily lives other than knowledge of the tragedy. Then rumors began to circulate among the city's inhabitants of what might come to pass. Actual, observable change was limited to the increase of military personnel in and around the city and a strictly enforced curfew when city gates were closed and barricaded. In fact, Matthias was somewhat taken aback by the lack of hard information about the death and any official observance to honor the young prince other than that after a period of mourning, the body would be entombed in one of the royal pyramids to the east of the city. Even Lady Asata remained away and left him to speculate on what was the proper protocol. Now he had an answer: he would meet the Candace face-to-face who would presumably communicate her expectations directly to him.

A door at the back of the room opened as the vizier walked out and made his way directly to Matthias, bypassing other anxious-looking officials.

"Come with me," Lord Harsiotef said abruptly to the young disciple as he turned and walked toward the living quarters.

Once beyond two large mahogany doors, Matthias felt a sense of *déjà vu*. Stripped of the multiple golden adornments that were painted on the walls or set on pedestals scattered about the room, the space was a near duplicate of that occupied by Prince Teritegas, only larger. To his left a large curtained area opened to a patio that fronted a canal, which ran parallel to the palace; to his right two ornately decorated beds stood side by side, with only a small bedside table separating both. Several tall brass stands topped with flaming discs cast a mellow light over the whole as various dignitaries and family members clustered in small groups as they spoke to each other in hushed tones. Matthias noticed that the man he knew as the Ethiopian was standing discreetly off to his right, as was Ibrahim, while the Candace herself was propped up in one of the beds with both her oldest son and consort hovering nearby.

Lady Asata's father, Lord Harsiotef, held out his hand for Matthias to remain where he stood as he made his way to the Candace and whispered into her ear. The Candace nodded as she pushed herself up in the bed and gestured for all to leave.

"The priests too?" her son asked.

"Yes, them too," the queen responded.

There was an awkward moment as those in the room hesitated before they began to comply, and Matthias caught the angry stares of several officials as they brushed past on their way to the door.

"Come here, my young prophet," the Candace said in a subdued voice as she gestured Matthias to her bedside. Both her son and consort took several steps backward but made no attempt to leave.

"I want you to know that I was truly impressed by your mission," she said. "I should have come sooner. However, I did not want to distract from my son's involvement. You may not know this, but he was very interested in your project. He believed that he owed his life to your god." Ibrahim interpreted as fast as the queen talked.

The Candace's voice cracked as she spoke. Nevertheless, with effort, she pushed herself against several pillows and signaled that Matthias should come closer.

"My treasurer tells me that there is a ceremony which binds you to your god." The Candace looked to her right and waved the Ethiopian to stand with Matthias. "I want you to perform that ritual with me."

"Mother!" Lord Amanikhabale interjected. "Do you think that wise?"

The Candace turned slowly.

"I don't expect either you or your priests to understand," she said very deliberately. "However, your brother intended to participate in this ceremony, and I wish to honor your brother." Then, looking at Matthias, she snapped, "Make it happen!"

Matthias turned to the Ethiopian for direction. The man took two steps to his right and bent to whisper in Matthias's ear.

"I believe she means baptism," he said. "That is possible, is it not?"

Matthias nodded his head.

"What do you need?" the Ethiopian asked.

"Water," Matthias answered.

The Ethiopian waved a hand at one of the attending slaves who hurried from the room. She returned almost immediately, carrying a brass bowl between both hands, and stood beside the Ethiopian.

"Ma'am," the Ethiopian said to the Candace, "he is ready."

"Good," the queen responded. "Proceed."

Both the son and the consort watched silently from a distance.

Matthias awkwardly approached the slave and cupped one hand as he scooped water from the bowl.

He then bent over the bed and let water drip onto the forehead of the Candace as he intoned, "I baptize you in the name of our Lord and Savior, Jesus Christ. Because of his sacrifice, your sins are forgiven." Again, Ibrahim interpreted.

The son very much wanted to say something but held his tongue. However, there was fire behind his eyes.

The Candace sat back in her bed and smiled as she wiped her forehead. Two slaves replaced the wet blanket and pillows with new bedding.

"Well, as ceremonies go, that needs improvement. Not much to talk about. I guess a little water and a blessing never hurt anyone. In fact, I think I feel better already. Lord Harsiotef, you will have to let the people know that I have done this. They should feel as good as I do," the Candace said, and she smiled again.

"And thank you, my young prophet. Now I would like to get some rest."

The queen settled into her bed as those in the room began to exit. Matthias was signaled aside by the vizier, who led him to the patio and out of earshot of the others.

"Be very careful, my young friend," Lord Harsiotef said almost in a whisper. "Although the Candace is pleased, you have made powerful enemies today."

"What was I to do?" Matthias asked.

The vizier held up his hand and said, "I understand. However, that does not change how Prince Amanikhabale and his followers, especially the priests of Amun, will react. You and your one god will be seen as a challenge to their authority."

"I have a mission to orphaned children and to those unable to care for themselves. I seek nothing else."

Lord Harsiotef nodded his understanding.

"Just be careful," he said. "The Candace will protect you today. However, she grows weak, and already her son is maneuvering to positions of power. Tread very carefully."

"I will," Matthias said, as much confused as anything.

He sought nothing from this kingdom other than to minister to the poor and less fortunate. He certainly wanted nothing to do with their politics. However, if the vizier was to be believed somehow, he had become the center of a storm. He could only hope that the path he had chosen was that contemplated by the Master. He could do no more.

Lady Ashad's role as principal attendant to the Candace had been difficult since the queen took ill. She never knew from day to day how the Candace would feel, even if she would want to rise from her bed. And today was no different.

As customary, Lady Ashad and her five slaves assembled outside the bedchamber with the queen's wardrobe, each slave holding a particular item such as a robe, sandals, jewelry, and so forth, waiting to be summoned to the royal presence. Then, as was her practice, Lady Ashad had the slaves remain outside the bedchamber as she alone approached the queen to await her sovereign's instructions.

"Your Grace, it is Lady Ashad," she said meekly as she walked over to the curtains that separated the bedchamber from the patio and began to let in the morning light. "What are Your Grace's wishes?" she asked with a hint of frustration.

There was no immediate response; although the woman could see a form underneath a soft white blanket.

"Your Grace…" Lady Ashad repeated as she approached the large bed. "It is…" she began as she reached down to touch what she supposed was the shoulder of a reclining figure.

Still no movement.

The woman bent again and began to pull back a blanket, which revealed a head with long braided hair. The eyes stared without blinking.

"*Oh, no!*" the woman was barely able to exhale before she dropped the bedcovers and ran from the room.

Once at the doorway, she stopped and looked at her five slaves. Her face was taut, and there was panic in her eyes. She attempted to speak, but nothing came.

Prince Amanikhabale entered from the hallway.

"Lady Ashad…" he said, noticing the woman's frantic demeanor. "Is something wrong?"

Ashad turned slowly.

"Your mother…" she stuttered, barely able to get the words past her lips. "Your mother has died! I need to inform Lord Harsiotef at once!" She tried to move, but the prince held her back.

"First come with me," Prince Amanikhabale insisted. "Maybe there is another explanation."

The two approached the bed hesitantly. Prince Amanikhabale raised the blanket. His mother's eyes still did not blink.

Both stared at the lifeless form for a long, silent moment.

"So it is true," the prince mouthed under his breath.

"Shall I notify the vizier?" Lady Ashad asked.

Amanikhabale thought carefully, finally nodded, and waved the attendant out of the room. He had long anticipated this day, and now it was here. So much needed to be done!

He sat on the edge of the bed and looked down at the still figure. His mother never really cared for him; it was always about his brother. How things had changed!

He stood slowly and turned. He would need to inform the high priest, if only to have the moral authority to act. But act he would.

Indeed, the very thought of what was to come quickened his step.

CHAPTER THIRTY-ONE

The sky crackled with bolts of lightning and claps of thunder as dark clouds rolled over the city. However, Matthias barely heard the midday threat as his attention was on children cared for by two women. This was when the toddlers scrambled for their portion of what was usually a piece of bread, some fruit, and water. Still, Matthias took his obligation seriously and enjoyed this special time. It certainly distracted from other events that engulfed not only him but the whole city of Meroe.

He was still in shock over the sudden death of the Candace as was everyone else. He had seen Lady Asata only once during the past several days and then only briefly, who reported that the palace was in disarray and government offices barely functioning. She said that her father was particularly concerned with Prince Amanikhabale who was anxious to take on the reins of power. Even the priests of Amun had begun to press for positions lost decades earlier. Lady Asata added that she was to remind him of her father's warning and to be especially vigilant during these uncertain times.

A clap of thunder jolted Matthias back to the job at hand.

As he was about to pick up empty mugs from four children sitting at his feet, he looked across the room and saw a disheveled Lady Asata standing in the doorway, looking shocked and disoriented. Her appearance frightened him.

"They have taken Father!" she gasped as her voice cracked.

"Who has?" Matthias asked, raising his voice to be heard above the storm.

"Prince Amanikhabale. The palace guards have aligned with him. I was barely able to escape!"

Matthias handed three empty mugs to a woman standing to his left as he walked to the doorway.

"They cannot hold him. He has done nothing wrong," he said.

"It does not matter," Asata replied. "He opposed the prince, and that is enough. You also need to take care."

"Look around you. How do I challenge him?"

"It does not matter," Lady Asata answered. "It is how you are perceived, and for some reason, you and your one god are seen as a threat."

Matthias did not know what to say.

"You must leave the city," Lady Asata warned.

"And you? Your father arrested and you barely able to escape! What are you going to do?"

"I'll find a way," she answered.

"So will I. Surely they will not harm children and defenseless women. It is you who need to be careful."

Unseen, the boy, Adda, entered the room, carrying wood for the fireplace.

"Adda!" Matthias snapped. "Come here, please."

The youth laid his bundle against a wall and hurried to Matthias.

"Where's your brother?" Matthias asked.

"He went to see Mother and will be right back."

"Lady Asata needs your help. Prince Amanikhabale has arrested her father and may want to take her into custody. She needs to leave the city immediately!"

As they spoke, the boy's twin, Attla, entered the room. Matthias acknowledged his presence and repeated what he had just told Adda.

"Can you help?" Matthias asked.

After some thought, Attla gave a suggestion, "We could try to get her to Mother's and then down to the river. We would have to be very careful, though. However, I think I know a way," and he looked at his brother with a half-smile.

"When?" Adda asked.

Matthias turned to Lady Asata and then back to the twins.

"I suppose *now*," he said pointedly. "At least get Lady Asata to your mother's. Can you do that? She needs to get beyond the city wall."

"I don't know," Lady Asata interjected. "My father is still at the palace."

"Yes, and under arrest," Matthias responded. "And you were fortunate not to be apprehended yourself. I am sure there will not be a second chance."

For the first time in Matthias's memory, Lady Asata looked less than confident.

"We can do it," Attla offered. "However, we have to leave as soon as possible. It was difficult enough to get past the guards at the gate, and I am sure that it has only gotten worse."

"And someone needs to move Lady Asata's chariot into the compound. Left outside it is a dead giveaway to her whereabouts," Matthias added.

"I'll take care of that," Adda said and left the room at a sprint.

"And what about you?" Lady Asata asked Matthias. "How will you protect yourself?"

"I will be all right. Dracus and I will find a way. Who wants to harm an orphanage?"

Lady Asata gave him a disbelieving stare.

"We will be all right," Matthias said again, trying to reassure her.

At that same time, Adda reentered the room from the garden.

"It is taken care of. Are you ready, brother?" he asked Attla.

"Yes. Lady Asata…" Attla held out his hand, pointing to the compound's main gate.

For an instant, the woman froze. Tears began to cloud her eyes. She took a step forward and hugged Matthias.

"You have been a good friend," she said, trying to hold her emotions in check. "Strange at times, yes. But a friend nevertheless."

Matthias reciprocated and then pushed away.

"This will not be permanent," he said with an attempt to show confidence. "We will see each other again." However, he felt as if something vital was being ripped from his very being and tried unconvincingly not to show the pain.

Lady Asata had no more words.

"She will need something to hide her identity," Attla said.

"Here, take this," Matthias replied as he slipped out of his robe. "It has a hood."

"Good, that will do," Attla said and handed the garment to Asata.

The woman slipped into the robe and flipped the hood over her head as the three started out of the room. Lady Asata hesitated only once as she turned back, and both she and Matthias attempted a smile. Then they were gone.

Matthias stood motionless. He understood the dangers; however, what could he do? Looking around the room and at the women and children who depended on him for virtually everything, he suddenly felt cold and angry. Surely Prince Amanikhabale would leave them in peace.

CHAPTER THIRTY-TWO

Lady Asata and the twins moved cautiously out of the compound and across the four streets that intersected in front of the southeastern gate. They were not alone as other shadowy figures hustled past the guards to unknown destinations within the city. A pall of gloom palatable enough to touch hung over everything. The sky rolled with thunder.

The three made it to the wall that ran northwest from the gate where they were partially shielded by slag and the ironworks. Their destination lay just ahead: a rivulet of water that ran between the shops and the wall whose source was a canal that paralleled the city boundaries. It was built for the iron factories; however, Attla and Adda had another purpose this evening.

Crouching low, the three silhouettes moved among the tall grass that edged the wall as they approached the canal.

"You need to take off your robe," Attla said in a whisper.

Lady Asata looked at the channel and stood erect.

"I'm going to get into that?" she asked. "It's filthy! Besides, an iron grate covers the opening."

Both Attla and Adda smiled.

"Perhaps not all is as it seems," Attla said in a whisper. "The builders only partially extended the grillwork into the channel. There is maybe an arm's length that has no barrier. We've been using this and the other opening as a way into the city for years. Can you swim?"

For an instant, Lady Asata was startled by the question.

"Swim? That looks more like sink and drown!" she snapped.

Attla's countenance suddenly turned serious.

"This is a matter of survival, ma'am. I doubt if you would be treated well at the palace. You can do it if it really is important to you."

Lady Asata's first reaction was to call the boy on his impertinence. However, everything he said was true. There were no other options.

A flash of lightening and a clap of thunder resonated at the northern end of the city as Asata took a deep breath with renewed resolve.

"Let's do it!" she said, slipping out of Matthias's robe. "Anything else I need to remove?"

The brothers discarded their robes, which left them in short tunics around the waist. They eyed Asata, which made her feel very uncomfortable. However, she said nothing.

"You will have to dive down about two body lengths to reach the bottom of the grate on both this side of the wall and the other. Are you wearing anything that might catch on the grate or slow your movement?"

Lady Asata thought for a moment. Now was not the time for modesty. She shed her tunic that went down to her knees, which left her waist and groin covered with a plain white cloth and her breasts restrained by a wide sash. Two gold bands circled her upper arms.

"We need to hide the clothing before we dive," Attla said; although his brother had anticipated the problem and found three large rocks around which the garments were tied and then quietly dropped into the channel.

"Let me explain what you need to do," Attla began. "Adda will go first, and I will follow. Take a deep breath, and when you're ready, pull yourself down using the grate as a guide. You swim under the bottom of the grate and then resurface as fast as possible. Don't panic when you find yourself in a tunnel. Swim over to the next grate and take a few breaths before you start down again. You will come up on the other side of the wall. Remember, when you pull yourself out of the water, do so quietly and stay low. My mother's house is not from there."

"Ready?" Attla asked.

Lady Asata nodded as Adda lowered himself into the pool of cool water and swam a few strokes before he took a deep breath and disappeared.

"Ma'am..." Attla said, pointing at the murky channel.

Lady Asata hesitated for an instant and then slowly lowered herself into the canal. The water was colder than she remembered. She then paddled her way over to the grate, looked back at Attla, took a deep breath, and dived. Her hands grabbed for the crossbars of the obstruction, which she used to pull herself down to the bottom of the waterway. Panic began to overwhelm her; however, she remembered Attla's words and that he was just behind her. So she maneuvered herself clumsily under the grate and made a sprint for the surface. As her head broke the waterline, she took in a breath of air and a mouthful of water. She struggled to stay afloat as Attla surfaced and held a hand under her neck and shoulders.

"Are you all right?" he asked. "Just stay calm. You only have to repeat this one more time."

Lady Asata nodded as she paddled through the dark tunnel toward the second barrier. Her muscles were sore, but she tried to put everything out of mind other than reaching the other side.

"Relax," Attla whispered. "Do it only when you are ready."

Lady Asata attempted a smile as she took in several shallow breaths. She then gulped in a large volume of air and dived for the bottom of the channel.

This time she anticipated the obstacles and moved swiftly through the water and under the grate, surfacing just as her breath expired. Adda was crouched on the opposite bank, holding an outstretched arm, which she swam to and grasped as he pulled her onto dry land. Attla surfaced right behind her and was quick to join them.

"We don't have far to go," Attla whispered.

"I know. I have been there before."

Attla thought for a moment and then smiled as he started toward the ramshackle community and his mother's shack. His brother and Asata followed, keeping themselves low and hidden by the shadows of the night.

Lady Asata made one quick turn and looked over her shoulder at the imposing wall that surrounded the city as another bolt of lightning illuminated the sky. Never had she felt so isolated from her adopted family and home.

Matthias and Dracus sat on a stone bench within the mission garden, awaiting events to unfold. It had been some time since they had heard from Lady Asata, and hopefully, all had gone well. A sense of foreboding had settled over everything.

"Have you communicated to the women the seriousness of our situation?" Matthias asked. "And that they will have to take care of the children should anything happen to us?"

Dracus nodded that he had.

"I don't know if anything will happen," Matthias added. "However, we have to be prepared."

Dracus again signed that he understood.

Matthias took a slow look around him.

"We have come a long way, my friend," he said. "I believe Peter would be pleased. However, I cannot help but worry about the children. You do think the women are up to it?"

Once again Dracus nodded as he put a reassuring hand on his friend's knee. A roll of thunder startled both men. Then another loud noise sounding something like thunder but closer drew both men's attention.

"Is that coming from the gate?" Mathias asked.

Another loud clash followed by men shouting as women yelled in panic brought Matthias and Dracus to their feet. Before they could start into the house a phalanx of guards, each wielding swords, entered the compound.

"What does this mean?" Matthias asked.

"Are you the one they call Matthias?" one of the advancing men asked.

"Yes..." Matthias responded hesitantly.

"Come with us!" the guard commanded.

"Why?"

"I have instructions to bring you to the palace. Come with us now!"

Matthias was momentarily stunned. Although the intrusion was not wholly unexpected, he did not expect to be escorted at the pointed end of a sword.

"Take care of the women and children," Matthias repeated. "I will get word to you."

By this time, the armed escort was pushing Matthias slowly toward the open gate.

Dracus knew not to interfere but to somehow blend out of the way if he was to be of any use in the future. Then he must act quickly. He had to discover what was at stake. However, who would help, he had no clue.

It did not take long for the armed guards with Matthias as their prisoner to reach the palace. They bypassed one entrance and made for the main gate where they passed under a grizzly display of the current state of affairs: five severed heads, two of which chilled Matthias to the very core. Illumination from a flash of lightening revealed one head was the vizier, Lord Harsiotef, Asata's father, and the other the man Matthias knew as the Ethiopian!

Matthias fell to his knees, as if a large rock had been hurled into his gut, and he had to be dragged to his feet. The reason for the detour was apparent. He was warned!

Dark shadows, indeed, had overtaken Meroe!

CHAPTER THIRTY-THREE

Matthias had made this trek through the palace hallways before, but under very different circumstances. Then he was a guest; now he was a prisoner to be interrogated as an enemy. The young disciple could think of little that had changed from then to the present other than his success with the mission. And perhaps that was it: the jealous envy of those neither as creative nor as dedicated as he and his associates. Whatever the reason, he would soon find out as he was being forcibly escorted by a contingent of armed guards from his prison cell to the private throne room. He nearly tripped over the buried visage of the Emperor Augustus as he was dragged by the guards from the chamber doorway to the far end of the hall and forced to his knees.

"And who is this?" Prince Amanikhabale asked, enthroned in the chair once occupied by his mother while on his head he wore a blue-and-gold crown with double cobras and held in his right hand a short golden rod.

One of the guards jerked Matthias's head up by pulling on his hair.

"Ah! Our young prophet," the prince pronounced, pointing his scepter at the prisoner. "I remember when we first met. In this very room, in fact." The ubiquitous Ibrahim had joined the prince on the dais and interpreted.

Matthias stared straight ahead. From what he could see, the prince was joined only by Ibrahim and the high priest who sat to his left. Matthias observed no others than the guards who surrounded him; although he had a sense that multiple pairs of eyes were focused on the confrontation.

"It seems that since that time you have come to the attention of many," Prince Amanikhabale continued. "Unfortunately, the reports are not all favorable."

Matthias noticed that with the last comment the prince looked over his shoulder and smiled at his priestly associate.

"However, what disturbed me most were your efforts to subvert my mother to the will of your god, *even* channeling your misbegotten ideas to her on her deathbed!"

"Your mother asked to be baptized," Matthias quickly responded. "I only did what she asked."

Prince Amanikhabale stood and glared at his prisoner.

"Only after weeks of intimidation!" he shouted. "Do you not think I know of her visit to your mission and her support of the same over the past year. And those now claiming to be converts to your god! Even my dear, departed brother was caught up in your schemes. Do you not think that I noticed my mother *died* soon after your witchcraft!"

"I don't believe..." Matthias started to say in his own defense.

"Silence!" the prince shouted.

Then taking a step forward and pointing at Matthias, he said, "You will pay for your arrogance. However, I am not quite sure what is most appropriate. Although your life means nothing to me, I do not wish to make you a martyr like that achieved by your 'god.'"

Turning away from Matthias and then back again, he addressed the guards.

"Take him and have him flogged! Thirty lashes should be sufficient. I will let you know if I have other orders. Now take him from my sight!" Ibrahim's voice quivered while repeating the pronouncement.

Matthias was again lifted to his feet and forcibly hurried out of the chamber. All his senses were numbed by the uncompromising vitriol of the prince and the man's blind disdain for the mission. Tears clouded Matthias's vision. Not for himself but for the women and children under his care. What was to become of them? He wept openly as the guards dragged him down the hallways of the palace to his cell. Matthias felt entombed in the very bowels of hell.

Prince Amanikhabale was unusually pensive as he stood facing his patio, which overlooked the canal that paralleled the city wall, with only the high priest as company. He suddenly walked to a large, narrow table positioned next to his friend.

"I am surprised how well everything has gone," he said, mostly for his own benefit. "I expected more resistance from my brother's supporters. Perhaps they were not as big a threat as I once feared."

"Perhaps," the high priest responded. "However, they were not expecting you to act so swiftly. A wise move on your part."

The prince smiled to himself.

"I probably did not have to be so aggressive with our young prophet. Nevertheless, he is an irritant, always preferred over me, and I wanted to make my annoyance clear. I believe I succeeded." A slight laugh punctuated his comment.

"I am sure you did," the high priest responded with a smile. "His presence is dangerous. It challenges our traditions. His end is inevitable."

"However, I am not sure that I want to make him a martyr. I am told that he has a following, even here in the palace, which could prove to be a nuisance. Although I am not a religious a man, his god appears to have some sway over events. What do you suggest?"

"There are ways to handle this," the high priest answered. "Let me take care of the problem. I also have an interest to see that his legacy dies quickly. You have other matters to consider such as your family."

"Ah, yes," the prince replied. "The family definitely needs to be brought around. Fear will probably convince most. Others will have to be eliminated. Although I need to proceed cautiously, as some have armed militia that are loyal to them only. My mother was very clever in this regard and how she used her many brothers and uncles."

"And the Lady Nasaisa, your brother's wife, and her young daughter, what of them? Remember, she is also my niece."

"Yes, the beautiful Lady Nasaisa," Prince Amanikhable answered as he stood again and walked back to the patio and canal. "As is the custom, I will take her as my bride. And the child will be raised as my own. My brother's memory will soon be forgotten. The good lady has already grieved too long!"

The high priest stood.

"You certainly have my blessing and the blessing of Amun," he said. "Now, while it is still fresh in your memory, let me handle that other detail. The Jew will bother you no more."

"Good. Let it be done. And quickly," the prince said as he returned to his desk. Then, as if his thoughts had changed added, "I have a marriage to contemplate."

The high priest started to respond, thought better of it, and left the royal chamber. He needed to act before the prince had a change of heart.

"The one you summoned is present, Your Excellency," a guard interrupted as the high priest laid a plate of figs on a tabletop in his ornately decorated reception chamber and took a sip of liquid from a golden cup.

"Good. Bring him to me," the priest said as he pushed aside a parchment scroll.

Without delay the guard returned with a tall, robed figure wearing a soiled turban and a weathered face that bespoke years of exposure to the sun.

The high priest wasted no time.

"I understand that you have a caravan about to leave the city for the east," the priest said matter-of-factly.

"Your Excellency is well-informed," the stranger responded bowing slightly.

"That is of no concern. I have a job for you. I want you to take a certain prisoner from the palace," the priest said as he turned back to his table. "I understand that you have others who are also prisoners and are to be sold in the east. This man should join them."

The stranger again bowed as he brought both hands up to his face.

"As Your Excellency wishes."

"And if this prisoner should not make it out of the desert, well, so be it," the priest added without looking at his visitor. "Do you understand?"

The stranger smiled.

"I understand perfectly," the man said.

"This might help," the high priest continued as he handed the stranger a small leather pouch. "And this conversation remains only between us. If I learn otherwise, there will be consequences."

"As you wish," the stranger replied, slipping the pouch of coins into the folds of his robe. "How and when will I take custody of this prisoner?" he asked.

"He will be taken from the prison guardhouse. Tonight, if you can. You will probably need two men to carry him out and some means for transport, as the prisoner will be bruised from the lash. He is just to disappear."

"Tonight then," the stranger said, thinking aloud. "Perhaps near the darkest hour just before dawn. I need time to arrange things."

"Certainly. And I will alert the guards. Until that hour," the priest said and extended an arm for the stranger to show obeisance by lowering his forehead to the outstretched hand. He was not disappointed.

The stranger was then escorted out of the room.

"You heard all?" the priest asked.

"Yes, Excellency," the unseen guard replied.

"Good. Go to the palace and arrange for our young prophet to be taken to the guardhouse after he is lashed. And wait there until he is taken by our friend and then report back to me. I want this to be over."

The guard bowed slightly and hurried from the presence of the high priest as the latter returned to his desk and his plate of figs. He had accomplished much, he thought to himself and smiled. His rewards were only beginning to come to fruition.

CHAPTER THIRTY-FOUR

Dracus knew that any attempt to contact his friend could prove disastrous. Not only would his association with Matthias be called into question but also his inability to adequately explain himself because he was mute. Therefore, he had to plan his moves very carefully and reduce the risks as much as possible. Not trying, however, was never an option.

In this regard, he waited out the first night within the confines of the mission, reinstructing the women on how to prepare for his absence. This proved to be more difficult than he first thought, especially when it came to the discussion of finances. However, he knew that the mission had support within the community and could rely on that resource. At worst, the children would be taken into individual homes. Then he had to map out in his own mind how and where to contact Matthias. He was certain that his friend would be confined within the palace prison. But how to get access?

No easy answer came to mind. The city was under a virtual lockdown. Therefore, Dracus decided that he had to confront the matter head-on, which meant that he had to get into the palace itself. However, to do this, he would need help; and there were few he could call on, especially as Lady Asata, her father, and other members of the royal family were themselves being sought out as enemies of the new order. Then one name came to mind: the interpreter, Ibrahim. The man seemed to straddle the politics of every occasion and would probably know Matthias's fate.

The best opportunity to enter the palace was just before dawn when workers assembled at the main gate. Therefore, Dracus cautiously approached the complex and hid beside an obelisk near the entrance, waiting for others to assemble when he chanced to look up and see the rotting heads of Asata's father and the Ethiopian impaled next to several other victims. This only strengthened his resolve.

While lost in thought, workers slowly began to congregate near the gate as the sky crackled with energy. Suddenly two large wooden doors opened with the way forward blocked by a cart occupied by three men, one splayed facedown on a bed of hay who, by all appearances, was dead. Two guards ran out of the compound, clearing a way for the cart as the driver turned on to the central thoroughfare and headed east. Dracus wondered how many times this scene had played out over the past several days as he moved with others into the palace grounds.

With no time to lose, he maneuvered toward the western annex of the complex and the room once occupied by both he and Matthias, knowing that Ibrahim's apartment was not far off. Darting into a doorway as rain began to pummel the city, he entered a hallway still dark and empty, making his passage to Ibrahim's rooms hopefully uneventful. Nevertheless, he kept the hood of his robe over his head as he hurried up to the second floor, passing three women who were too engrossed in their own conversation to give him any notice. Once at Ibrahim's door, he tried the latch, which fortuitously was unlocked, and he entered. A cool breeze blew curtains that concealed a balcony, with Ibrahim asleep just off to the right.

Dracus crept silently up to the interpreter's bed and reached for the reclining figure as he covered the man's mouth with his hand. Ibrahim woke, startled and confused as he flailed unsuccessfully at the hooded stranger. Dracus pulled his disguise back as he continued to pin the man to the bed. He then slowly began to release his grip.

"What are you doing here!" Ibrahim said under his breath. "Don't you know there are guards everywhere?"

Dracus nodded and then pointed to himself as he tried to communicate his search for Matthias.

"Although I must admit, I am not surprised," Ibrahim added, pushing himself up on the bed. "You're looking for Matthias," he said matter-of-factly, staring at Dracus.

Dracus nodded.

"That's a little complicated," Ibrahim replied, "and I fear we may be too late." He suddenly turned away from his intruder. "The Prince brought him to court yesterday," Ibrahim continued, "and Matthias did not fare well. Our friend was ordered to be flogged before returning to his cell. I was there, and it frightened even me."

Dracus took a step back, held up both hands, and mouthed, "Where is he now?"

Ibrahim thought for a moment.

He then replied, "Where is he?"

Dracus nodded.

"I would guess in his cell," the interpreter answered. "I really do not know much more."

Dracus signaled at the doorway.

"You want to go there?" Ibrahim asked.

Dracus nodded.

"Now?"

Again, Dracus nodded vigorously.

Ibrahim shook his head.

"I don't know what good that will do," he said. "I don't even know if they'll let you anywhere near your friend. But I suppose we can try." With the latter, he pushed himself off the bed and grabbed a robe that hung across the back of a chair. "Follow me," he said. "And don't do anything foolish. At least I should be able to get you into the prison."

Both men hurried out of the room and down a nearby stairwell where they exited into an arbor. The rain was still pretty steady; although the rolls of thunder had stopped.

"We have to get to the other side of the palace," Ibrahim said as he began a run across the courtyard. Dracus followed. Once there they stopped at a gatehouse, which Ibrahim approached alone.

"I'm afraid I have bad news," he said when he returned.

Both stepped under an eve out of the downpour in order to be heard.

"It seems that after our friend was flogged, he was released to one of the caravans. They picked him up by cart not long ago."

Dracus stared at Ibrahim, as if in shock.

"Did you hear what I said?" the interpreter asked.

Dracus nodded as he slowly returned to the present. Could the cart he saw earlier have been the one? he asked himself. Whatever, he needed to act fast and pointed at the gate as he made a run toward it.

"Wait!" Ibrahim shouted. "I need to get you past the guards!"

However, Dracus refused to be slowed as Ibrahim finally caught up to the man at the guardhouse.

"Wait here!" Ibrahim insisted. "I'll see if I can get you out. Then you are on your own!"

Ibrahim disappeared into a small, protected building where moments later a guard appeared and began to open one of the gates. Dracus did not hesitate but ran out of the courtyard, splashing through puddles and down a central thoroughfare toward the eastern perimeter of the city. His mind was set on only one course: to rescue a friend.

CHAPTER THIRTY-FIVE

Lady Asata was awakened by the roll of thunder as she returned to the conscious world of today. She still could barely comprehend all that had transpired during the past twenty-four hours, including her own narrow escape from palace guards and reports of her father's death. On her instruction, Attla had returned to the city to revisit the mission, only to discover that Matthias had been taken prisoner. Attla also attempted to infiltrate the palace and somehow managed to make it as far as her suite of rooms, where one of her slaves said everything had been confiscated. He did not dare press further.

Asata pushed herself up from a makeshift bed inside the shanty and stared blankly into the dark space of the single room. She had barely slept, conflicted by both an overwhelming sense of grief and the need to survive. What cataclysmic event had so entangled the city that her world was now upside down?

Consumed by this question, she stood and wrapped a musty, ankle-length robe around her cold body. If all had gone as planned, the brothers had left to secure a cart, which she financed by giving up one of her armbands. And the rain would help to cloak their effort. Still, she could not shake the feeling of being forsaken; although the risk to their own safety undertaken by the twins and their mother was not lost on her.

The blanketed entry to the shack was unexpectedly pushed aside, and two rain-soaked boys hurried through the doorway as their mother and grandmother joined Asata in the middle of the hut.

"We need to go," Attla said, walking quickly to a pallet that was his bed where he gathered up some things into a small cloth bag. His brother did the same.

"The workers start about now, and we want to join them on the road out of town. This will draw less attention to ourselves," Attla explained.

Lady Asata nodded and started to move toward the door. However, the boys' mother stopped her with a hand on the shoulder.

"Take care of my sons, please!" There was the unspoken mother's concern with each word.

Lady Asata knew she could say nothing to adequately alleviate the woman's fear, so she just reached out and touched her arm and nodded knowingly.

Fortunately, Attla stepped between the two women who barely understood the other's world.

"Go to the mission if you need anything," he reminded his mother.

Again, the woman tried to fight back the tears.

"Be careful!" she said, stretching out her arms.

"We will," Adda replied as he and Attla embraced their mother and then moved to the doorway.

"Coming?" the young man asked.

Both Asata and Attla nodded as they exited into the stormy morning. A donkey and cart waited just beyond the threshold.

Lady Asata climbed into the bed of the vehicle alongside Adda as Attla took the reins and snapped the ends on the hind flank of the animal. The cart jerked and began to move slowly through a muddy trail that fronted the ramshackle community and led south away from the city. Lady Asata wondered if the twins really understood the full import of what they were about. Indeed, she wondered the same of herself!

Dracus ran down the abandoned streets as he splashed his way back to the mission. He could not stay long. However, he needed to gather up a minimal of necessities, especially his bag of herbs, and again reassure the women of their competence to handle the situation. Then, after blessing the children with a silent prayer, he headed back to the streets and for the eastern limits of the city where the caravans assembled.

Dracus came to an intersection where a road that fronted the ironworks met the city's main thoroughfare and came to a halt. To his right was the eastern gate, which framed a bazaarlike conglomerate of shops and animal pens.

Dracus thought this was perhaps the best place to start and slowly made his way up the thoroughfare toward the gate, carefully eyeing everything which might point to the whereabouts of Matthias. However, those who could understand knew nothing about an injured man in the bed of a donkey cart. Therefore, he continued to walk through and around the enclosures that made this an important part of Meroe's economy until he neared the farthest stalls, where herders were busy maneuvering animals into some semblance of order. Still, nothing really caught his attention. Finally, one of the young herders stopped and asked if he could help.

Not able to speak, Dracus did his best to sign that he was looking for a particular person. The boy just shrugged and stared blankly ahead.

"Maybe I can be of some assistance?" an older man in a long, dark robe tied only at the waist said as he stepped between Darcus and the boy, shoving the latter out of the way with a weathered hand. "What is it that you want?" the man asked.

Dracus again attempted to explain but could see that he was getting nowhere. He then spied several stationary carts, walked over to one, and put his hand into the bed of the vehicle. Gesturing what he wanted, even getting into the cart itself, he awaited a response. The man slowly began to comprehend.

"You're looking for something that came in a cart like that," the stranger said.

Dracus nodded.

"Another man," the stranger added.

Dracus nodded again.

"Well, not here," the man replied. "However, there was some activity earlier this morning at another caravan down the line. It looked like they dragged a man out of a cart and put him in with the other slaves. What's he to you?"

Dracus held up his hands, nodded his thanks, and hurried off without waiting for further inquiry. He just hoped that he was not too late.

He did not have far to go. Dracus splashed through several large puddles and cart tracks before coming to a stop at a large graveled area where at least a dozen camels and several donkeys grazed. Herders darted in and around the animals, loading supplies and goods for the long journey east.

Then, out of the corner of one eye, he saw him, Matthias, head bowed but braced and seated upright against what appeared to be large baskets and surrounded by at least a dozen men! Matthias's legs were shackled with a wide leather bracelet strapped around one ankle and chained to at least six other prisoners. One of the prisoners hovered near Matthias with a bowl of food while two robed men with short scabbarded swords watched suspiciously.

Dracus's heart raced. However, he knew that to interfere would be fruitless, probably costing both men their lives. He then noticed a large tarpaulin anchored about midpoint within the caravan and started in that direction, knowing he had probably only one chance at success.

"Help you?" a gruff voice asked from his rear.

Dracus turned to confront a tall, gray-bearded man with a large white turban and a worn red-and-brown robe that dragged the ground. His face was weathered with a mouth full of decaying teeth, which showed prominently when he spoke. However, it was the man's dark, predator-like eyes that held Dracus's attention.

Dracus reciprocated the man's stare with his own as he pointed to the caravan and mimed an interest.

"What is it you want?" the bearded man asked.

Again, Dracus pointed at the camels and herders then to himself and silently mouthed the word "go."

The other studied Dracus for a long moment before he responded, "You want to join the caravan."

Dracus vigorously nodded.

"Can't you talk?" the man asked.

Dracus shook his head and pointed to his severed tongue.

After a moment, the stranger said, "Wonder what you did to deserve that."

Dracus just stood his ground. After another long moment, he grabbed his bag of herbs and held out some dried leaves. He then attempted to mouth the Meroitic word, "trained."

"I think you're trying to tell me that you know how to use that stuff," the man said and looked slightly interested. "However…"

Before he could complete his thought, Dracus had rummaged into his second bag and pulled out the golden band given to Matthias by the Ethiopian on their journey to Meroe. The object had an immediate effect on the stranger.

"Let me see that!" the man said, grabbing the armlet out of Dracus's hand. "Where'd you get this?" he asked while carefully studying the object as he let his figures outline the profile of the lion's head chiseled into the design. "Never mind. You willing to give it up?"

Dracus nodded but also pointed at the assembling column.

"I understand. I understand," the man said. "If I agree to take you along, you will have to travel with the herders. Bed down and eat with them too."

Dracus nodded that he agreed.

"And there may be times I'll need use of your special talent." The turbaned stranger reached out and tugged at Dracus's bag of herbs. "In fact," he added, "there's already one of my slaves who could use your particular skills. I'd forget about him, but the locals want him out of their city, so I can't just leave him behind—alive or dead," and the man laughed. "See what you can do."

Dracus continued to stare, astonished by his good fortune. He then started to turn away and walk to Matthias when the other put a strong grip on his shoulder.

"You'll need someone to tell the guards that it's all right for you to examine my property," the man said and whistled at a young herder who was passing by.

The herder stopped.

"Take this man to the slaves and tell the guards that he is to look after the one we brought here this morning. After that, I'll expect you to find him a place in the caravan. Now, both of you, get going! We leave midmorning."

Dracus anxiously followed the young man down a muddy path to the hobbled prisoners. His thoughts raced in anticipation of what lay ahead. Hopefully, he was not too late! Then his anxieties began to settle as he considered that everything had happened so providentially! How could he have ever doubted?

CHAPTER THIRTY-SIX

Dracus's breath grew short as he approached Matthias. His escort had gone on ahead and made contact with the guards who turned and looked suspiciously at the anxious Greek. Undeterred, Dracus advanced toward a circle of hobbled men, all squatting with what looked like a bowl and a piece of bread in their hands. At first, he did not see his friend. Then, to his left and braced against some large baskets, he spied Matthias still sitting with head bowed and legs stretched out in front of him as another hobbled man squatted beside him and ate from his bowl with two fingers.

One of the guards held out his arm.

"Before you approach," the man said very deliberately, "know that all these men are property of the caravan. Do what you've come to do and then leave." The man not so subtly placed a hand on the hilt of his sword to emphasize his point.

Dracus indicated that he understood and hurried to Matthias, where he stood at the man's feet. A nearby slave looked at both curiously.

"Can you help?" the man asked haltingly with a nod at Matthias. "He has suffered much."

Dracus did not respond but knelt as he used two fingers to lift his friend's head. He looked at the other with pain in his eyes and muttered something very guttural so that it was obvious he could not talk.

As if instinctively knowing what Dracus wanted, the hobbled slave put his hand on Matthias's left shoulder and gently shook him.

"Someone to see you," the man said in barely intelligible Meroitic. "Wake up!"

There was a brief moment before a faint groan came from deep within Matthias. Then his eyes opened slightly, and he squinted at the two men kneeling next to him, dazed by the bright sun.

Dracus took Matthias's right hand, pressed it against his face, and held it there.

Matthias began to stir.

"Dracus!" Matthias finally exhaled in a graveled yet excited voice. His eyes opened wide as they swelled with tears. "You have come! But how…"

The two friends attempted an embrace, which caught Dracus off guard as Matthias drew up in pain and then collapsed into his arms.

"It's his wounds," the slave to their right interjected. "He was lashed pretty bad by the whip."

Dracus nodded and started to pull the tunic over Matthias's head. At the same time, the herder who escorted Dracus to Matthias made an appearance and reminded Dracus that they needed to establish his place in the caravan.

Dracus answered by splashing his hand into a puddle, pointing at the water.

"He wants water," the slave said, now standing. "Clean water!"

Dracus nodded as he continued pulling at Matthias's tunic.

The herder looked perturbed. However, deciding not to argue with someone under the protection of the caravan leader, he ran off to find water. The hobbled slave smiled in momentary victory.

"Let me help," the slave said in broken Meroitic as both he and Dracus leaned Matthias forward and removed the man's garment.

Dracus then came around to the rear of his friend as the slave held Matthias upright, and Dracus had his first examination of Matthias's wounds. The man's back was almost stripped of all flesh, with scabs covering most of the welts. Blood still seeped from several of the wounds, with puss outlining many of the scabs.

Dracus let out an audible gasp. At the same time, the herder returned with a full goatskin.

Dracus immediately grabbed the bag from the boy, took a tunic out of one of his two bags, and soaked it with water. He then gently began to work the cloth over Matthias's wounds as he washed away as much filth and puss as possible. Dracus then pulled his remaining clean tunic over Matthias's torso while gathering up and tucking away the two soiled garments which he would use again. He looked at the slave and attempted to communicate that he wanted to keep his friend upright and free from the filth that surrounded them. Surprisingly, the man understood.

"I'll do what I can," the slave said hesitantly.

Dracus felt a tug on his sleeve.

"We need to go," the young herder said as he tried to lead Dracus away.

Dracus reluctantly released Matthias into the arms of the slave and followed the herder. However, before leaving, he turned and looked pleadingly at the man who held his friend.

"You'll be back," the man said in a heavily accented tongue. "Go do what you have to do. We'll be right here." There was a slight smile with the last comment.

Dracus smiled in response. He wasn't going anywhere either.

Lady Asata reclined awkwardly in the bed of the cart, still unsure why they had to attempt the ruse of her being pregnant! The brothers had even gone so far as to roll up a discarded piece of linen found in the bed of the cart and insist that she place it under her robe to confirm the pregnancy. The story was that Asata was going home to Arborepi, located about fifty miles south of Meroe, to have her baby, and the pregnant belly would only help to confirm the tale. Lady Asata decided to play along.

In point of fact, she and her two coconspirators were presently stopped on the roadway that fronted one of her favorite sites just on the outskirts of Meroe: the wild-animal pens. She was vague on the reason why they had stalled. However, it at least gave her the opportunity to inspect a couple of the stockades, especially the one enclosing the elephants whose size and obvious intelligence fascinated her.

It was not until early afternoon when the signal was finally given that the caravan of carts could move south again, generally following the course of the Nile River. Adda explained that he had discussed their dilemma with one or two of his coworkers, and they had enthusiastically volunteered to join their small band of travelers. Lady Asata even began to relax in her role as a pregnant woman, finding humor in it all. However, her thoughts would eventually slip to the events of the past several days and the horror at the loss of her father. Unlike her usual temperament, she let the tears come at such moments, knowing that in Arborepi, at least, she had friends.

The caravan of more than two dozen camels, four carts, and at least twenty men on foot started out slowly from the eastern boundary of Meroe, headed for the great sea beyond the desert. It all seemed haphazard at first. However, the skill of the caravan master seated on his camel with one leg slung around his saddle horn, and a loud, sharp voice accented with the wave of a hand brought order out of chaos as the assembled band headed past the pylon-fronted pyramids of dead rulers and Meroitic grandees. One disruption, though, needed immediate attention.

Near the far end of the column where the dozen or so slaves were confined, three men broke away from the others and stood motionless around the body of another lying prone on the hot sands. At first, the master did not know what to make of the situation.

"What happened here?" the master asked.

One of the guards answered, "It's the new one. He's unconscious."

The caravan master pushed himself back in his saddle. He had suspected all along that this particular prisoner was going to be trouble. Nevertheless, he had taken the priest's money, and they were not far enough from the city to leave the slave behind.

"Get me that mute who's traveling with us," he ordered.

The guard ran up the line of camels and shortly returned with Dracus.

"It seems your patient has relapsed," the master said. "Can you do anything for him? We need to keep moving!"

Dracus looked at Matthias who was still unconscious and instantly hurried to his side. He held his friend's head upright and gestured that again he needed water.

"Get him some water," the master snapped. "Anything else?"

Dracus slowly raised Matthias's tunic and examined the wounds. Although improved, blood still seeped from several of the deeper gashes. A guard returned with a goatskin, and Dracus poured water onto a dry rag as he began to worked it around Mathias's mouth and forehead. Matthias began to respond.

"Good," the master said. "When he comes to, get him back with the others. Find someone to help carry him."

Dracus pointed at himself.

"You?" the master asked. "Why would you want to get involved? Remember, he's my slave."

Dracus, however, paid no heed but began to pull Matthias to his feet with the help of one of the prisoners. When upright and with one of Matthias's arm slung around his shoulder, Dracus looked up at the caravan leader.

"All right," the man said, adjusting himself on his camel. "Have it your way. However, you'll have to walk with these men. And it won't be pleasant."

Dracus nodded and then carefully led Matthias to their place with the other prisoners as the master rode to the head of the column. It was not long before the march east began again in earnest.

For Dracus, he had accomplished much: Matthias was now under his personal care. Everything else, including thoughts of escape, would have to wait.

CHAPTER THIRTY-SEVEN

The journey east from Meroe was touch and go at best. Stumbling across the coarse, hot sands of the open desert, deliberately avoiding the occasional forested outcroppings, was discouraging enough. However, to do so with an injured companion clinging to your shoulder who at any moment could lose consciousness was almost too much, and all done under the watchful eyes of four guards, each looking for any excuse to chasten their less-fortunate charges with the sting of the whip. Nevertheless, Dracus pushed on one step at a time, knowing they were that much farther from Meroe and its prince.

The caravan sheltered the first night on the edge of a wooded ravine, where Dracus used the opportunity to scour the basin for a fallen limb, which he fashioned into a crutch. That same night and the nights which followed, he was also able to smuggle goat meat and dry bread out of the herders' camp and bring it to his friend who devoured it heartily. Still, each day's march took its toll, and Matthias was exhausted by nightfall.

Now, seven days into their trek, the caravan of camels and donkey carts took a much-needed rest at an oasis, which sheltered a walled community of nearly a half-dozen mudbrick buildings centered around a large open square. Other caravans did the same as all competed for access to two small pools of fresh water surrounded by date palms, as each replenished supplies and tended to their stock.

Being late arrivals, Matthias's caravan had to camp some distance from the watering holes. However, there was enough shade from the clusters of palm trees and other foliage to give a modicum of comfort. And the animals had a direct path to one of the two pools of water. Therefore, after early grumbling, the caravan master along with his principal herder and four guards accepted their lot and erected three tents near the tethered animals, which meant that everyone else had to scramble for whatever shade was left. Ironically, the slaves' encampment was located at one of the better sites, most likely because of its proximity to the armed detail.

Dracus was grateful for any respite, especially as Matthias's wounds were finally starting to heal, and so was the man's recollection of events.

"I cannot believe how fast Prince Amanikhabale changed everything after his mother's death," Matthias said to Dracus. "It's as if he wanted to erase all memory of her."

The guards had yet to hobble the slaves, including Matthias, even letting them congregate around an open-pit fire.

"I doubt the mission will survive," Matthias continued.

Dracus stepped in front of his friend, made a sign that indicated a woman, and then held his right hand about two feet above the ground.

It took Matthias a few seconds to assimilate the message; however, he translated as best he could.

"The women will see to the children," he said.

Dracus nodded.

"I hope so. They have been through so much." And then, thinking further, Matthias added, "And what of the twins…and Lady Asata? I hope she wasn't there to witness her father's execution." He barely stammered out the latter.

Once again, Dracus stopped to answer with signs that the three had escaped on foot. However, he knew nothing more.

A long, silent pause then passed between them.

"And you, how did you escape the wrath of the prince?" Matthias asked for at least the third or fourth time.

Rather than respond immediately, Dracus finished doctoring Matthias's wounds, noticing that most of the bleeding had stopped, and all observable scabs looked healthy.

"Well, however you were able to do it," Matthias said with a winch as Dracus pulled down the tunic, "you certainly saved my life. I cannot imagine what the Master must have endured when he suffered his flogging. And to bear his own cross to the site of his crucifixion! The pain I have suffered is nothing compared to what he had to endure."

Matthias began to tear up as Dracus put a hand on his friend's shoulder and looked deep into the man's eyes with a sincere understanding of what he felt. Matthias took a deep breath.

"Now somehow we've got to address our present circumstance," he said almost in a whisper, still trying to hold back his emotions. "Any ideas?"

Dracus squatted in front of his friend and thought for a moment. He then looked at Matthias and nodded. Matthias looked surprised.

"You do?" he said.

Dracus held his two hands to the side of his head, as if sleeping, and then pointed a finger at both himself and his friend.

"Tonight?" Matthias said.

Dracus again signed "yes" while looking for some contradiction.

Matthias sat back for a moment and thought.

"You know," he began, "that may not be such a bad idea. Right now, everyone is pretty worn out. Even the guards are a little lax in their duties," and he pointed to his ankle restraint. "They probably figure that we are in the middle of a desert, so why bother? Where is there to go?"

Dracus smiled his agreement. He still wanted to hear an explicit approval. It was not long in coming.

After a moment of hesitation, Matthias said in a whisper, "Let's do it!"

Dracus again gave the sign for sleeping and then pointed to himself.

"You'll get me when you're ready," Matthias interpreted.

Dracus nodded.

"I imagine I'll be right here," Matthias responded with the hint of a smile. "What about the guards?"

Again Dracus pointed to himself. "You have an idea there too," Matthias guessed.

Dracus just smiled.

"You know," Matthias began, "if we get caught, it will probably mean our lives. We have no friends in this place."

Dracus shrugged, as if to say, "What choice do we have?"

Mathias leaned forward and put a hand on his friend's knee.

"Do what you have to do. I wish I could help more. Until tonight then," he said, leaning back.

Dracus stood and put his two hands together as he brought them up to his face.

"Oh, yes," Matthias replied immediately. "I will pray too. However, I have always felt that the Master has never been far away."

Dracus drew in a deep breath as he crouched low into the shadows of the camp and approached the rear of the three tents. It was well past midnight, and he had already pilfered a goatskin of water hanging loose from one of the carts. Now the precise execution of his plan would determine the fate of everything.

To this purpose, he had gathered some dry grass and dead fronds into his herb bag, which he carefully removed and built into a small mound directly beside the wall of the large white tent occupied by the four guards. He then scrutinized his immediate environment, looking for anyone who could raise the alarm. One person still crouched at the central firepit; however, Dracus decided he would take his chances. It was not unheard of for herders to come and go from the community pit, with some taking an ember to start their own fire. Therefore, he stepped out from behind the tent as he approached the unsuspecting herder.

Walking slowly up to the fire, he smiled as he pulled his usual piece of stolen meat from his bag and bent beside the open pit. The other looked at him curiously for a moment and then continued to eat.

Holding the pilfered meat in one hand, Dracus removed a small ember of burning wood, smiled again, and started back toward the tents.

Still no alarm.

Taking no chances, he hurriedly buried the smoldering ember under his pile of grass, saw what he thought was the flicker of a flame, and ran crouching toward the slave encampment.

It seemed only seconds before someone hollered, "Fire!"

However, this was precisely the reaction Dracus wanted as he ran up to Matthias, nudged him on the shoulder with the tip of his foot, signaling that they needed to move quickly, as the camp was suddenly alive with activity. Even the guards on duty had run to help put out the flames which, again, was exactly as Dracus had hoped.

For a second time, Dracus tapped Matthias on the shoulder, who hesitated for a moment; however, once fully awake, the man awkwardly pushed himself up and looked to his friend for direction. Fortunately, the guards still had not shackled anyone. A tug on Matthias's arm alerted him to a companion slave who pointed to the far end of the caravan.

This same slave wasted no time and began running, using the shadows of the camp for cover as Matthias and Dracus followed, believing that any direction was as good as another. When they finally came to the end of the encampment, near the point where the oasis began, the slave stopped and turned. A half-moon silhouetted the man's face.

The slave mouthed something incomprehensible as he pointed north. He again repeated himself and then signaled that they should make a run for the far side of a nearby ridge of dunes.

Not waiting for a discussion, the man turned and ran, as did Matthias and Dracus. Once safely beyond the dunes, Matthias wanted to rest. However, their slave benefactor would have none of it and continued his race to the north. Matthias and Dracus stumbled behind, keeping the slave in sight if for no other reason than that his haphazard dodging was their best hope.

At the campsite itself, the caravan master reluctantly stirred, discovering that the fire had been quickly contained with damage only to the guards' tent and its contents. And almost at once the culprit who set the blaze was identified with both this mute stranger and the wounded prisoner gone.

The guards wanted to give chase. However, the master emphatically refused. He had had enough of the troublesome duo. Even when it was reported that another had run off, he would not give the order to pursue. Where would they go, he asked himself, being as they were surrounded by desert? Let the scorpions and jackals have their fill. Besides, he had what he wanted: gold from the high priest and gold from the mute traveler. A chase profited him nothing.

CHAPTER THIRTY-EIGHT

City of Arborepi, South of Meroe

It was early afternoon on the third day out from Meroe when the cart carrying Lady Asata and the twin brothers entered the city of Arborepi and began to roll past a large walled complex that was familiar grounds to Asata. Their journey along the well-traveled road south out of Meroe had proved relatively uneventful, with only two incidents where militia stopped the caravan and questioned their movement, which was easily put to rest with the ruse of Asata's pregnancy and the artful banter of the twins. In fact, it was the constant chatter of the two brothers, including several garbled songs sung loudly during their three-day journey, that seriously wore on Asata's nerves. Consequently, it was with considerable relief when the silhouette of Arborepi rose on the horizon as the caravan of carts slowly advanced.

"My father and I would visit this city when the Candace located her court here for an extended term," Lady Asata said with a degree of nostalgia as her eyes surveyed the rambling mudbrick buildings. Large palm and fruit trees dominated the interior of the largest structure which was the palace. "It holds good memories for me."

Adda, who was seated with his legs extended into the bed of the cart, nodded politely as his brother maneuvered along a congested thoroughfare toward an intersection with a large public square centered by a tall obelisk.

"Where do we go now, my lady?" Attla leaned back and asked.

Lady Asata thought for a moment and then directed that they should pull to one side of the intersecting roads. Women with baskets balanced precariously on their heads had to step aside while

Lady Asata smiled, as if recollecting some familiar past event. She then pointed toward the western gate.

"Elephants!" she shouted to the startled brothers. "Aren't they wonderful? Working logs cut from the forest down to the river. I forgot how many there are in Arborepi."

"So is that where you'd have me go, my lady? Follow the elephants?" Attla asked.

"Don't be impertinent!" Lady Asata replied, leaning back against the hard wooden side of the cart. "No, head for that temple." She pointed southeast to another mudbrick structure flanked by two large pylons, each with lion-headed figures that dominated the skyline of two and three-storied shops and dwellings. "I just hope it is as I remember."

Attla snapped the donkey on its hindquarter with his reins as the cart maneuvered into the crowded intersection and headed east, sidelining any pedestrian who was unfortunate enough to get in his way. Detours for any reason were out of the question.

Lady Asata took a deep breath before entering the temple, careful to study the two lion-headed gods painted in multi colors and chiseled into each pylon surrounded by lesser Egyptian deities. She had entered through this portal on several occasions but had never really taken the time to admire the workmanship that went into such monumental building. It was built to impress, and for once in her life, even she was overwhelmed.

Once through two large, open wooden doors, the interior of the temple was an exposed rectangle with monumental columns on either side of a central corridor illuminated by wall sconces. At the far end stood a golden statute of the same god depicted on the pylons centered on a stone altar, which itself was elevated above the central corridor. Behind the altar were other representations of the lion deity mingled with elephants and other Egyptian-inspired gods. A fragrant haze permeated everything in the temple.

Lady Asata thought she heard voices to her right and abruptly slowed their progress. Approaching the end of the central corridor,

Asata turned and was confronted by a group of six individuals huddled together, around two young white-robed men holding what looked to be a bowl of red liquid. A third older male, obviously a priest, with a lion skin wrapped around his shoulders and the jaws of the lion covering his head, reached into the bowl, wetted his fingertips, and then sprinkled the liquid onto the forehead of an infant held by a young man and woman. Throughout the ceremony, the older man mumbled some indiscernible incantation. A previously unseen male stepped from behind one of the columns to stop the intruders. He also signaled for silence. The ceremony ended when the priest held up his hands, turned on his heels, and stared suspiciously at the three interlopers.

"This is a sacred place," the priest said, obviously perturbed as he pushed the jaws of the lion off his head. "What business do you have with the temple?" As he spoke, he carefully studied each intruder.

Lady Asata's demeanor was suddenly less self-assured.

"Do you not remember me, Lord Karkamani?" she asked. "I have visited before with my father."

The priest looked at Lady Asata, puzzled. Recognition was not immediate. Then his eyes flashed.

"Asata..." he said, taking a step out from the shadows and into the light. Placing both hands on the girl's upper arms, he continued, "My child, how you have changed! The last time I saw you, you were many years younger. And now look at you, a young woman!" He shook his head and smiled as he focused on Lady Asata's pregnant belly. "What brings you to Arborepi? And how is your father?"

Lady Asata stiffened as she fought back tears.

"Father is dead," she stuttered.

The priest took a step back as he collected his thoughts.

"I... I didn't know. Do you need to sit down?" He clapped his hands to get the attention of an aide.

Lady Asata immediately understood, reached under her robe, and pulled out a wadded linen cloth.

"This was necessary to hide my identity," she explained as she held up the ruse. "I did not know if I would be able to escape." Then, turning to Attla and Adda, she added, "Nevertheless, with the help of my two friends, we made it this far. I was hoping…" and she hesitated.

"Yes, child?" the priest asked.

"I was hoping that you might be able to help."

"In what way?" Lord Karkamani responded.

Asata again hesitated as she took a deep breath.

"I… We need to leave the kingdom. It is urgent that we do so at once," she said very deliberately, with her eyes clearly focused on the priest.

Lord Karkamani put the back of his hand up to his mouth as he thought.

"You know," he finally responded, "your father is responsible for me having this position: high priest of Apedemak, an equal to Amun, some say even greater. And to your dilemma, child, yes, I will do what I can. However, we need to talk of this further, but at my residence, which is just across the courtyard. The temple is far too public with many ears," and he swung his arms wide. "Have you eaten?"

Lady Asata closed her eyes and sighed. It was the first time since leaving Meroe that she truly began to feel that circumstances were finally turning her way.

Lord Karkamani's residence was a modest, two-storied structure built adjacent to a well-maintained garden with multiple groves of fruit-bearing trees. The scent of jasmine and wild lilies hung in the air.

Passing under a canopy that extended from the temple to the residence, the party of four entered the home through a narrow wooden doorway and were immediately led to an upstairs room that had no furnishings other than two chairs, a small rectangular table, and a mat rolled neatly against the far wall. Two small windows with wooden lattices opened to an exterior street.

"I am sorry that I cannot offer more," the priest said. "However, this is the best accommodation I have, and it is for you to use. Your friends will have to sleep with my aides." The latter was said with obvious embarrassment.

"After what we've been through," Lady Asata said, "this is wonderful. Attla and Adda expect no more than you offer. This will do just fine," and she smiled at her benefactor.

The priest nodded as he turned to leave, saying, "And I expect you and your friends to join me for dinner. We will talk there. However, take the time necessary to wash," and he clapped his hands, summoning two aides who were instructed to bring basins of water and clean robes to each guest. "Your friends need to follow my associates," which both Adda and Attla did willingly. "And I will see you at dinner." Lord Karkamani then left the room.

It did not take long for a large basin, two clean robes, and two tunics to be brought to Lady Asata's room. She enjoyed her moment of privacy and the opportunity to wash away all evidence of her escape. However, she knew that her father's friend had more to discuss, so she dressed as quickly as she could, adjusting one loose-fitting robe to her form, drawing it tightly around her narrow waist. She then proceeded to the lower level and was directed to a large rectangular room where Adda, Attla, Lord Karkamani, and three others she did not know circulated in front of a dining alcove set in the Greek fashion.

On seeing her, the priest directed all to be seated, with Asata positioned to his right. He then clapped his hands, and a communal meal of hot meats, fruits, and bread was served.

"Do you have everything you need?" Lord Karkamani asked.

Lady Asata nodded as she noticed how much older the man appeared now that he was without his robes of office.

"Then let me introduce you to people you have not met," he said, and his hand pointed to his left and to two males seated directly across from her.

"This is Jaibal, a priest from the islands in the high lake many days journey from here, and the other is his aide, Moire. Next to them is my aide, Piye. Jaibal and Moire have traveled a great distance, and the reason for their journey may concern you."

Lady Asata bowed slightly at the three strangers and then turned quickly to Lord Karkamani. He had her full attention as well as that of Attla and Adda.

"Jaibal comes to us from the Temple of Apedemak located on an island in Lake Tana," the priest began. "Have you heard of Lake Tana?" he asked.

Lady Asata shook her headed.

"It is a beginning to the great river. Far from here," Lord Karkamani explained. "And Jaibal comes with a request." There was a definite pause, which was calculated to add to the speculation. "His temple wants recruits, specifically priests from Arborepi, who know the fundamentals of the old ways."

Lady Asata attempted to look politely interested but wondered why she was being told this.

"You look confused, my child. Let me explain," Lord Karkamani said. "Not many want to give up what Arborepi offers. However, you and your friends are of a different circumstance, as you have reasons to leave Meroe."

Lady Asata scowled as she tried to comprehend the priest's words.

"You mean," she began, "you want us to go to Lake Tana?"

"Precisely!" Lord Karkamani said.

"But we are not versed in the ways of your temple," she countered. "Besides, I am a woman, and your priests are all male."

Lord Karkamani smiled and said, "That would be an obstacle. However, you're a clever girl, and with some 'adjustments,' we might be able to overcome that inconvenient fact, at least until you are safely beyond the reach of those in power."

"What 'adjustments' are you contemplating?" Lady Asata immediately shot back.

"We'll have to bind your breasts, although what we wear"—the priest tugged at the front of his robe—"is loose fitting in itself."

Asata gave a hesitant nod.

"And you'll have to walk more upright and not so…so…"

"I understand," Lady Asata said, finishing the man's thought. "I can try. I can also try to talk at a lower pitch."

Lord Karkamani was silent for a long moment before continuing, "And each of you will have to shave your head. Priests of Apedemak are bald." He emphasized the point by rubbing his own bald scalp.

Lady Asata shook her head vigorously while turning to Adda and Attla.

"What do you think?" she asked the brothers. "You've got as much at stake as I do."

A look that only the brothers understood passed between them before Attla spoke up.

"We can do this. But can you?" he asked.

Lady Asata thought for a moment.

"Do you really think it necessary to shave our heads? Won't the rest of the disguise be sufficient to fool anyone?" she asked.

Lord Karkamani smiled and said, "It is if you truly want to escape. You are probably safe here even if you only do part. However, once you leave and go on, especially up the big river, you will be on your own. And if discovered, I cannot help."

Lady Asata took a moment to consider her options. Actually, she only had two: to remain in Arborepi or to go on. To remain meant that Prince Amanikhabale's reach would tighten and increase the chance that she be discovered; to go on meant that she had a chance to be free of the new order. But to do so, she would have to undertake an elaborate ruse. There wasn't much of a choice.

"I'll do it," she finally said. "However, what do your priests think of the scheme? After all, they'll have to work closely with me. And this puts them in jeopardy too."

"We have talked this over, and they are in total agreement. Jaibal and his aide, along with Piye from this temple, will travel with you and your friends. They all feel that you will be a blessing."

"Then we had better get started. Tomorrow we'll make the necessary changes and start for the river the following day. Is that too soon?" Lady Asata asked.

"No," Lord Karkamani answered. "Even I have noticed the growing presence of the militia and the subtle change in politics taking place in the city. Two days from now will not be too soon."

"Good," Lady Asata said, comfortable with the decision. "Then let's finish this excellent meal and get some rest. A long journey awaits."

CHAPTER THIRTY-NINE

Savannah Grasslands, East Northeast of Meroe

The two exhausted, weather-tempered men huddled closely under the protective branches of an acacia tree, succumbing to the balm of sleep while a third volunteered to stand watch. For eight days they had endured the fires of hell; now it was time to enjoy the rewards of survival.

At first, the escape was far easier than Dracus had anticipated. Although they could not help but look over their shoulders as they struggled across the dunes, no one followed, perhaps believing that the barren landscape sealed their fate. However, this failed to take into account the resolve of the three men and their inherent will to survive. Even Matthias, who began each day exhausted, pulled himself together sufficiently to keep with the pace set by their slave companion as they headed farther through the seemingly endless desert. Yet it was this same slave who gave Matthias his shoulder to lean on when necessary, and when Dracus's goatskin ran dry, it was the slave who knew where to find water.

Matthias tried to communicate with their companion through means other than body language or pointing at what was of interest. However, the best either he or Dracus could manage was an incomprehensible response, which Matthias translated into the name "Omanga-ji," which seemed suitable to all. In any event, the slave now called Omanga-ji was their lifeline to survival, as for days they fought the battle of sun and sand until they finally reached a savannah where the terrain was more forgiving and offered the occasional meal of a bird or a lizard, which Omanga-ji would catch at the sharpened end of a tree branch and cook over a fire ignited from the spark of two rocks. Yet water was the commodity most in demand. Only now others were also in search of this same resource: they had entered the land of predator and prey.

Omanga-ji let his companions sleep as he surveyed a darkening sky splintered with the occasional bright rays of a morning sun. The odd smells of dry grass and animal dung hung in the humid air as a stiff breeze began to blow from the east, where peaks of ragged mountains began to sprout on the horizon. They had chosen this site because of its foliage, including the large acacia under which Matthias and Dracus now slept, which was one of several in a grove of trees that grew atop a shallow gully. Other outcroppings of foliage scared the open grassland.

Movement across the gully caught Omanga-ji's attention, and he stiffened in response. A small herd of gazelle began to graze along the perimeter on the opposite bank, eating whatever grasses and leaves they could find as the herd moved cautiously along the dry waterbed. However, Omanga-ji knew that gazelle also signified something more sinister—lions!

He slowly stooped and put a hand on both Matthias's and Dracus's shoulders.

The two woke with a start as Matthias began to say something. Omanga-ji put a hand up to his mouth and pointed across the gully.

Matthias looked but could see nothing that warranted concern and started to speak again.

Omanga-ji hit Matthias harder on the shoulder as all three stared at the grazing herd of gazelle. A flash of lightening illuminated the savannah as finally both Matthias and Dracus spied what was troubling Omanga-ji.

A pride of a least four female lions was following the gazelles as splatters of rain cascaded across the plains and rivulets of water began to stream down the dry waterway. Omanga-ji knew precisely what this meant.

Shouting something incomprehensible, their companion sprinted out into the now-rain-drenched savannah as lightening flashed and thunder crackled overhead. Matthias and Dracus could only interpret this one way: move!

The three sprinted across the savannah toward a distant ridge of jagged mountains. Matthias only once looked back at their abandoned camp and was alarmed that the placid gully was now a torrent of boiling water which lapped almost at the base of the acacia under which he slept. And for a moment he also thought he saw a lion standing on the bank, roaring at the retreating threesome. In the future, he would have to give more credence to the instincts of their new friend.

Dockside on the East Bank of the Tributary to the Nile River, City of Soba, South of Arborepi

The six white-robed, bald-headed individuals sat cross-legged in a circle on the pebble walkway near the bow of a boat that was to transport them upstream on this principal tributary of the Nile River. A goatskin of water was being passed hand to hand as each finished their morning meal of cheese and unleavened bread. For Lady Asata, the past seventy-two hours had been quite challenging.

For one, she had reluctantly undergone the personal indignity of having her head shaved completely bald. Then she had to endure the discomfort of having her breasts bound as she assumed the role of a priest, including an attempt to mimic male gestures. And although she did not think of herself as better than the others, she was accustomed to more differential treatment, including the communal living she had to endured on their two-day journey to Soba. Even their one night at a local temple continued the ruse of her male identity as she ate and slept in the same confined quarters with the other five.

One thing, however, kept her motivated. Although stopped and questioned a couple times, the disguise worked, and her escape was that much more likely. Nevertheless, Asata felt sad not only for her personal losses but also for her homeland. The future of Meroe seemed to be uncertain with a pervasive sense of panic. Nothing really tangible, although there was a noticeable presence of militia along the roadways and at various checkpoints. Everyday people, the men and women who made up what was the community of Meroe, seemed to be on the move, trying to escape whatever dark events were forthcoming. Even here, while eating their communal meal and waiting to be summoned to board a vessel headed upriver on this branch of the Nile, Lady Asata watched the crowded pier as people jockeyed for passage away from perceived dangers. She understood all too well.

"Open up here!" a gruff voice ordered from the fringe of their circle.

All eyes turned toward the interloper who was an armed soldier accompanied by two companions. The three pushed their way to the center of the circle as they scrutinized each of the six priests.

"What is your business?" the obvious leader of the three asked.

As was agreed, Jaibal answered for all.

"We travel back to our temple on Lake Tana and are waiting for permission to board," he said while pointing to a boat docked to his left.

The solider with questions responded with a short, sarcastic burst of laughter as he continued to scrutinize the six.

"You've a long way to go then. And what treasures are you trying to steal away from Meroe?" he asked.

Jaibal looked indignant.

"Nothing!" the young priest replied. "We are priests, not thieves!"

"We'll see about that," the man said as he took his sword out of its scabbard and poked at a bag slung over Jaibal's right shoulder.

"What's in that?" the man asked. "Open it and let me see."

Jaibal hesitated at first and then opened the top of the bag, which revealed nothing but extra robes and vestments.

The soldier grunted his disappointment as he moved to each in the circle.

Finally coming to Lady Asata, he stared at her for a long moment and then asked, "And what have you got hidden in your bag?" He poked at it like the others with the tip of his sword. Then the sparkle of something on Asata's right arm caught his attention

"What's that?" he asked as he brought his sword up to the sleeve of her blousy garment and pointed at the source of his curiosity.

Lady Asata caught the stiffening of both Attla and Adda, as if preparing to strike, and held up the palm of her left hand to stop them.

"Pull up your sleeve!" the soldier ordered.

Lady Asata hesitated, so he ordered again, only this time he used his sword to move the sleeve himself. Revealed was the remaining golden band with the chiseled figure of a lion.

"Well, now," the sword-wielding soldier said as the tip of his blade touched the armlet and outlined the lion's head. "This is a little fancy for a priest. I doubt if you'll be needing it where you're going. Give it to me," he ordered.

Lady Asata slowly raised her left hand and unsnapped the object. She then held it up to the soldier.

"That's more like it," the man said as he let the armband slip down the length of his sword. "Anything else like that?" he asked.

"And what if he does?" a new voice asked. "How does that make it of interest to you?"

The soldier and all others in the circle turned to confront a new intruder who stood only an arm's length away. Recognition suddenly altered the sword-wielding man's demeanor.

"My lord!" the man blurted, bringing the flat of his blade across his chest.

The intruder smiled as he slipped the armlet off the sword and held it in his hand.

"I don't think you really want to take this from the priest, do you?" the intruder asked.

"No, my lord!" the man answered.

"Good." Then, looking at the other soldiers, the intruder said, "I believe your efforts can best be served by infiltrating more likely candidates than a circle of priests. Move on!" he ordered. "And use better judgment next time!"

"As you wish, my lord," the most vocal soldier replied as he and his two companions stepped quickly out of harm's way.

The intruder watched for a moment and then turned to Lady Asata.

"And you, I want to talk to you...alone."

Lady Asata took a deep breath and hesitantly stepped away from her companions and into the crowded walkway along the pier.

The intruder pointed to a collection of baskets waiting to be loaded on a boat.

"Over there," he said, pointing. "You don't recognize me, do you?"

Lady Asata stared without response.

"Lord Nastasen, Lady Asata. You, I, and Prince Teritegas met once before when you came to hunt lions. We haven't seen each other since that time. However, I proudly served with the prince and miss him. Much has changed."

Lady Asata closed her eyes with the mention of her name, and her apprehension increased.

Lord Nastasen saw the change in demeanor.

"Don't worry. I will not give away your secret. You and Prince Teritegas were very kind, and I can only attempt to repay the favor. Actually, if I had not spent time with you before, I would not have recognized you. Your disguise is very effective," he said as he rubbed the top of his head.

Lady Asata sighed and said, "I know. That was the hardest part," and she smiled.

"However, you need to keep as low a profile as possible. I have heard your name mentioned a couple of times, and there are those who would give much to take you into custody."

"So I understand."

"Oh," he said and held out the golden armband, "take this, but keep it hidden, at least until you are well upriver."

"I will," Lady Asata replied. "I only wish I could repay..."

Lord Nastasen held up his hand.

"Payment is not getting caught. Our kingdom will need people like you when the times are right again."

Lady Asata smiled as she took the armlet and hid it in the sleeve of her robe.

"Now I suggest you return to your fellow priests," Lord Nastasen said. "And I promise that I won't be far away until your boat sails. The best of luck, my lady."

Lady Asata touched the man's arms and then stiffened as she walked back to her five companions. Fortunately, the boat's pilot signaled that those traveling upriver should board, and she dodged all questions as they found their places on the crowded vessel. Hopefully, this experience would be the worst of it.

Foothill of the Mountains East of the Kingdom of Kush

Matthias and Dracus lumbered up the steep incline spotted with yellowwood trees and junipers interspersed with clumps of grass and various flowering plants. Every so often the landscape would give way to an open field of boulders and rock, which Matthias and Dracus now approached and were seduced by its relative tranquility.

"I need to stop," Matthias said as he leaned against a large boulder which offered shade from the ever-present sun. "Our friend can go on," he said, pointing up the mountain. "However, I need to rest. Not for long but enough to catch my breath."

Dracus squatted next to his friend, who sat with his back braced against a large bolder. One thing they both enjoyed was the cooler weather and the frequent access to water. Their more resourceful companion, Omanga-ji, was also able to snare more variety of game since they had entered the mountains, especially hares, which helped their overall physical condition. Nonetheless, Matthias had never fully recovered from his wounds, and therefore, Dracus did not object to the temporary halt in their climb out of the desert. Although Omanga-ji would not be pleased, Dracus gambled that the man would acquiesce once he understood the circumstance. Besides, he also welcomed the respite.

Dracus put a hand on his friend's knee as a signal that he agreed and was more than slightly amused to find that Matthias had already fallen asleep with his head barely touching the rock. Careful not to disturb his friend, he wadded a tunic against Matthias's leg and did the same.

It seemed only minutes before Dracus felt the heat of the sun again warming his legs, where once there had been shade as he squinted his eyes open and felt a tug on his bag of herbs. Instinctively, he brushed at the strange sensation, which was followed by another tug, only augmented with loud chatter.

He woke and sat upright, as did Matthias. Two small brown baboons froze in the space between them. Dracus heard another loud chatter, only this time there was an element of a cry with the noise.

The two baboons immediately responded and ran in the direction of an older baboon standing on the alert not far from the reclining figures while exposing his fangs as a warning.

"Look," Matthias said, pointing farther down the clearing toward the tree line. What had caught his attention was a whole troop of baboons moving in their direction.

Dracus attempted to push himself up as Matthias strained to do the same. Although rested, both were still challenged to go on. A large, shapeless shadow suddenly blocked the sunlight again, and Dracus turned slowly to its source.

There, standing only an arm's length away, was a tall, gaunt man with a fierce expression, pointing a metal-tipped spear at both Dracus and Matthias. Two others, both equipped with spears and shields, stood to one side with Omanga-ji between them.

The warrior nearest to Matthias shouted something incomprehensible; however, the thrusts of his spear clearly meant that Dracus and Matthias were to follow.

Once again, they were prisoners!

CHAPTER FORTY

Mountains of the Tigrayan People, East of the Kingdom of Kush

The trek up the mountainous slopes was almost as challenging as the forced march across the desert perhaps in part due to the altitude and the precipitous footing they had to endure. Narrow footpaths and toehold climbs between tight spaces were almost routine as they navigated around towering cliffs and through gorges riddled with rocks and boulders. Distant valleys of lush vegetation seemed merely a mirage; however, they could be thankful that the climate was temperate.

The march into the mountains was short, as on the third day of their captivity, their small band of six stood at the mouth of a large gorge that opened onto a relatively flat plain where, in the distance, specks of white structures came to view. As they moved closer, the "specks" became substantial round huts of whitewashed adobe with thatched roofs and small, well-maintained gardens. Wooden corrals were interspersed among many of the structures with what looked like a communal fenced area located at the far end of the village. At least fifty or more buildings constituted the community that was well located between towering mountains with sloping green pastures and occasional streams cascading down slopes that originated at some of the higher peaks.

Shunted by spearpoint down the central axis of the village, Matthias noticed the absence of young men with one curious exception being a light-skinned male dressed in the Roman fashion, exercising two near-white horses at one of the outlying corrals. Nevertheless, a crowd of spectators quickly began to congregate until, when they reached the far end of the village, the number of curious had grown so substantial their captors had to push the overzealous onlookers away. Everything quieted when a tall male stepped out from one of the whitewashed huts dressed in a bright-yellow kilt that hung just below his knees with a leopard skin draped over his shoulders. The man also sported a feathered headdress fringed with gold beads and carried a scepter ornamented with carvings of various animals. He was escorted by an entourage of three females dressed in multicolored robes with an abundance of bracelets and necklaces and a young male wearing a simple tunic who distinguished himself with an elaborate, seemingly molded hairdo.

The older man held out his scepter as he said something incomprehensible, which precipitated the three captors to push Matthias and his companions forward. Matthias also took note that several men armed with spears and shields had entered the semicircle that now surrounded them. However, the person who interested Matthias the most was the young male who stood alongside the chief.

Attention again turned to the captors, who began what could only be an explanation for their interruption of village life with special note given to Omanga-ji. When the three talked of him, they would push Omanga-ji at the shoulders to which the encircling warriors would respond with loud cries and thrusts of their spears above their heads. Matthias became concerned for the man's safety.

"Leave him alone!" Matthias finally stuttered with some difficulty. The agitation in his low-pitched voice was obvious as he struggled to remain upright. His torn clothing and disheveled appearance reflected the pain of his unhealed wounds compounded by the strain of their climb up the mountains.

The chief turned to Matthias with a perplexed look.

"Why do you speak for our enemy?" the chief asked. "The captors say they found him surveying one of the herds, grazing on the new grass in the mountains. What is your part in all this?" the man asked as he pointed his scepter at Matthias.

Matthias understood nothing but that he had called unwanted attention to himself.

"Let me help," a new voice said in the Meroitic tongue as a hand touched Matthias on the shoulder. "What is it that you want to tell the old chief?" the man asked, coming to the right of the young disciple.

Matthias turned abruptly. It was the man dressed in the Roman fashion that he observed as they entered the village.

Suddenly all breath went out of Matthias as he placed his hand precariously on the man's arm.

"Aristotle…" he said, dumbfounded. "What…" A hand reached out to touch the other's face.

The stranger took a step backward as his jaw dropped with a look of disbelief! The chief demanded an explanation.

"My young Jewish friend with the strange ideas! And his companion! This is unbelievable! What has happened to you?" Aristotle said, and he ran his hand up and down, as if tracing Matthias's silhouette.

Matthias shook his head, saying "There is much to tell. At the moment we have to help this man," and he pointed at Omanga-ji.

The one called Aristotle held up his hand and turned not to the chief but to the young male standing to one side. The two had a brief exchange in the native tongue, which resulted in the same reaction as that which jolted Aristotle.

The young man immediately began an animated conversation with the chief and pointed several times at both Matthias and Dracus. He then took Matthias by both arms and shook him, all the while speaking in an incomprehensible tongue. A broad smile broke on his face.

"Matthias… That's your name, right?" Aristotle asked.

Matthias nodded.

Then pointing to his left, he added, "And Dracus. Of course. Do you not recognize our gladiator friend?" he asked coyly.

It was Matthias's turn to look with disbelief. Once recovered, he turned to Dracus and explained.

"I would never…" Matthias began as the young man who stood next to the old chief beamed.

"He cleans up rather well, wouldn't you say? He's the oldest son of this chief," Aristotle added. "And what's that?" the man asked, pointing to the leather slave anklet.

Matthias closed his eyes before answering, "It's part of the story. But what of our friend?" he asked, indicating Omanga-ji with a tilt of his head.

"I see he has one of those too," Aristotle commented as he turned to engage the young man known as the gladiator. As he did, Matthias had reached the end of his endurance and collapsed. Dracus immediately bent to minister to his friend as the chief's son also took a step forward.

"What is wrong?" Aristotle asked.

Dracus looked up as he used both hands and arms to indicate that he needed space.

"Will he be all right?" Aristotle asked.

Dracus struggled as he attempted to balance Matthias in order to raise the tunic and reveal the multiple wounds.

Aristotle jerked back in shock, as did the chief's son, who clapped his hands and signaled for some of the onlookers to approach.

"No, take him to my hut," Aristotle said. "He will be more comfortable there. How did this happen?" he asked to no one in particular.

Dracus gave no indication that he heard the man, however, giving his full attention to the four men carrying Matthias to the outskirts of the village and to Aristotle's hut as the chief dismissed the crowd. Omanga-ji, though, was still in custody and was escorted to a tall, fenced area near the far side of the village. There were issues yet to be resolved.

Matthias woke cold and sweaty in the dark interior of Aristotle's quarters with two strange women in long, colorful robes and turbans, each crouched on their legs, ministering to him. Several oil lamps attempted to light the space with a rug that covered the entryway pulled back for additional light and ventilation. Dracus was not far away, boiling water and herbs on a low open fire at the large open center of the structure. Matthias immediately complained of a tremendous headache.

"What happened?" he asked, rubbing his forehead.

Dracus signaled for the women to leave and took their place.

"How did I get here?" Matthias asked, still barely conscious.

"With a lot of difficulty, my friend," Aristotle said as he entered the hut. "You starting to feel better?"

"I don't remember much. How long have I been like this?" Matthias asked.

"Three days. But who's counting?" Aristotle answered with an attempt at a smile. "You've been very sick. I think whatever happened caught up to you. And what did happen?"

Matthias attempted an explanation of the flogging and subsequent trek across the desert. He also gave a short rendition of his life during the past two and one-half years. However, talking began to wear him out, and both Dracus and Aristotle discouraged further discourse.

"I think you have explained enough. You need rest," Aristotle said. "Fortunately, I am in the village of our gladiator friend to trade for whatever they may have of value. As you entered the village, you may have noticed the magnificent white stallions I have been fortunate enough to acquire."

He was interrupted by the chief's son, the gladiator, who hurried past the Greek and stood over Matthias with the same two women who earlier had been nursing him.

"It seems that our young prophet will recover," Aristotle said by way of explanation.

The chief's son approached, put a hand on Matthias's arm, and smiled.

"What of Omanga-ji?" Matthias asked with evident concern. "Nothing has happened to him, has it?"

Aristotle translated for the young man, who immediately responded. Aristotle repeated what he was told.

"No, he is safe. The chief and his council decided that because you saved his son, they would do likewise for your companion. Although he is of an enemy tribe, he is yours to do with as you like. He will be set free."

"You mean he is my slave," Matthias responded.

Aristotle thought for a moment.

"I guess you could say that. More like your property, perhaps."

"Well, I will certainly let him return to his people. He has suffered enough."

Matthias groaned as he started to lie back. Both Dracus and the chief's son helped to lower Matthias to the blanketed mat.

"That's all to be discussed later, my friend," Aristotle said. "For the moment, you rest. As I was beginning to tell you, I will be in the village a few more weeks. Use that as a time to recuperate. Then I will personally escort you back to Egypt. Can you believe the coincidence of our meeting in this remote place?"

Matthias did not hear the latter, but Dracus did and smiled. His friend had lost consciousness; however, it was a healing sleep, not one that threatened death. As to Aristotle's point, Dracus thought of his friend and how he would have responded: simply put, "To *Him*, all things are possible."

CHAPTER FORTY-ONE

On the Bank of Lake Tana, Source of the Principal Tributary of the Nile River

Lady Asata stood with her feet buried in the cool waters on the shoreline of Lake Tana as she scrambled to unravel the turban that had covered her head for weeks and shake loose her partially regrown locks of hair. A cool lake breeze invigorated her as she bent to splash water over her face and arms. Freedom!

It had been a long and difficult journey through dense tropical forests, narrow gorges rimmed with jagged cliffs, rapids too innumerable to count, and spectacular waterfalls the most recent located only a short distance from Lake Tana. However, their small band of six had made it safely. She was proud of her escort, especially the twins, Adda and Attla, who never lost sight of their principal objective which was to protect her. Although more accustomed to a city environment, they adjusted well to their circumstance and participated with the others in establishing campsites, hunting game, and when necessary, transporting their boats, which now numbered two past seemingly insurmountable obstacles. Now, after weeks of hardship, their goal was at hand.

"My lady," Adda said, coming up on her right within her shadow. "Come eat before it is gone."

She turned and smiled. She knew the entire crew was exhausted, having just portaged past the expansive falls not far from the lake. However, she wanted a few moments to herself.

"I'll be right there," Asata said as she rubbed the outline of the lion's head on her golden band, which she had reattached to her upper right arm and returned her gaze to the placid lake. A setting sun skimmed rays of light across a surface that sparkled on the crest of waves like stars at dusk.

She knew she had to endure one more long day crossing the lake to an island chosen centuries earlier by priests as their sanctuary home. Now it would be her sanctuary too. Of course, grief still overwhelmed her when she thought on the loss of her father and all the others she knew and cared for. However, this was home now, and like her twin friends, she would adjust. She had truly escaped.

Harbor of Adulis on the Red Sea

Matthias stood alone at the stern of a modest ship as the crew maneuvered two sails into place and slowly left the harbor to enter the waters of the Red Sea. The stimulating smell of salt air reminded him that the promise of Egypt and safety was just over the horizon.

He really did not realize how torn his body was. However, it took the three weeks they remained at the mountain village of their gladiator friend for him to fully recover. In the interim, Aristotle amassed quite a collection to take with him to Egypt, including the two prized white stallions—all of which were now safely boarded as they began to lumber up the coastline to a more-familiar topography. For his part, Matthias journeyed with both a sense of loss and regret.

His thoughts could not move beyond the question of just what had he accomplished during the nearly three years in the Meroe? Had anyone really listened to his message? And how would he explain to Peter? These and other questions played on his mind constantly. At least he was able to save his companion, Omanga-ji, who he freed as they journeyed to the sea. But what of the twins and Lady Asata, what had become of them? His body might have recovered, but not his spirit.

"Deep in thought again, I see," Aristotle said, coming up silently from the middle deck of the ship.

He was startled to see tears in Matthias's eyes. A silent moment passed as both looked back at the retreating harbor.

"You know," Aristotle finally said, "you did what was asked of you. Even more."

Matthias stiffened but remained silent.

"Isn't it you who says that your god works in strange ways?" Aristotle asked. "How do you know that all that has happened is not part of his grand plan? It takes more than one lifetime to change the world."

Matthias took a deep breath and turned. He nodded hesitantly as the tears stopped.

"Come. Let us join the others," Aristotle said, leading Matthias by the arm.

The young disciple did not resist as he placed one foot in front of the other and walked with his Greek friend toward the bow. The way was forward, with the past but an unchangeable, bittersweet memory.

EPILOGUE

Island of Tana Qirqos, Lake Tana—Seven Years Later

Attla faced his brother and Lady Asata with some trepidation. He had made his decision and would not be turned back. He also knew that those who stood with him on a pier that jutted into Lake Tana were not yet convinced.

"Are you sure this is what you want, brother?" Adda asked as one of his two small daughters came and wrapped their arms around his leg. "You know the dangers that lie ahead of you."

"Yes," Attla replied, "it is. And I am fully aware of the difficulties I will face. But surely you see that I must do this."

Attla was respectful but firm in his response. Adda had found peace on Qirqos and had settled in nicely with the local population, marrying one of the local merchant's daughters and rearing a family. He even built an orphanage much like the one Matthias had established in Meroe. And from time to time, both brothers used the orphanage as a platform to tell the stories taught by Matthias of a Jew who gave his life to save others. And this was why he must leave: the Jew about whom Matthias preached, both confused and fascinated Attla, and he wanted to learn more. Much more!

"I will miss you," a female said from behind Adda's active family.

"And I you, my lady," Attla said, straining to make eye contact with Lady Asata.

The woman had fared well, Attla thought to himself. Her position within the Meroe royal family and her knowledge of the culture of Apedemak made her a favorite with the community of islands. She was the uncrowned queen, the Candace of Lake Tana.

Attla could wait no longer. It was time to go.

He nodded to the oarsmen who would convey him in their small reed boat across the lake to the shore where the main tributary to the Nile River began. He had a long journey ahead, but he had conquered it once before. At the end of his pilgrimage was Meroe and another life. Only this time he was girded with the words of the one Matthias called Jesus.

City of Apsaros, Colchis, on the Coast of the Black Sea—Date Uncertain

A lone, middle-aged male stood apart from an angry crowd, which was spewing epithets and accusations instigated by local priests. Then one in the crowd picked up a large rock and hurled it at the defenseless man followed by another, then another, and another until the man's lifeless body fell buried by a mound of bloodied stones.

Matthias had passed. He would never know the consequence of his work and that upper Sudan and Ethiopia would be among the first to accept Christianity.

ABOUT THE AUTHOR

Don Schofield is a retired attorney who with his wife are longtime residents of West Texas. He has had a lifelong interest in history, earning two degrees in the subject. Don is particularly interested in the first-century Mediterranean cultures that impact even today.

CPSIA information can be obtained
at www.ICGtesting.com
Printed in the USA
LVHW031241270521
688665LV00007B/159